THE SINGALONG TRIBE

KENT ASHFORD has spent his adult life in journalism. From a cadet with the Newcastle *Herald* he rose to the position of finance sub-editor on *The Australian* before branching out into freelance work.

He was in Laos during the collapse of the Souvannaphouma coalition government and the takeover by the Communist Pathet Lao in May 1975.

Now divorced, Kent has two children and when not at home in rural New South Wales spends his time travelling as a stringer in the Philippines, the United States, France, Britain and Spain.

KENT ASHFORD

THE SINGALONG TRIBE

First published in Britain in 1986 by GMP Publishers Ltd,
PO Box 247, London N15 6RW.

British Library Cataloguing in Publication Data

Ashford, Kent
  The singalong tribe.
  I. Title
  823[F]   PR9619.3.A7/
  ISBN 0-85449-001-9

Cover art by Chris Corr
Printed by The Guernsey Press, PO Box 57, Braye Road,
          Vale, Guernsey, Channel Islands.

TO THE MENDERS

· PROLOGUE ·

Before the Great Revolution, December in Manila was the month of firecrackers. Hardly had the eleventh page of a calendar been turned when explosions shook the Philippine city. At first they were few and, as noise was the object of the exercise, confined to spaces where resonance was greatest. Crowded Manila then had many narrow streets ideal for such public mischief. It also had an army of jobless for whom any diversion was a holiday from tedium. Day by day the noise would escalate and by the end of the third week few streets in the metropolis of four cities and thirteen towns had escaped the firecracker fever that would climax in a mad symphony of tribute to another New Year.

One of the last locations affected was wide and affluent Roxas Boulevard. It skirted crescent-shaped Manila Bay and, for most part, had become a showcase of concrete and glass towers. The occupants of this veritable ghetto of the rich enjoyed a reassuring seaward view. Beyond the sculptured shoreline a varied collection of pleasure craft lay moored at a marina or rode at anchor on a glistening bay, the shapes of commercial shipping in the far distance. Boxy structures containing a culture palace, convention hall and a prestige hotel occupied a blunt tongue of reclaimed land lined with swaying palms. Vendors rang bells as they wheeled icecream trolleys along a waterfront promenade and gardeners tended vivid flower displays in the busy boulevard's median strip, seemingly like a floral morse code from a height. The illusion of heaven on earth had appeared almost real. Especially if one had chosen to ignore a panorama of poverty behind the line of towered wealth.

Not surprisingly, the thoroughfare was the officially designated route by which taxi drivers had expressed impressed and perspiring foreigners into the tropical city from an international airport in the southern suburbs. The visitors had usually alighted a little short of Rizal Park and outside one of a score of hotels in a tourist belt. The bed trade, and particularly the five-star establishments, had previously done well in December. This particular year, though, it

1

was different and, to the alarm of hotel management, nothing like the boom days of the preceding seven years when getting a room without a forward reservation tested travel-worn tempers, as many of the American, Japanese, Chinese, Arab, Australian and German visitors had found. This time it was not only easy to get a room but also one with a nice view of the bay or the park with the walls of the Old City and Pasig River somewhere behind.

Proximity to the park had undoubtedly been a plus for tourists. It spread over the equivalent of six city blocks and stretched inland in a fragmented green wedge from the bay. Large crowds had attested to its popularity. At first acquaintance it had been difficult to see why. The flora was nondescript and the boulevard and another major road cut the park into three sections — bayside, central and eastern — eliminating tranquillity in peak traffic hours. Two buildings with columned facades, housing the government ministries of finance and tourism, alienated large chunks. Another building serving as a repository for the national archives, a car park and defunct planetarium encroached elsewhere. Trees were confined largely to park perimeters and not infrequently were a cover for muggings or temporary shelter for the homeless.

To the further detriment of the park, the termite-ridden city's eternal love affair with concrete and masonry had left its imprint. Benches, litter bins, garden surrounds and bird lofts abounded in the drab materials. A large concrete pool featured green concrete lumps. Only from an elevated concrete platform did the shapes reveal themselves as a map. Numerous concrete paths had led to various pavilions and statues, the widest path to the park's central section where on a massive stone block a sightless form faced seaward, its back to an obelisk. Armed soldiers were always at its side then, changing guard every two hours.

However, none of this had deterred tourists. Indeed, the monument had served as a lure to the curious. The stone figure of a man standing, a book in hand, was a likeness of Jose Rizal. He was a Filipino writer shot dead on the very spot by a Spanish-supervised execution squad on December 30, 1896, just two years before revolutionaries overthrew the hated colonisers, only to be trumped by an expansionist United States posing as a Filipino ally. Since death, Rizal had reigned supreme as the people's first hero, though his days on that particular pedestal were destined to end with the upheaval the Great Revolution would bring. It was Rizal's poem "Kundiman" that had helped damn him to oblivion at his military trial where he was accused of being the living soul of the Filipino insurrection. The twelve lines of self-indictment read:

2

In the Orient beautiful
Where the sun is born
In a land of beauty
Full of enchantments
But bound in chains
Where the despot reigns
The land dearest to me
Ah! that is my country
She is a slave oppressed
Groaning in the tyrant's grips;
Lucky shall he be
Who can give her liberty

Rizal's thirty-five years of life had been ones of remarkable achievement. His genius had been evident as early as three when, under his mother's devoted tutorage, he mastered the alphabet. Two years later he could read the Spanish version of the Vulgate Bible. Aged eight, he wrote a drama in his native tongue of Tagalog. By fifteen he was a poet, painter and sculptor and at twenty-four a physician. He was credited with speaking twenty-two tongues, four of them used in his homeland and one — Chinese — in keeping with the generally unmentioned fact that part of his blood was of their race. Great as these attainments were, it was Rizal's role as a gentle apostle of nationalism that had been responsible for his place of honour. Armed only with a prolific pen he was, by his mid-twenties, in the vanguard of those forces struggling to free the country of Spanish enslavement. The ardent patriot and literary general produced poems, essays, pamphlets, newspaper articles and novels which often as not were banned by authorities and thus read secretly at night by oil lamps behind closed doors and windows. That he was successful in the end, despite the mortal victory of his enemies, was evident when, a few years after his execution on the field one day to become Rizal Park, a fellow Filipino poet, Cecilio Apostol, was able to write:

Oh redeemer of an enslaved country
In the mystery of the grave, do not cry
Heed not the brief triumph of the Spaniards
Because if a bullet destroyed your cranium
Likewise you destroyed an empire.

Away from this sobering stone reminder of the archipelago's turbulent history, the park actually had provided a number of pleasant diversions. Most popular was an outdoor cafe run by a charity for the deaf and mute and staffed by its beneficiaries. Customers would place written orders for light refreshment

3

including the celebrated *halo halo*, a tall mixture of icecream, fruit, coconut, beans and ice. Elsewhere, coloured balloons were on sale and a Chinese garden provided picnic spots. For camera clickers there were ocean sunsets of postcard fame and a fairyland of lights. And, much to the pleasure of thousands sitting before an outdoor podium or drifting along the many paths, there were the strains of a concert orchestra and the voices of guest choirs, for music was then a food to the people and the park an escape from another life, almost certainly a hell on earth.

This illusion was seen later to have been an important part of the park's appeal to the masses. Like the candle world inside the musty churches of the then overwhelmingly Catholic nation, the park was a refuge from overcrowded, slummy housing, high rents, dry taps, foul toilets, blackouts, cockroaches and mosquitoes. So bad was the situation at that time that there even existed an inflated market for the sale and purchase of the illegal shacks of rotting wood, rusty iron, plastic sheets and cardboard, collectively called home by an epidemic plague of squatters.

And the squalor within dirty walls had extended into streets too. Footpaths, if provided, were in disrepair. Rotting garbage lay uncollected in random piles, the home of flies and rats. Sedans rattled over rutted secondary roads frequently pockmarked with heaps of earth around deep trenches abandoned by defaulting contractors. Buses and passenger jeepneys belched fumes into an already smelly atmosphere. In some streets manhole covers had disappeared, stolen by scavengers hunting for saleable scrap metal. Truly, the metropolis of Manila had become a blindman's nightmare.

Of course, exceptions had existed. A fraction of the ten or so per cent who lived above the poverty line had had retreats, not only along the boulevard but in high-rise apartments crowning a new commercial cloudland known as Ayala Makati and, even further inland, in a scattering of walled estates. These enclaves, patrolled around the clock by armed security personnel, were choked with mansions, swimming pools, limousines, bodyguards, chauffeurs, maids, house boys and gardeners. Many of the residents were from the provinces where security had not been the best for some years, with a resurgence of the banditry and guerrilla activity stifled in the early seventies. Consequently, families of sugar barons from the central Visayas, timber tycoons from southern Mindanao and mineral kings from the high Cordilleras of northern Luzon had rubbed shoulders behind protective walls with the rest of Manila high society, while outside another world prevailed.

It was here again that Rizal Park had come to the rescue of some

4

in that underprivileged world, as it was a possible avenue of escape, not just for a night but a lifetime of nights. Young Filipinas had been particularly aware of this and came in droves to what was, for them, a meeting place with the world beyond the seas, represented by the tourist. They had learned by the experience of others that romances with foreigners had begun on park benches and had led to new lives in the United States, Canada, Australia and Europe. They knew dreams could really come true amid the statues if fate got a big enough push. And to snare a foreigner with the words "I do" was to have all one's prayers to the Virgin Mary answered.

For their part foreign visitors had quickly sensed this availability, which was not confined to Filipinas and, enjoying their status as temporary stars, regularly frequented the park during their stay in the metropolis. Unfortunately for intending brides quite a number of the male tourists were not so much interested in marriage as sexual souvenirs, male and female. So, girls who were willing to settle for much less had also mingled with the crowd. If they sensibly kept a low profile during the times police vehicles patrolled inside the grounds, a good living had been theirs for several years before the eventual rejections. Much more difficult had been the plight of those boys who hung around the park in what was an apprenticeship in sex before they graduated to the nearby discos and gay bars in M.H. del Pilar and A. Mabini Streets. Park police, though not exclusively heterosexual—as some fairer-skinned *mestizos* had discovered while waiting patiently on benches for clients—had been less inclined to tolerate the activities of their own sex. Inevitably, many of the boys saw the insides of police cells.

The all-night station usually host to them was two blocks from the park. Only in the severest of typhoons had the doors of the building ever closed. Some of the older boys had been more familiar with its layout than had the khaki figures who worked inside. This was because police personnel were never posted there for more than a month at a time. And it was by no administrative accident. Somehow their superiors had known of the temptations in a tourist area and had devised a rotating roster. An offshoot of this policy was that it resulted in a certain urgency and abuse in the administration of the law. And particularly so late at night.

As one callboy had said to another, also leaving the brightly-lit building in haste, "What did it cost you?"

"My wristwatch."

"Huh!" scoffed the questioner. "I gave them mine the last time."

5

"Then what did you do tonight? Give money?"

"I didn't have enough."

"So . . ."

"What else? I let a couple of them have me."

The other boy had not been surprised. He had heard such tales before. He was curious about one thing, though. "Where did they take you? That place was like a madhouse tonight."

"To a back room," he said, suddenly laughing.

"What's so funny?"

"Oh, nothing really. We had some trouble getting out of the room. The door knob fell off."

They had approached an intersection and a parting of ways. The boy who had lost his watch that night had said, "Maybe I'll see you at the disco tomorrow."

"Okay," the other had replied, drifting away. Then, in an afterthought, he had half turned and called back, "Enjoy yourself while you can."

It was advice that seemed to be the motto of those times. It was also advice certain to bring a little closer the day of reckoning. But such perceptions were strangely absent from many, many minds that particularly noisy December of yesteryear . . .

· CHAPTER ONE ·

Zacarias Campora was early. To kill time he took a stroll along the river bank. Or rather the bitumen and stone surface that lined the southern shores of Manila's Pasig on the last bend before it mingled with the South China Sea. Today the river's murk was relieved by patches of water hyacinth. Moored craft hugging both sides had snared the green and purple growth. So had the pylons of the nearby Jones Bridge which gently arched to a Chinatown wedged in the commercial clutter of the north bank. Like all the city bridges spanning the serpentine waterway it was a busy crossing and especially just then—a little before eight in the morning.

Zacarias was waiting for the Central Post Office to open. He had come early because, as everyone knew, with only three days to Christmas the place would become hopelessly crowded as the day lengthened. And it was a dreary place to spend time.

The post office had its back to the river, almost fully occupying a space between the southern approaches to the Jones Bridge and, further upstream, the MacArthur Bridge. The big building was distinguished at the front by the elevated portico of Grecian columns. From its shelter the view was of a plaza of dying trees fronted by the grimy statue of a man with a sword at his side, the lot corralled by aggressive, fuming traffic.

Though the post office doors had not yet swung open, a gathering had assembled nearby. A good many were vendors who had set up various displays. There were little stands of envelopes, pens, pencils, erasers, peanuts, soft drinks, sweets, chewing gum and tubes of glue, usually necessary to affix the post office's somewhat unsticky stamps. There were also fixers who lolled against the columns waiting for business.

All bureaucracies in Manila had fixers at the front door. Their function was to cut or circumvent red tape. Quite often they were part of the bureaucracy. In the case of the post office the role was sometimes performed by armed security guards. Anyone calling at the post office to collect a registered letter had to first produce proof of identity. No proof, no letter. Identity cards could be obtained as a result of employment, enrolment at a college or university or service with the armed forces. All outside those categories, like the unemployed, in number equivalent to at least a quarter of the city's workforce, were in trouble. They could get a residency certificate but the post office, in its wisdom, did not recognise it as sufficient even though another bureaucracy, the City Hall, issued it. So fixers thrived. For a fee they would handle everything, taking the client to the right window, signing the necessary papers and handing over the registered letter.

Zacarias, or Zac as he had been called for most of his twenty-nine years, was one of the city's unemployed. But as he ambled back to the portico in good time for the eight o'clock opening he muttered a silent prayer of thanks that he did not have to deal with people he regarded as vultures. He could ignore them because he had a passport.

Seconds after the big doors swung open Zac entered the lofty interior. He descended a stairway to the basement and went to a window where registered letters from overseas could be collected. The window was a smallish opening in a curved metal wall comprising hundreds of locked mail boxes. To Zac, it seemed to have been made for dwarfs. He stooped and peered inside to a semi-circular office. People were at work but no one was attending the window. He straightened and patiently waited.

Zac was tired. He had not slept well and as a consequence the dark patches under his spaniel eyes gave him the look of a fallen angel. Yet, despite the blemishes which had been with him since youth and the fact that now his black tousled hair was thinning ever so slightly on the crown, he still turned heads in a street.

Zac had been woken that morning by firecrackers ignited under a canal footbridge near Singalong pension where he had been living the past two months. The canal was a favourite spot for such happenings because of the resonance it provided. At this time of the year only odd puddles of foul, black sludge lay on its floor. In six months all that would change abruptly as the first of the season's typhoons swept in from the Pacific and the canals overflowed, flooding the squatter shanties lining the banks.

But even before the crackers exploded Zac's sleep had been patchy. Mosquitoes had been active, for one thing, though a more likely reason was his unresolved thoughts about the prank he would play in eight days. It had seemed harmless fun when Jojo first told him of the idea. And his friend needed an extra pair of hands. Zac had *really* wanted to be in it too, and actually begged with mock humility to be the chosen one. He was celebrating a homecoming. He was back from a Europe that, in a noisy, bustling Manila street choked with jeepneys, paled as righteously stuffy, lacking exuberance. A Europe that, despite surface appearances of incorruptibility and affluence, had disillusioned him, especially after the incident. In the days following his return he had revelled in the sights and sounds of his Manila. He had visited old friends and old haunts, discos and inexpensive hideaway restaurants. He had tasted anew the delights of the mango, inhaled the perfume of the delicate sampaguita flower, heard the clip-clop of work horses in Chinatown and watched a Manila Bay sunset. It had been a feast of the senses.

And then the days became weeks and he realised he was in another Manila but this one, conjuring up old fragmented feelings that had subconsciously lain dormant while he had been half a world away. He saw with clarity the street faces betraying weariness and resignation. Smiles were masks. Laughter was a diversion from reality. Even those few of quick, purposeful step and intent expression seemed on their way to hustle or make a buck while they still had a chance. Money or the promise of it, or even the whiff of it, was the oil that kept a suddenly shabby Manila going. Almost everyone had a problem: a train of woes and wants strung together by the common need for money, and preferably black-market American dollars, not the sagging peso. He had been regaled with countless chance-in-a-lifetime business schemes. Did he have money to lend? Sorry to ask but . . . No? Really? Didn't everyone make money before coming home? C'mon, you must be kidding! And he had heard so, so many who just wanted to get out of the country if only they . . . After an awkward silence he would learn that their sisters had married Americans, Australians or Germans and were living in Sacramento, Gulgong or Frankfurt. Maybe they could get shoe-ins as relatives. And tell me Zac, they would ask with slightly puzzled expressions, just why did you come back?

In the streets, too, Zac could see more beggars than he remembered and evidence of growing joblessness in stand-bys who lolled against walls, all the while appraising opportunities in the passing parade and giving sly digs in the ribs of companions. When he had begun job hunting and had met with nothing but disinterested responses, he had gradually realised he was now one, too. He did not admit this for several weeks, deliberately hurrying from job queue to job queue and trying not to dwell on thoughts of his dwindling funds and the rent now due at Singalong pension. But from the day he did come to terms with his situation, a creeping lethargy began to permeate his spirits. He did not go out so much. He spent more time in thought, stretched out on his hard bed or browsing through old magazines borrowed from fellow boarders.

He often visited Jojo's room in the pension when his friend was not working at the nearby San Andres markets. The prank would usually crop up in the conversation and on one occasion its planned execution was refined a little. Zac was always involved, yet with the knowledge that somehow he did not have the same initial feeling. Jojo appeared not to notice. Lately though, Zac had begun to mildly regret having committed himself, but as he was the one who had almost forced himself into the partnership did not say anything. Besides, Jojo was a friend, despite the difference in life style. For unlike Zac and just about all his other friends, Jojo was not gay.

Zac had no doubt as he stood in the post office that morning, the registered letter awaiting his signature and some action by the tardy staff was from one of those friends. Or, to be more accurate, from his former lover Ian in Spain. The previous day a notification card had been delivered to the Singalong address in Zac's absence. He had been out till late afternoon and then had no time left to get across the city. He hoped the letter had in it what he expected. What else could it be?

Zac was about to check the low window again when he felt a finger prod his stomach. He bent down to see a rather sour face framed in metal.

"I don't have all day," the clerk muttered.

Zac handed over the card.

"And your I.D."

He took a black passport from a pocket and watched the clerk scan the pages, making in addition an unnecessary inspection of visas which traced a path that had taken him to Spain and home again. Manila re-entry was dated October twenty-two.

"Wait," the man instructed, moving away from the window to a table on which were open cardboard boxes containing registered mail.

Zac glanced behind at a lengthening queue. After some minutes the man returned with an envelope.

"Thanks," Zac said affably. "And a Merry Christmas too."

The clerk was unmoved. "Next," he snapped.

Zac was still smiling as he boarded a jeepney heading south towards Singalong. The letter had been from Ian. It also contained a welcome and expected cheque, the belated proceeds from the sale in Spain of the Filipino's stamp collection. But Zac was

10

smiling for another reason. He was remembering Ian's vow never to return to a country he had called "beastly and full of bounders". He had said some other things too. However, Ian had changed his mind and, further, wanted Zac back. Ian was like that and apparently could now afford his whims, Zac mused, quite without envy.

*   *   *

Ian's surname was Essex. This would automatically cause most people meeting him the first time to assume he was English. Actually, he was a Scot, though his accent said otherwise. Ian had disliked the Scottish voice for most of his thirty-five years and in particular abhorred the pronunciation of the letter "r" with a trill of the tongue. While working in London he had taken the opportunity to shed his shame, cultivating something closer to the upstairs conversation at Buckingham Palace. Only in rare moments of excitement did he ever lapse. On his thirty-first birthday he switched his home to Villablanca on the east coast of Spain and thereby completed the break with Scotland, except for infrequent visits to a widowed mother who lived in Edinburgh. She wrote regularly but her only child was a poor correspondent.

The mailman in Villablanca thought, incorrectly, that there were two Ians living at the same address. Some days the man would deliver letters from London to Ian Essex and other days letters from Edinburgh to Ian MacPhee. The explanation was simple. Ian had legally changed his name in London but had never told his mother and relatives. Neither had he told them that he was gay. "None of their business," he would pronounce to himself. To his new friends he never mentioned his origins, and with his acquired accent they never would have guessed. In any case the two groups had never met and Ian intended that they never would. He was determined to keep his secrets and, when Zac was in Spain, always insisted on being the one to check the locked mailbox downstairs in the lobby of his apartment building. Zac only knew Ian had a mother living somewhere in Britain.

Ian's selection of a new name had not been easy. Before his final choice he had entertained Forsythe, Windsor, Buckingham, Kingsley, Churchill, Wellington and Drake. He discounted Drake after realising that it might not go down well in Spain, which he already had an eye on as a future home. Besides, on further reflection it also had an animal connotation. He dismissed Wellington as it, too, might be a controversial choice for the

Continent. Churchill was crossed off the list because of its potential to attract unwanted attention from British tourists, especially those from Edinburgh. Kingsley was very much in favour till he had an argument with a doctor who happened to have the same name. A last minute failure of courage on his part eliminated Buckingham and Windsor. So, Forsythe seemed the winner. Then he had doubts as to whether it should have an "e". He could not decide. He was about to go back to Kingsley when he saw his future name on a map.

Ian's olive skin and dark hair strongly suggested that one of his ancestors might have been a survivor from the Spanish Armada sent against England in fifteen-eighty-eight and partly claimed by the stormy Scottish coastline. In Spain the assumption was often made that he was one of their own. The Scot was aware of this too and, like a conquistador of old, had on his chin a hairy, pointed embellishment. However, the moment he uttered his first syllable all such thoughts by Spaniards would vanish. Ian had never bothered to come to grips with the language. In the four years he had lived in Villablanca he had got by quite satisfactorily, relying on the broken English of others.

By profession the man practiced accountancy and by nature frugality, in startling accordance with the national stereotype. The single exception to this creed was a peculiar passion for five-star hotels and superior cuisine while travelling. In his more honest moments of reflection, the Scot knew this one lapse from a strict budgetary approach to life was a manifestation of nostalgia for his childhood. His father, in the twilight years after retirement from government service, had with his wife and pubescent son travelled Europe extensively on the proceeds of superannuation. The choice of destination and accommodation had been left to the young Ian. His father had permitted the oddity, and approved wholeheartedly of the selections, partly as a practical lesson in geography and partly out of sheer laziness. They had seen most of Europe when he suddenly died. The death was a shock for Ian and his mother, but the depleted state of his father's bank account and subsequent adjustment in living standards an even greater one. Resentful of what he saw as his father's failing, Ian had taken a vow of frugality. In the adult years since, it had cost him many friends. It did not matter. He would *not* desist from his course. He would walk rather than ride, usually read discarded newspapers and live on porridge. If he had overnight guests in his high-rise apartment on a hill behind a beach in Villablanca, the hot water was switched off the minute they left. One visitor who suggested his shortsighted

12

host was being vain in not publicly wearing spectacles found the water cold hours before departure.

In keeping with all this, the Scot's wardrobe was a sparse collection of items, some borrowed from friends and never returned. In time, neither did the friends. As well, the occasional guests forgetfully left behind socks or underpants, or both, to the delight of Ian. Zac was a contributor too. He had the misfortune to be the same size, right down to the shoe fitting, and had lost to the wardrobe a pair of sneakers and jeans, a bathrobe and several shirts. The Filipino had even been asked to lend his watch temporarily when Ian had business appointments. Ian had owned a watch once. It was a bargain he had picked up at a Spanish bus station from a man who said he was a traveller needing money to get home. Two weeks later the watch had stopped. It had been taken to a repair shop in Villablanca where the owner had contemptuously glanced at it and pronounced it dead.

Ian always practiced travel economies too. One of the brief visits to his mother had been by what was advertised at a Villablanca tourist agency as an express coach. Normally he travelled by air after carefully shopping around for agencies selling cut-rate tickets. Ian soon discovered Villablanca had few. As nothing had been available at the time required he had opted for a seat on the cheaper bus. He suspected he had made a terrible mistake when a fat man returning home to Manchester squeezed into the space next to him. It was not surprising that his had happened, for the Scot seemed to have the regular misfortune of acquiring undesirable travelling companions. Ian had sat next to mothers with crying babies, compulsive talkers, sufferers of halitosis, garlic breaths, farters and so on. One queasy stomach had even emptied its contents over his trousers. Soon after the Villablanca bus to London got away the Manchester traveller had slipped off his shoes and added smelly feet to the list. Ian had buried his nose in a paper bag of food taken along to save money. However, the supply of boiled eggs, salted crackers and fruit had run out soon after the French border. Thereafter he had refused to pay what he considered exorbitant prices at roadside cafes and steadily grew weak from hunger. At the Channel crossing, a full day after leaving Villablanca, he had taken up the Jewish cry of "Never again". On the return trip to Spain he flew and forthwith avoided mention of the painful experience, putting it on a growing list of distasteful subjects which, not surprisingly in view of earlier events, was headed by poverty. Such talk could even anger him, like a red flag is supposed to enrage a bull. To friends and lovers he made his attitude plain enough. "I don't want to hear about those sorts of things," he would announce from the comfort of his Villablanca apartment while focusing binoculars on a luxury motor yacht moored in a Turneresque sea.

Villablanca was an Iberian Miami if one could disregard the lack of waterways and the addition of a curved backdrop of rugged, barren mountains. Skyscrapers had sprouted almost the entire length of its crowded beaches which flanked a low rocky headland, like wings on a seagull. The rock supported the old quarter, a jumble of roof tiles and alternately sun-drenched and shadowy walls from which balconies jutted over chasms founded on steep, zigzag steps. Where the old quarter bordered the new, touristy shops and restaurants flourished, serving both flanks of the resort.

Foreign tourists tended to congregate in national patterns. The northern end attracted the French, Belgians, Dutch and Swedes. The British could be found immediately on the southern side of the rock with the Germans at the extreme south. There, skyscrapers gave way to expensive villas. The Spanish lived on the rock or behind the line of skyscrapers that now hid their Mediterranean and blocked its balmy breeze.

Ian's rejection of his motherland had a curious aspect because in some ways Villablanca was not unlike home, weather aside. It was hard not to be so reminded at least once every day in the tourist resort, on even the briefest excursion out of doors. One could ride a bus and hang on to support straps while hearing familiar voices from Edinburgh, Manchester or London. An English-language weekly provided news of Villablanca happenings involving resident and holidaying Britons, a lengthy column on Westminster skull-duggeries, the latest doings in the royal nursery and recipes for Anglo-Saxon palates. On the animal front, kennels operated night and day and regardless of silly fiestas and siestas. Mobility could be obtained at Victoria Rent-a-car. Meals could be eaten at fish and chip shops, the Merry Magpie and the Geordie Tavern. A night out could be had in the dining room of the Hotel Titanic, a place which had, aptly enough, a colour scheme amounting to a gastronomic disaster.

While Ian had no objections to this white-anting of Iberia, he most certainly held strong views on the fee charged by a Villablanca bank in converting a sterling cheque to pesetas. He had complained to a teller and the man had just grinned. Back at the apartment he had brooded at his treatment till Zac had said, "If you feel so strongly about it, why don't you write to that local paper?" Ian had done so immediately and was particularly pleased with the punch line, "I had always believed before this outrageous episode that bank robbers operated from the customer's side of the counter." Ian had posted it off the next day and later even bought succeeding issues but it had never appeared. Only his beloved summer routine had helped him to forget what he believed to be a slight.

The Scot's day began around nine. After a shower and spartan breakfast he would don swim shorts and thongs and set out on his a.m. walk. On the way to nowhere in particular, he would meticulously inspect restaurant menus displayed in window fronts, looking for culinary bargains. After that he would head for the beach where he loved to feel the sun on his tanned back, the soft sand under his feet. Next, a quick dip and back to the shore where a few minutes of standing in basking rays would substitute for a towelling. And all the better if probing toes found coins beneath the beach's trodden surface. The afternoons were reserved for business, mainly property deals financed with capital acquired from the estate of a forgotten and late uncle and the modest savings of a short career in accountancy. And so the years had gone by. Then, restless for a mate, he had visited Manila where he met Zac at a disco. A mutual attraction had quickly developed and Ian had not found it difficult to persuade the Filipino to give up his bar job in a Manila hotel for a life in Spain. Six months after the Scot's return with Zac, the bottom fell out of the property market and, in time, Ian's bank account. Too many quarrels later, the pair's relationship was in a similarly depressed state. Inevitably, came a break-up. Now, suddenly, Ian had written of extraordinary luck. Everything had sold. Money was rolling in and the Scot was returning in the new year to Manila to talk about a fresh start. "How about it, old chap?" he had written.

*   *   *

Zac lurched as the jeepney driver deftly swerved to miss a young road vendor. None of the passengers said anything about the incident. It was too commonplace. Then, the jeepney was squealing to a stop for a red light. Zac watched the youths weave between vehicles with their wooden trays of cigarettes, armfuls of newspapers and sampaguita necklaces. A boy wearing a towel like an Arab sold cigarettes to the jeepney driver. He was one of the luckier ones because sales had been few. Soon a clickety-clack rhythm loudly asserted itself as the unoccupied, grinning figures slid back and forth the slotted lids of money boxes affixed to every tray. To

Zac the spectacle had always held a certain fascination and now, after his time in Spain, he saw them as child matadors who daily battled masses of metal bulls to the accompaniment of castanets. Impatient drivers were suddenly blaring horns, the light having changed to green. The jeepney was moving forward again, the clickety-clacks fading and the vendor incident quite forgotten. Instead, Zac was remembering that other incident months earlier in an office in Spain . . .

For Britons, Villablanca had one drawback. It did not have the services of a British consulate. The nearest one was in the even larger city of San Fernando. Getting there from the resort meant ninety tedious minutes in a bus or train. The buses were air-conditioned, a necessity in summer. The trains were not and, worse, seemed to suck flies into the carriages from the barren countryside that separated the two centres. The train was cheaper, which probably explained why Spaniards occupied nearly all the seats. The only tourists were either adventurous or ignorant and in the latter case, not for long.

Zac had to journey to San Fernando too, being in need of a visa for a planned London stopover on the way home. Riding an early morning bus on which every seat was taken he entered the city as inhabitants trudged to work. From the bus depot he passed along narrow back streets, frequently having to press against walls as cars edged past. Suddenly he was out of the meanness and into a sunny plaza. He found the consulate in a newish building on the far side. A lift off a small lobby did not appear to be working so he mounted an unlit stairway to the second floor. The first thing he noticed as he entered the office was a sign on the counter, "Official receipts must be given for all transactions." Then he saw behind the counter a pasty-faced man, possibly in his early thirties, wearing a rumpled pinstriped shirt with a loose black tie. A matronly woman with dyed blonde hair typed in the background. Zac stated his business and was given a form to fill in, which he did in the comfort of a chair by a potted palm. Back at the counter, the man quickly eyed the form and Zac's passport and said, "You'll be interviewed shortly." Twenty minutes and several glossy magazines later, the man motioned Zac to follow. The Filipino went through a swinging gate at the side of the counter and past the typist, then through a side door leading into a carpeted office.

"Take a seat," the official said, closing the door before taking one himself behind a large desk.

"You're a long way from home, Mr Campora."

"Yes, er —"

"Didn't I say? Pardon me, Miller."

"Millet."

"No, Miller. With an r."

"Oh, sorry. I'm not yet use to English names."

"Well, you'll have your chance with a visa, eh?" Miller laughed politely, revealing bad teeth. "Now, Mr Campora, how long do you plan staying?"

"About a week. I'm visiting a friend. It's all in the form."

Miller shifted papers on his desk and studied the application. "Hmmm," he murmured. "Your Spanish address is Villablanca, I see. Nice little spot."

"Yes. A friend's place."

"How long have you been there?"

Zac calculated. "Nearly a year."

"How *nice*," Miller said almost as if pleased. "Is your friend, er—"

"Mr Essex," Zac replied, immediately regretting it, though not knowing why.

"Yes, Mr Essex," the man repeated. "Is he a resident?"

"He's lived in Spain for years."

"He has a very English name. I suppose he's English."

"That's right," Zac replied, wondering what this could possibly have to do with his visa application.

"Actually a lot of us Britons live here now," Miller was saying. "Can't blame them really. And it's a lot cheaper by far." And after a pause, "What does your friend do for a living?"

"He has business interests," the Filipino said guardedly.

"Ah, yes. A great place for business."

Zac was silent. He glanced at his watch, doubting there would be time to catch the midday bus back to Villablanca. He would have an hour's wait for the next.

Miller was studying the form again, his free hand abstractedly tapping the desk. Then he looked up at Zac, cleared his throat and asked, "Is Mr Essex gay?"

The Filipino sat stunned. He could hardly believe what he had heard. At home, he would have expected this sort of question. Nothing would surprise him there. But this was Europe. This was a British consulate.

At length when he felt able to reply, he said coldly, "You'll have to ask him that."

Miller politely laughed again. "You're lucky having friends in Europe, aren't you?"

"What do you mean?" he replied tersely.

"Well, it's a good place to have friends, isn't it, if you like to travel."

"I suppose so," Zac agreed, deciding his want for a visa was greater than his anger at the conversation.

"Of course," Miller said, getting to the point, "*before* I issue a visa I'll have to telex Manila to check your credentials, a necessary routine. Naturally, the telex will have to be paid for."

"Naturally," the Filipino said, feeling he was already in Manila.

Miller flashed his rotten teeth. "Could you pay now, Mr Campora? Then we can avoid delays. You can give me a ring in about a week. Everything should be ready by then."

Seeing Zac's wallet at the ready, Miller cooed, "That will be three thousand pesetas, thank you."

Zac handed over a wad of notes and in exchange was given a slip of paper torn from a receipt book. Outside in the square, as pigeons fluttered overhead, he unfolded the slip and read, "Twelve hundred pesetas on account of visa fees."

* * *

Singalong pension retained a reasonable air of outward dignity in what was a scrappy, crowded neighbourhood. The elongated, two-storey structure had arisen from a shattered and smouldering Manila soon after the Pacific war. So had the pension's immediate neighbours, though by the accumulated evidence of unpainted surfaces overlain by decades of dust and grime, a much greater antiquity could be assumed. The area, like most of the city south of the Pasig, bore little resemblance to what had once existed there. It had been the preserve of the well-to-do, especially nearer the bayside which had boasted a fine collection of gracious homes set in gardens of bougainvillea, oleander, flame and banyan trees.

If the cream and green pension exterior had any claim to being an echo of that past, the interior did not. From the moment of passing under a line of fern baskets decorating the slab-faced entrance, all pretensions vanished. Downstairs and upstairs it was a maze of passages off which were tiny rooms. Some had no windows to the outside. Toilet and shower cubicles were tucked away without pattern in odd corners or partly under stairways. Back rooms had a view of a canal and footbridge, front rooms of the street and building opposite. On one flank windows had no views, just the wall of a large warehouse. On the other side was a laneway linking the street and canal footbridge.

Zac had just crossed the footbridge and was turning the corner of the lane into the street when he almost bumped into Luz.

18

"What's the hurry?" he asked the fat woman.

"I'm going to get the police this time," she spat, her beady eyes almost lost in a contortion of brows and bared teeth.

Zac suspected the reason. "Do you think you should?" he cautioned, secretly alarmed that almost anything could happen once the police were involved.

"It's the only way. If I don't do something now I'll never get my money."

"Why don't you have a word to the manageress about it. She might—"

"Pah! Perla?" she exploded. "I've just been to see her. A waste of time. Do you know what she says? It's not her business. And she says I can't collect debts in the pension. Probably she wants first peck for unpaid rent."

"Maybe," Zac conceded, though unwilling to say anything too critical of Perla, whom he liked. And to soothe Luz, "The trouble really is that you are too kind. Why do you do it? Let them buy their food somewhere else."

"I know, I know," she cried, a little mollified. "But they come to me and say they are so hungry and they haven't eaten all day. Stories like that. What can I do? I give them food and they promise to pay as soon as they can. And the next time it's the same story. Till I suddenly stop seeing them."

"Yes, it's happened to me too," Zac lied. "I lent one of the boys some money and haven't got it back."

"Oh?" said the vendor with interest. "What are you going to do?"

"Well, Luz, it's Christmas and that's their best time. I know I'll get paid so I'm waiting a little longer."

"That's all very well but you're not owed as much as me."

"Better to wait than bring in the police. At least you'll get your money in time. How does it help you if they're arrested? They can't earn anything in jail."

"That's where they should be," the woman retorted. "All of them."

Zac laughed. "The jails wouldn't be big enough."

Luz was silent in thought. "Perhaps you're right. I'll wait a few days longer. And if they don't pay by then, God help them," she said and waddled off down the laneway to the footbridge.

*　　*　　*

Zac's room was at the back of the pension. It seemed to him what a prison cell might be like. It was small with a mean, barred window at the end farthest from the door. Through smudgy, louvred glass

19

he could see the canal rim and footbridge. On one side of the room was a bed, high over which protruded a varnished shelf holding three paperbacks and an empty cup. Behind the open door was a closet which Zac always locked when he was out of the pension, such was the rate of thievery. By a grey wall opposite the bed stood a wooden chair and electric fan, its plastic blades partly obscuring a black framed print of a hero, handsome Jose Rizal, hair sleek and moustache clipped, above high collar, coat and tie.

Zac switched on the fan. A soft whirr filled the room as he stripped to his briefs and draped an already sweaty shirt on the back of the chair. He flopped to the bed intending to only rest, but found himself drifting towards sleep, his mind revolving around and around Ian and the apartment in Villablanca and, for some reason, the abnoxious, teenage son of the caretaker whose rudeness was the talk of all the tenants. Good mornings were greeted with surly stares; a visit to the caretaker's rooms—to have a message passed on to his temporarily absent father—with a slammed front door. The boy did not care how loud he slammed the door or how close to it you were standing. Bang, bang. He had no feelings for others. Bang! Bang!

Zac sat up with a start. The noise seemed to fill the small room. He felt whoosy, having risen too quickly. He braced himself with a hand against a wall. He became aware of shouting outside and, getting up, looked beyond the window. Two figures were leaning over the footbridge railing, apparently peering under the structure.

Zac heard one say, "Go somewhere else. Not here. Some of the boarders are night workers." He knew that voice, and when the man lifted his head was not surprised to see Jojo. The other man, however, he did not recognise.

A youthful chant of, "Killjoy, killjoy," floated to the window.

"Forget it," Zac heard Jojo's mustachioed and balding companion say. "*Gago.*"

Jojo spat over a railing. "Was I ever so silly, Laya?"

The other laughed gruffly. "How would I know?"

The pair moved on in the direction of the pension and passed from sight.

When Jojo entered Zac's room a few minutes later he was unaccompanied and apparently exasperated.

"How long has the water been off?" he asked Zac, who by now had donned shorts and was back on the bed re-reading Ian's letter.

"I didn't know it was. I haven't been back long myself."

Jojo threw a newspaper to the chair and sought a space at the end of the bed. He sighed and ran a mutilated hand back over a

20

closely cropped head that seemed largely composed of high prominent cheek bones. Jojo was an Igorot, a people whose homeland was in the mountainous north.

"I only have an hour. I wanted a shower before I go back to the markets," Jojo said.

Zac studied the sinewy form at the end of the bed. Lugging sacks had certainly kept Jojo in shape. That and his friend's stint in the army. He watched as Jojo got a cigarette out of a pack and deftly lit it. The loss of those fingers on his left hand made little difference. Most things he did seemed unaffected. Only when it came to tying knots did he admit difficulty. Of course, the Igorot said nothing but curses had been heard more than once. "There's hardly any pressure even when it's running," Zac said, in consolation. "I had to use a bucket this morning."

Jojo shook his head in disgust and flicked a spent match floorward.

"It must be a blackout in an area affecting the water pumps," Zac suggested. "The power is okay. The fan's working."

"For now."

"Yeah, that's right. We're having three or four blackouts a day in the pension now."

"And everywhere else."

"No, not *everywhere*," Zac said, enjoying a puzzled face opposite. "Not in the tourist belt."

Jojo laughed. "Or the palace."

Their merriment filled the room. Then Zac said, "Why are we laughing? God, it's no joke."

A silence followed, with each lost in unspoken thoughts. Gradually the wail of passing sirens intruded, replacing the fan's whirr. Jojo exhaled smoke slowly and, gesturing at the opened letter on the bed, said, "Ian?"

"Uh-huh. He says he's coming back for a visit."

Jojo nodded. He knew about Ian and something of Zac's affairs. He did not care about Zac's orientation one way or another. Manila was like that. "When?"

"Oh, maybe next month. You know what Ian's like. Changes his mind every day."

Jojo did not really know Ian that well, but had heard enough bits and pieces to form a poor opinion of the man. In any case, he did not like foreigners. The ones he had met seemed crazy or were full of their own importance. Self-centred and arrogant. He remembered that American on the bus to Angeles City where a lot of off-duty servicemen went. They hadn't been on the road five minutes when

21

the man shouted to the driver to turn down the music. "Can't hear myself damn well think," the American had loudly complained. Everybody had been humiliated and the driver the most. He had turned off the music rather than just keep it low. No one would have been able to hear it like that anyway. The bus rattles would have drowned the sound. Who didn't want music when they travelled? What did these foreigners have in their blood? Who did they think they were? The masters?

"Ian says he's back in the money now," Zac continued. "Business has picked up. He wants me to return with him to Spain."

"Will you?"

"A few weeks ago I would have laughed at the suggestion. The way things are turning out here I'm not so sure. I'd better get a job soon or I'm going to be in trouble."

Jojo flicked ash to the floor, not very impressed with what he was hearing. But he said, "You might find work soon. There's still some about."

Zac sat up a little straighter. "Work? Where? I can't even get a hearing. Maybe I should have rich relatives who can pull strings."

"That would help," his companion admitted.

Another silence developed before Zac said, half in jest, "Probably I should copy Luz." And as an afterthought, "If I can find a space in the streets. There're so many now they outnumber everyone else."

Jojo got up and went to the window where he threw out the cigarette butt. "She does more than that."

"What do you mean?"

"She lends money."

"With interest?"

"Why else? She doesn't do anything for nothing."

"But that sort of money lending is illegal."

"So's corruption."

"But she could get caught. Someone's going to complain eventually."

"So she has to grease a few palms, put aside a little for *pulis* expenses."

Zac remembered the morning's conversation. "Right now she's thinking of getting them on to the boys. They've got her upset again over unpaid meals. I managed to talk her out of doing anything for a few days. It'll give me time to warn them. I don't think they realise just how worked up she is. If they could have seen—"

"Wait," Jojo said, his hand commanding silence.

22

"What is it?"

"Wait."

Zac looked around, seeking an indication of what was going on.

"There," his companion said, rising from the bed. "The picture. It's moving." Rizal was indeed moving, gently rotating against the wall.

"Let's go outside," Zac advised. "It's safer out there."

Outside the fern baskets they waited with others for the tremor to pass. Inside, it was more eventful. The pension acquired a new crack. A vase broke in room fifty-one. Lop-sided pictures were everywhere. The newspaper that Jojo had thrown to the chair in room seven slipped to the floor. In so doing it unfolded, revealing a downpage item of considerable importance to the man it most affected. The ribbon heading read, "Editor under house arrest for subversion."

· CHAPTER TWO ·

Jojo Bangse-il's room was upstairs on the side furthest from the footbridge. Its window faced the warehouse wall of galvanised iron and consequently a naked light bulb dangling from the ceiling worked overtime. Though Jojo had been living in the pension for thirteen months, none of the other boarders knew much about him. Even Zac's knowledge of Jojo's background was so sketchy he would have been surprised to learn his friend had once been a runaway. He did not talk of it but in his fifteenth year the Igorot had left a village home near Bontoc, seeking brighter lights in the mountain city of Baguio. He had stayed less than a year before drifting to the lowlands and Manila. There he found survival tough and, lying about his age, enlisted in the army where he adopted and kept the cropped hair style. The Igorot had been glad to leave four years later with an honourable discharge, even if it was at the cost of three fingers lost through another's incompetence at a rifle range. He was glad, because by then he was certain he was saying goodbye to an organisation that was anything but honourable: the infantile yet cruel initiations, the arrogance of officers, the rackets . . . the disturbing stories he had heard. Once he had been posted to an illegal night-time checkpoint on a country road used regularly to transport farm produce. The officer-in-charge, Captain Fernandez, and Sergeant Batobato had organised an unofficial toll collection, "a *tong* party" they jokingly called it. Afterwards Jojo had refused his share and Captain Fernandez had reacted with a long, cold stare at the shaven private. Jojo had never been detailed similarly again. He was excluded and he was glad. He had no desire to be an *aswang*, sucking the blood of the helpless.

Jojo had told Zac of some things after they became friends while serving behind the same bar in a Manila hotel. However, Jojo had dropped one too many glasses and had moved on to other jobs before manning the San Andres market stall owned by a Chinese. The pair had continued their friendship despite the separations and often had some prank in mind. The best had been when they threw a headless mannequin off the Jones Bridge and later, from the river bank, watched a police rescue drama unfold.

24

But there was *much* more that Jojo could have told Zac whose life, from the moment of birth in the farm community of Baza, near the west coast of northern Luzon, to his experience in Spain, was truly an open book. For one thing, the Igorot could have explained why he shunned films and TV; why his room shelf never held a book or even a paperback; why he never talked about his home and relatives as other boarders often did to bored room neighbours who had heard it all too often before.

The reason went back to Jojo's Baguio days. He befriended a man who planted ideas, though it would take time for these to work themselves to the surface of the Igorot's mind and gradually be put into practice. The friend, whose first name he remembered as Leo, was perhaps fifteen years older and in his early thirties. They met at a cock-fight, secretly organised in an outer *barrio* behind Castro's canteen. Later Leo had shown him a red book of quotations. Leo said it was the thoughts of the Chinese revolutionary, Mao Tse-tung, whom Jojo had vaguely heard of but forgotten. Leo had sworn the youth to secrecy, much to the latter's unconcealed amusement, saying possession of the book was illegal. It was such a *little* book and Jojo had reasoned his friend was exaggerating. Jojo had found the contents interesting enough, but it was not till he was well into his army service that remembered snatches seemed suddenly *indelible* in his mind.

Particularly the words, "Power comes out of the barrel of a gun." Time and again he saw its truth: the fearful faces of *provincianos*, strikers in picket lines, detainees arrested on presidential command and held in army compounds. Yet drunken soldiers discharging rifles in cafes escaped censure. People were too afraid to report them. And if a few did, the worst thing that usually resulted was a transfer to another area where the same incident would occur again. Yes, *he* really knew where power came from.

Another remembered quotation had puzzled him initially. Why should "Too many books drown the mind?" What did it mean? How could it be? Hadn't he been told often enough it was the way of the future? That if books were read, one day he would be a leader of men? And then it was while on leave in Manila one evening, in a nearly-empty beer garden, that he became aware of the most beautiful sunset he had ever seen. The sun was sinking into Manila Bay and the water appeared on fire. He had a sudden urge to share the moment and mentioned it to an unoccupied waiter who had his head buried in a book. The waiter had looked up briefly, said nothing and resumed reading. Jojo felt almost insulted. He checked an impulse to pull the head up by the hair and force him to look. Jojo felt angry, then just disgusted. He spat on the ground and left. After that he had looked at bowed heads and understood. He even got a little contemptuous of books and universities, lumping them with TV and movies. He didn't want to read or sit before images. He wanted to *do* things.

The brutal truth of the third dictum, "Blank minds make superior canvas," had not become apparent till the time he was stationed at Camp Aguinaldo in Quezon City. In a washroom he had had a chance meeting with a relative and learned his grandfather was dying. He got compassionate leave and made the bus journey back to his mountain village. He was grateful that he had those final days with the old man and for something else on the return trip: the realisation of just how stupidly gullible, how *tarantado*, relatives and villagers had appeared to him after all those years. A lot of *provincianos* were like that and he knew he had been one of them, a blank mind. How many untruths had he been told? How many superstitions? He used to believe in the power of the *anting-anting*. The army had changed that. When a bullet fired by a drunken soldier smashed Corporal Pilapil's brain the *anting-anting* didn't save him. All the believers who saw the bloody amulet strung around his neck walked away different men. No one who had seen the evidence told midnight stories, in the dark of bivouac tents, about the power of the *anting-anting* again . . .

As a consequence of these somewhat different thoughts Jojo did not have much to do with the other boarders. Zac was the single visitor to Jojo's room, which was entered via a small recess off a hall. Despite the restrictions, the space allowed a long, narrow mirror. It was a popular spot for Jojo's immediate neighbours to gather. This always happened in the daytime because the halls were poorly lit at night when, in any case, these particular roomers were at work. They usually returned in the hours before dawn and rarely got up much before midday.

Jojo's neighbours were callboys, a loose description of any male capable of selling his body for sex. There were so many in rooms off that section of hall that other boarders often referred to it as Queen Street.

Jojo's contact with them, usually on his day off, was as an unseen audience to hallway conversations.

"Darling," a Narcissus would coo before his reflection. "I had an awww-ful time last night. Aww-ful. Nothing happened."

"Same here," the other would yawn.

"How long is this going to *continue*?"

26

"Should get better soon."

"God, I hope so. The rent's due next week."

Another yawn.

"My God, is that a grey hair?"

"Uh? Let me look." Silence. "Move your head a bit. No, not that way. Yes, that's better."

"Well? Is it?"

"Yup."

"My God! Pull it out. Quick."

"Oh, everyone has a freaky grey hair or two."

"No, pull it out."

"Okay, okay."

"Ouch."

"Well, darling, you *told* me to."

"My God, you seem to be *enjoying* it."

Laughter.

"What's happening?"

"Oh, Carlo. You're up early . . . for once." Giggles. "Lito has been torturing me."

More laughter. More voices. Noisy and unintelligible.

Some of the boys had small dogs as pets and their yaps would add to the commotion, though they were never present long. While the pension manageress—known to all as Perla—had no prohibition on them, factors like disease and hunger culled numbers. Other things happened too. One puppy was washed, combed, perfumed, cuddled and kissed every day for a week till on the eighth day of residence it mysteriously vanished, about the same time as a group of visiting callboys departed.

And dogs were not the only creatures in residence. One boy kept an aviary on the sill of his top-floor window. He was distressed one morning to discover that in his absence, some birds had failed to survive an overnight typhoon. On another occasion three birds had simply disappeared from the cage, and the suspicion was that someone in the neighbourhood had shinned up a drainpipe to put dove on the family menu. The thought was voiced that Singalong's cats might have been responsible till someone laughingly pointed out the absence of bloodied feathers.

The skinny cats roamed the halls as unpaid ratters. Their numbers varied according to the ratio of births to deaths. It was never less than ten and once seventeen were counted. The kittens would emerge into a vicious world of competition for food and survival. They would wander halls and meow pathetically at food odours coming from the slit between floor and door. Some boarders took pity on the shaking bundles of fur and bone and would throw a few scraps. Older cats lurking in the shadows would dart forward and snatch the offerings.

Some cats bore tell-tale signs of battle. Torn ears were common. Two had tail stumps and one had lost an eye. At night the fights and fornications in the halls and stairways would keep wakeful minds off mosquitoes swarming in from the canal. For boarders who worked in the day and needed their sleep it was often too much. In murderous mood they would rise from sweaty beds and fling buckets of water in all directions, turning corridors into carpets of bedraggled fur. The peace was temporary. By the time a boarder had returned to bed the refreshed animals were usually at it again. However, none of this ever seemed to bother the boys, probably because they kept similar hours to the cats.

Their work day began in the afternoon with a shared taxi ride to one of the airconditioned shopping centrès. There they joined hundreds of rivals from other callboy colonies and an even greater number of novices, some playing truant from the schoolyard. All were looking for prospects, preferably moneyed foreigners. The callboys were more brazen, dispensing knowing winks and suggestive tongue movements, and usually triumphed over the amateurs. On odd occasions they even recognised former foreign clients laden with parcels to take home across the sea. The men would consult watches, mentally juggle holiday timetables, and say, "Come over to my hotel suite at four o'clock." Apart from the financial reward, the boys were only too happy as the assignation meant indulgence in all the things life denied them: hot showers, air-conditioning, television, telephone, refrigerators and comfortable furnishings. At night the scores of gay bars and discos in the tourist district of Ermita adjoining Rizal Park were home for the boys, though the colony had a preference for El Torro gay bar and the nearby Milky Way disco. There, they would drink or dance while hustling business. Later, luckier ones would go with preferably foreign partners to air-conditioned hotel rooms while the rest pooled pesos for a taxi through dark, dingy streets to the pension where they would endure another sweaty sleep.

*   *   *

The boys often shared rooms at Singalong to reduce the cost of rent, the payment of which was a constant struggle. From time to time a few did achieve single-room status if they had a generous lover. Or if their room mate took a holiday with a client at an out-of-town resort. But generous lovers had a nasty habit of becoming

28

mean or unfaithful, or of simply fading from the scene, and holidays always ended. A contract, which each boy had to sign before moving in, stipulated that the maximum room occupancy was two. This condition was often broken, with as many as five crowding in for the night. Boarders had to pay a month in advance and another month's rent as deposit. This would be refunded only when they left the pension and if the room was in satisfactory condition. If they fell behind in rent the room would be locked and all possessions inside were forfeit till they were out of arrears. Further, they would be expelled from the pension if they were found to have broken any of the many house rules. Thus, concealment of transgressions became quite an art.

Unlike most other tenants in Singalong the boys were always changing rooms. Sometimes it was a purely geographic move. Rooms downstairs were regarded as inferior. Those upstairs caught the faint night breezes which made sleep easier. Rooms near toilet and shower cubicles were unpopular because of smells and were always vacated if something better came up. The front and the back rooms were the ultimate because they had views. Usually, however, the moves were the result of shifts in relationships. A room mate could eventually become a bore, a thief or a liar, too untidy, miserly or gossipy. Someone else could become a confidant, understanding, cooperative, reliable and even desirable. At some time or other just about everybody had shared a room with everybody.

The youngest in the colony was Jessie, just sixteen. Like most of the others he had begun his trade in Rizal Park when twelve. His experience was common enough. Jessie was absorbed in a comic when an elderly European approached and began a friendly conversation. Within the hour Jessie was in the man's hotel room overlooking the park. The boy was given alcohol. After two glasses Jessie felt dizzy and lay down on a big, soft bed. When the European began undressing him with fumbling, cold hands, Jessie did not object. Compared to what the boy had previously endured in his short life, the experience was merely a curiosity. At that time Jessie was living with his parents, six brothers and three sisters in a squatter's shack on the northern side of the metropolis in the slum hell of Tondo. The collection of scrap materials called home was in a spot shunned even by most squatters. It was next to a dump. When the wind blew from the south an overpowering stench made life almost unbearable. Nevertheless, for Jessie's family and hundreds of others it was a means of survival. Daily, after the dump trucks had disgorged their stinking loads, the families would rummage through the piles, ignoring swarms of flies, cockroaches and rats. They would look for bottles, plastic containers, wrappings or anything of minute value. When they had amassed enough the lot would be sold to junk merchants in Chinatown. The dump had enabled Jessie's family to survive the seven years they had lived on its perimeter, refugees from poverty in the provinces. When Jessie graduated from the park to El Torro he shifted to Singalong pension so he would not have to explain to his parents why he kept such late hours. Jessie's biggest triumph so far was to be given more money than he had ever seen by a trusting Swiss intern. "For your education," the sleek, handsome callboy was told. Jessie lost the lot at a casino in one night. "There'll be more," he casually philosophised later. The Singalong boys called him the new Superstar.

Tommy was nineteen and an exotic youth even by the standard of a nation as diverse in racial makeup as the Philippines. His mother was half Japanese and his father quarter Spanish. The mixture had resulted in a striking appearance, the eyes hinting of samurai, the golden skin and bronzed hair suggestive of a young pharoah. As Tomas he had come to Manila from Cebu about eighteen months earlier for a commerce course at one of the city's many business colleges but had quickly become bored with his studies. However, he did not find Manila's night life as dull, especially the gay scene. Increasingly it became the focus of almost all his activity to the dismay of an uncle and aunt with whom he was staying. The youth was sitting in a street cafe one night with his friends when a foreigner of Arab appearance wandered over from a nearby table and said to him, "Excuse me, are you a boy or girl?"

Tommy was not offended and laughed. The foreigner introduced himself as Feisal, a businessman from Baghdad, and invited Tommy and his friends to the hotel where he was staying. In Feisal's suite the boys were introduced to several other Arabs from Baghdad. Feisal proposed that the others go with their partners to their various rooms. Tommy and Feisal were soon alone. Feisal produced an unfamiliar tube and invited the youth to inhale its contents. He was reluctant at first, but after repeated assurances of its harmlessness did so. Tommy remembered becoming extremely light-headed and bathed in sweat though unaware a now-naked Feisal had undressed him. He did vividly recollect being sat on the Arab's lower belly and almost simultaneously registering an excruciating pain that caused him to scream. Feisal, however, ignored him and gripping the youth's torso began bellowing so loudly that Tommy temporarily forgot the agony. Afterwards the Arab gave him a lot of money.

The youth thought again of his experience when he got a letter three weeks later from his parents in Cebu saying they were ceasing his allowance as they were aware their son was not attending classes and that he should return home immediately. Tommy did not worry unduly. He had found another way to get money, much more than the amount his parents had sent each month. When Tommy's concerned uncle questioned him a few weeks after the arrival of the Cebu letter as to how he was managing to survive so well the youth decided to move out and a day later did. Tommy roomed in various boarding houses but found them either too dear or too lonely. A gay friend suggested Singalong pension and, though he regarded the place as no bargain, found it handy to his night haunts and moved in. It was inevitable in Singalong that the other boys soon became aware of Tommy's popularity with Arab visitors. Thus he became known as the Camel.

Martin had been pensioned off that year after an affair with an American engineer. For two years the two had lived on the seventh floor of a comfortable hotel run by a Chinese syndicate. Long-term guests got a generous cut. The night after Martin's twenty-third birthday, which was celebrated at a restaurant on del Pilar, he was given a golden handshake and the first instalment by cheque of a monthly allowance, sufficient for him to live in a boarding house. The engineer, who said he yearned for the crisp air of his native Vermont, shifted away from city smog to a select housing estate where the air was more tolerable. To Martin's surprise they continued to meet every two weeks or so for a luncheon where Roderick—he did not respond to abbreviations like Rod—talked casually of an eventual return to Vermont and Martin of life at Singalong pension. What Martin did not say was that he had slid into debt and had resorted to hustling for business at El Torro and gay discos. Lately the luncheons had been on a monthly basis and Martin had been worried at the implications.

Santiago was the pension's good guy. Everyone liked the boy with the Prince Valiant haircut, his good nature and easy ways. An old Spaniard who owned an art gallery on Mabini had gradually come to recognise the young man's worth when the latter dropped in every now and then to talk to his parrot. The bird had many visitors. After all, it was practically famous for its vocabulary especially the screeched word, "*Bakla*," Tagalog for gay. The old man had decided to take Santiago "under the wing", as he liked to quip, and pay the boy's tuition fees at a business college. Santiago was doing reasonably well with his shorthand and typing, when he managed to wake in time for afternoon classes. As the cheerful Santiago was prone to burst into melodious song in the halls of Singalong pension and as he was, in a way, being kept by the old man, the other boys called him the Bird.

Lito and Ace had been lovers. These days they just shared the room rent. Ace was booked to fly to Jogjakarta on Christmas Day to join his Chicago boyfriend Nelson who had sent an airticket and money for an overnight stay in Jakarta. Ace had spent the money already, some of it on his brothers, sisters and parents, who all knew of his life and enjoyed its occasional fruits. His boyfriend, a field officer with a United Nations agency, would have been outraged if he knew. "God damn," he had once screamed at Ace in a Manila hotel room after a spending binge by the Filipino on his family, "I don't give a shit about them." Ace was hoping to pick up some quick cash to cover his splurge with the Jakarta funds. The Filipino suspected that Nelson was his final chance. Ace was right. At twenty-four, premature white hairs were starting to pepper his thick, black crop and an unattended ear infection had dulled the hearing on his right side.

Lito, like Ace, sometimes took drugs that were beginning to erode his skinny good looks. The little pills he favoured helped him forget problems for a few hours or a night. But of late he was less choosy and often popped anything that looked promising into his small mouth. Once, with a callboy friend, he had gone to a Frenchman's room at a hotel in Mabini for a sex orgy. Afterwards he enjoyed a hot shower. While towelling his brown body he spied an interesting packet on the bathroom shelf. Inside was a small sheet of foil containing tablets. He quickly tore off three and, with a handful of water from the sink tap, swallowed. Hours later he had experienced no effects, except that his urine in the toilet bowl was unusually yellow. His Filipino partner in the orgy had later told him that the Frenchman's tablets were anti-malarial.

Bongbong was among those boys on the sermon list. The sermons came from clients who had been to Manila during their annual, paid holidays. Not a few were married. Without exception, sermons came after the event or late in the relationship, if it survived the usual one night. Letters were a popular medium of reproach.

Dear friend, (former clients would chorus from Ballarat, Australia and Bakersfield, California)

Thank you so much for your letter. Excuse my failure to write sooner but pressure of work at the bank has kept me very busy. I don't think there will be time this year for a holiday in Manila. Instead, we're having a family reunion at Christmas in our holiday house by the beach. I was interested to hear of your weekend in beautiful Mindoro with a companion but sad that you apparently haven't broken free of your old life. As I've told you before, you must change your ways and get a decent job. Remember when we visited that show village outside the airport last time I was in Manila? Well, you told me how you liked the country air and had once thought of living away from Manila. Why don't you get a job in a country town? Save your money and in time look around for a small farm. It would be a good life. Nothing ventured, nothing gained my friend. Well, all the very best. Have a Happy Christmas and a Prosperous New Year.

Your pal, John.

PS: Enclosed is a picture of the new car.

Such appeals by foreigners did not worry the boys too much. They were amusingly tolerated, like bald heads and pot bellies. However, one recent letter really *did* disturb Bongbong. It came from Mike, a San Francisco hairdresser who had kept up a spasmodic correspondence since holidaying in Manila the previous year. After a few personal references to the good time they had together, Mike continued, "I don't know what crap is being put in your newspapers now—it was movie hype when I was there last year—but have stories been carried about this big scare going on now over here? A lot of gays are dying of a horrible disease called AIDS. First it seemed to be something that affected only the fastlaners and druggies but now it's shaping up to be much bigger. Over here, it's really hysterical. Even kissing is supposed to be taboo. Sure as hell it's coming your way if it's not already there. Man, get out of that game. You're in the front line. It isn't worth it . . ."

Bongbong had talked about the letter with some of the other boys and soon a wave of panic swept over the Singalong colony. Then, someone had said it was probably peculiar to America because they knew of no one in Manila with such a disease. That had reassured many of the boys. Several had said that to play safe they would not have sex with Americans anymore. The atmosphere had become much more relaxed. Gradually the subject had dropped from sight at Singalong, aided hugely by official vetting of health reports damaging to tourism. And in any case, negative statistics were never compiled.

If Carlo had one outstanding feature it was probably his general unpopularity with the other boys who saw him as stingy. Hallway conversations were always turning, in the absence of Carlo of course, to the latest instance. His usual transgressions were in refusing small loans to needy roommates and sponging free taxi rides without later returning the favour. To the boys this was an outrageous violation of an unwritten rule in the colony. Only stealing was ranked worse. Other boys had refused their friends a few pesos too, but they prided themselves on at least having the grace to lie about their ability, thereby saving face all around. It was readily assumed that Carlo had accumulated a small fortune because of such meanness, though there was little evidence to support this. However, Carlo's possessions were supplemented by several items not usually found among the boys of the pension. He had a set of weights and a chest expander. Carlo obviously had put the equipment to good use, having a well-developed body. Like the other boys he did not eat a lot of protein and so had escaped the appearance of being muscle-bound. He wore skin-tight clothing that did nothing to hide his proportions and seemed to enjoy a reasonable popularity with macho foreigners at gay bars. The boys could have chosen to call him Muscles or Superman but they did not. After flirting with the Manila Gorilla they settled for Dumbell.

Max had been to Australia and had an album of coloured photographs taken in Sydney and the Snowy Mountains as proof. His fresh, regular features had helped in getting through stringent screening procedures at the Australian Embassy in Manila. That, and a six-week course in choreography at a Sydney dance studio. Embassy staff stamped a capital A in an applicant's passport in the event of rejection, a common happening. The A was the mark of Cain in the immigration bureaucracies of the English-speaking world. The Americans had a similar system. Unsuccessful applicants at the Manila Bay embassy had their passports returned with the lettering MNL on a blank visa page. The Americans insisted it simply meant Manila in abbreviated form. Thousands of rejected Filipinos believed it stood for Must Not Leave.

Max had enjoyed two months in Australia, living for most of the time in an old, gracious house with big windows overlooking Mosman Bay in Sydney Harbour. After his host left for work by a double-decker cream and green ferry, Max would walk the scented bush trails behind lapping water to nearby Cremorne Point. There the Filipino would marvel at the opposite view of the young city and sail-roofed Opera House. At the week-ends he would stand with his host on windswept clifftops rising above tiny secluded beaches and watch hang-gliders hovering over a blue ocean speckled with white seacaps. Sometimes the gliders would dive at the frothy waves surging shoreward and then, like modern-day Icaruses, soar towards the dazzling sun on multicolored, triangular wings. On the southern alps, Max indulged in exhilarating snow fights and toboggan rides, amazed his brown hands and ears could get *so* cold. Back at Singalong pension, he had talked of nothing else for months and the others now referred to him as Aussie Max.

Efren was the pension stayput, being content to collect a monthly cheque in the mail from a lover in Adelaide, South Australia. The cheque helped pay the rent and half fill his flat, firm stomach. However, Efren had other ways of supplementing the windfall. His modus operandi was to stand by the entrance of the pension and wait for visiting clients seeking safer ground than a hotel suite. Hotel detectives at the stricter establishments were often responsible for the exodus. One detective liked to hover by the ground floor lifts and intercept likely boys on their way out. The detective would take the suspect to an office and demand that he empty pockets. When the boy produced a single note of large denomination the detective knew that once again he had scored. The money was confiscated and the boy told to keep away. If the boy objected, police were called by the detective who would slyly return the money before they arrived. The guest was left uninvolved but boys often telephoned the room and relayed details of the incident. Feeling uncomfortable about outside knowledge of his sexual bent, the guest would change hotel or rendezvous with boys some-where else. Quite often that was Singalong pension. To foreigners used to a better lifestyle, the pension was a maze of hallways and steps. The curly-headed boy's guidance was always appreciated. "I like y'laddie," a middle-aged gentleman from Christchurch had confided one stormy night in a dark hallway. The New Zealander then promptly changed his plans and disappeared into Efren's room. Subsequently, he was known as the Usher.

* * *

Like Efren, Jojo of late did not go out so much, work aside. It had been very different once. Then there had been Pricilla. He had met her just before the accident and its happening had made no difference. It may have even helped in the beginning of the relationship and the transition to civilian life. Sometimes they had just sat on the edge of the bay before a sunset. They would linger there at night as well, the breeze carrying wavelets into a stone wall below and ruffling Pricilla's hair. Sometimes they would see a movie, though Jojo was always restless almost from the minute the two took their seats. Once, after a lover's tiff, he had told her he

35

did not want to see any more. And he had not relented. Differences, however, were smoothed over later to the point where Pricilla had asked him to visit the provinces and meet her family. Jojo had eventually made the trip with Pricilla who also took along a distant relative of hers from Manila as a chaperone. Pricilla did not want to upset her parents by arriving home in the sole company of a strange man. Of course, as was the growing trend with provincial girls who came to Manila, she had had sex with Jojo. For a long time she was reluctant. So he desisted in his advances. But eventually one night in a moment of surging passion she had accompanied Jojo to a cheap short-time motel and ended forever her virginity. It seemed to Pricilla that the relationship had thereafter developed into a never-ending series of assignations. An animal passion had taken over, though she, too, had felt unable to do anything but be swept along in its powerful tide. Then one day she had found herself pregnant. She had later told Jojo. From that time everything had changed for the worst. At first he had been almost angry, then sullen. Pricilla could not understand why he was so reluctant to marry. Jojo had instead suggested an abortion. Pricilla had cried. Their last few weeks together were replays of the same scene. Surprisingly to Jojo, she got a secret abortion. Jojo had attempted to rekindle the relationship of old but Pricilla would only hear of marriage first. The pair had a final, bitter parting.

Zac had asked about Pricilla on his return from Spain. Jojo had not been forthcoming and had quickly changed the subject. Her name had not been mentioned since. Zac had heard of no new interests and consequently decided to ask his friend to spend Christmas at the farm in Baza with Aunt Maria. She had been the protector of the Campora boys since the time they had lost their parents and she her sister Josefina and brother-in-law Pablo. The spinster had suffered a stroke while Zac was in Spain but on his return he found her cheerful and able to get around. Only her voice was affected. She could not speak.

Jojo had met the old woman once and they had got on well. So when he declined the invitation Zac was mildly surprised.

"At least have a Christmas drink with me tonight at El Torro," he insisted the day after the tremor.

Not wanting to offend twice, the Igorot said, "Let me pay."

And Zac, wondering just how long his stamp money would last, feigned a reluctant acceptance.

*   *   *

The barman at El Torro carefully placed two drinks before his only stool customers.

"It's dark in here," said Jojo, who less than a minute before had been in the commercial razzle-dazzle of M.H. del Pilar.

"You'll get used to it," Zac replied. "When you do you might recognise some faces."

A soft tinkling came from somewhere in the smoky gloom. Gradually in the depths the form took the shape of an apparently blind pianist in dark glasses, caressing a keyboard. Huddled figures occupied less than half the tables paralleling the long bar. Laughter broke out among one group. Zac and Jojo saw Martin stand and walk away, joining shadowy shapes at the back.

"I don't see so many foreigners," Jojo said. "Is that usual?"

"No, it's not. Particularly at Christmas. The boys tell me it's the slowest one they can remember."

Jojo watched them at work. Their memories wouldn't go back that far.

The other laughed. "No? Some of them have been working the bars for six or seven years."

"That long?"

"Ummm," Zac nodded, "And still hanging on for as long as they can."

The two sipped their drinks before Zac continued, "It's sad because every year brings fresh faces, more competition. Just kids. Maybe they have dropped out of school or maybe their parents don't care. Usually the parents don't know. The kids cruise the big shopping centres, streets, Rizal Park and if they can get away with it, the bars and discos. Tourists are what they want. They pay best. If they can't get one, a Filipino will do."

Zac looked into his glass. "The boys get a bit of money, think they've struck it rich, tell their friends and the word gets around. Pretty soon everyone is trying it. Why not? they say. They can't get jobs. Pretty soon the successful ones become hooked on the life and all that goes with it. Good times, good food, drugs if they want them, and they usually do. Before they know it they're into their twenties and have no hope of being anything."

"What happens then?"

Zac shrugged. "A few can't take it. Some of the street crazies you see wandering around once worked the game. Most go back to their families or become street hustlers or pimps. You know, 'Hey Joe. Wanna nice girl.' The pimps even run kiddie gangs. One's operating in Rizal Park."

"How young are the children," Jojo asked quietly.

"Seven or eight."

A group of youths came in from the street and made their way to the back. Zac could recognise none of them. The pianist began another tune as Zac looked for Martin but was unable to distinguish him from the others. In better lighting he would have easily made out the callboy's slender figure and delicate facial features which, as Martin had already confided to Zac, had earned him the schoolyard name of Sampaguita. He had confided more too: he wasn't taking his situation with Roderick at all well.

Zac gave up the search and said to his companion, "Martin told me recently about a German who wanted him as a guide to Pagsanjan Falls. When Martin asked why not just catch a bus the German said he wasn't interested in a tour. He wanted young boys and the younger the better. The boys in Manila were too old for him. He'd heard all about Pagsanjan."

"How old are they there?"

"Five, six."

Jojo froze, glass almost to his lips.

"It's *true*. I've heard about it too. There are thousands in it. Father and son teams as well."

Jojo slammed the glass to the bar, slopping the contents. "Animals!" he exclaimed, turning heads. "Must they have the children too!"

Zac was startled at his companion's vehemence but hastily nodded in agreement. He could see pallid, foreign faces still turned in their direction.

"It has to stop," Jojo said. And after ordering another drink, added, "It must."

"Yes," Zac said lamely.

"Of course it must. But why doesn't it?"

"*I* don't know."

"And a lot of other things."

"Umm," said Zac, a little embarrassed at the drift of events. How he wished those faces would mind their own business.

The drinks arrived and the two sipped, seemingly submerged in thoughts.

Jojo broke the awkward silence. "When are you going to Baza?"

"Morning bus," Zac replied, glad to affect normalcy. "I might go back home through Baguio this time. I owe the judge a visit."

Jojo nodded. He had heard of Zac's friend since the days of the inquiry into the Baza deaths.

"I should get to Baza late tomorrow night."

"Take a jacket. It's cold in Baguio now."

"I won't forget," Zac said mechanically, wondering how he could keep the new line of conversation going but glad at least they weren't being watched anymore. He gave up the effort, lightly tapping a foot to the music. By unspoken acquiescence they continued their silence, this one lasting till Martin and others emerged from the shadows. The callboy broke away and joined Zac and Jojo at the bar. His young companions drifted outside.

"Your first visit to a gay bar?" Martin asked.

"Yes. And my—"

"We're having a Christmas drink," Zac interrupted, having hastily decided they were on the conversational path back to Pagsanjan and wanting to keep as far from there as possible. "I'm going home to the provinces tomorrow and won't be back for a few days. Our last chance." And then quickly, "What are your plans for Christmas?"

Martin shrugged. "It depends on Roderick." He paused, giving Zac a resigned look. "The usual situation."

"You should tell him how you feel," Zac said.

"He knows."

"So you're going to continue this way."

"I haven't much choice if I want to see him occasionally. A bit is better than nothing."

Zac leaned towards Jojo and said, "Roderick's the one we saw waiting in the red car outside the pension."

Jojo frowned in unsuccessful recollection.

"With a face like Abraham Lincoln," Zac prompted.

The frown vanished. Everyone remembered *that* face.

"I don't understand," Martin was saying. "There doesn't seem to be anyone else. I'd know sooner or later. He couldn't hide it forever. But how can I change things?" He looked at his long fingernails reflectively. "Sometimes I really hate myself for letting it drag on this way."

"It's a strange way for him to behave," Zac said sympathetically.

"Not for a foreigner," Jojo murmured, before draining his glass in one long gulp.

Zac and Martin exchanged glances.

"I'm off," the Igorot said, touching Zac lightly on the shoulder. "Enjoy Baza," he added and was gone.

*   *   *

Under a street light outside El Torro, Jojo met Ace.

"No business," the callboy shrugged. "I'm going back to the pension."

The two set off along del Pilar in the general direction of Singalong, every now and then glancing backwards for approaching transport. Jeepneys were infrequent after twelve and this night was no exception. All the same, to Jojo the street appeared curiously quiet. Where were the pimps, the painted girls, the standby youths, the drug pushers? Why were the doors closed to the nightclubs, bars and strip joints? They were doing business. He could tell that by the muffled throb of rock and the humming of air-conditioners feeding pools on the narrow pavement.

Jojo forgot about jeepneys and looked instead for a taxi.

"What's going on?" asked Ace, who had been mindful only of money problems up till then but suddenly found himself sharing his companion's apprehension.

"Something," said Jojo, quickening the pace. On the other side of the street a figure approached and in similarly brisk step passed on. They heard a motor behind and turned to see a speeding taxi half a block away.

Jojo stepped to the road and raised a hand. The vehicle's horn blared, its high-beam lights dazzling him. Then he realised it was not going to stop. He leapt back feeling the car whoosh by.

"My God," gasped Ace. "That was close."

"*Putang ina mo*," Jojo swore.

They pressed on in a half run till they were approaching a dark side-street that was more of an alley. They had almost reached it when a tail-less cat darted out and across to the far side.

Jojo stopped just short of the corner, pulling back Ace with a low, "No."

But it was too late. Forms emerged and with shouts of, "Hoy, some more," had the two struggling futilely in their many grips.

"What's the hurry?" they were asked, hands now pulling, pushing and shoving them towards a street light.

The forms moved back and the light revealed a ring of grinning men. They parted momentarily to admit a short, bald man with a bespectacled monkeyish face. He assessed the two from bottom to top and, his spectacles inadvertently catching the light above, demanded, "Well, why were you running?"

Jojo looked down on what he assumed to be a *barangay* captain and wondered when these snoopy pests ever rested. Lording it over their city block or village *barrio*. And those *tanods*, the captain's goons. *Pulis* lackeys and informers the lot. They seemed to infest the place like lice in a chicken yard.

"Sir," he said with polite concern. "We thought hoodlums were following us."

The *tanods* looked back along del Pilar. "No one in sight, captain," one reported.

"Then we must have outrun them."

"Yes," echoed Ace, catching on. "Or they saw the *tanods*."

The *barangay* captain considered his next move. He was inclined to accept the explanation. The area was full of villains. But he had to be careful. "What is your business here."

"A party," the Igorot said. "We were saying farewell to an engineer friend going to California."

Ace, surprised at the other's unsuspected talent, added, "He's flying out next week."

The *barangay* captain adjusted his spectacles, a little impressed. Well, they certainly didn't *look* like trouble makers or callboys. One stood almost like a soldier and the other had silver hairs.

"Show your ID's and you can go," he said.

Jojo looked at Ace. The callboy's face confirmed what he suspected. How could he have one with no job? Jojo cursed silently. He had left his at the pension. Only in the bar had he realised that.

"I'm sorry sir," Jojo replied. "We forgot to carry them."

The *tanods* grinned anew. They looked down on the dome of block authority, knowing what would come next. They had seen this scene many times. Such a worn story!

The *barangay* captain stamped a booted foot on the pavement. "No excuse," he snapped and, pointing downstreet, "to the vans."

Gripped anew they were led two blocks farther along del Pilar and around a corner. There, police stood by five vans, all partly open-sided and two packed with silent figures.

"Room for more trash," barked an officer holding a truncheon. "One in that van, one in this."

"Hurry up," said the officer, prodding them. "We don't have all night."

Jojo moved towards the back of a van, a tangle of arms and legs inside.

"Don't you know how to hurry," the man hissed, bringing the truncheon into the small of the Igorot's back.

Jojo winced. Then he felt the truncheon again, but much harder. He gripped the van's door-frame lest he collapse and lifted himself in. He heard one engine splutter to life, then a second.

"Take them away," someone outside called.

Jojo became aware of his body rocking with the van's motion, a

41

hand gripping his shoulder and a voice, "Are you okay?" But he did not reply. He was incapable of speech. He could only feel a cold rage.

*　　*　　*

The desk sergeant at the police precinct two blocks from Rizal Park looked askance on the scene from his elevated perch.

"In the name of God," he muttered to an offsider, "how many more?"

"Maybe another hundred," he was told. "Another five vans are supposed to be on their way."

The sergeant threw a pen over his shoulder in exasperation, thought better of the action in view of the lieutenant's presence at the station that night, and bent backwards on his chair to retrieve it.

On the other side of the sergeant's high desk was a confusion of faces, the Igorot among them and towards the back. He was looking for Ace and, when he could not see him, through the large glass doors of the station. A van arrived and disgorged its load. Ace was among the new arrivals escorted in.

"Why so long?" Jojo asked when the two were together.

"We had a *pulis* detour on the way. We stopped in a side street and those who had money bargained for their freedom."

"How many were let go?"

"Seven I think. I didn't have enough pesos."

"Not for crocodiles," the Igorot said almost inaudibly in the din.

Then, on the other side of the room the desk sergeant rose and bellowed, "Shut up! Shut up! Give me some silence!" And as the noise quickly died, "Right, that's better. Now, I want the males to go into that room over there. Yes, over there! Hurry up! Get a move on!"

Several khaki figures awaited them. One said wearily, "Okay, get it all off, everything."

Most began to comply but there were also mutterings. Someone protested, "What right do you have to do this?"

The Igorot thought the sing-song, Cebuano lilt familiar and looking past heads saw it was Tommy. Let the youth carry the banner, he decided coolly.

Tommy was ignored so he repeated the question, but louder.

"Do as you're told," he was harshly ordered.

"We shouldn't even be here," Tommy persisted indignantly. "It's not legal. We were arrested by *tanods* and they aren't supposed to do that. They don't have the power."

"No, no. They don't," offended voices chorused.

"And," said Tommy, not put off by the sight of authority angrily moving towards him, "some of us were hit."

"That's right," someone farther behind said.

"I know my rights," Tommy continued. "This is illegal. I was just walking down a street, that's all. The next thing I know the *tanods* grabbed me and my friends from behind and marched us to a van."

A red face confronted Tommy. Suddenly the youth was slapped hard on the cheek.

"My God!" Tommy gasped, a hand to his face. "How dare you!"

The man ignored him. "Separate this troublemaker from the others," he instructed an offsider. And addressing the silent faces around, "Now, clothes off!"

Ace whispered as they stripped, "They're looking for tattoos to see if we've ever been to prison."

After cursory inspections they were told, "You can all get dressed and go back to the next room. Someone will interview you."

In minutes they were back in the charge room. At length Jojo was processed, then taken along a passageway to a small office where he was sat before a desk at which a lieutenant opposite was scanning papers, a hand shading bespectacled eyes from a fluorescent light above. On the uniform breast pocket the name Felipe C was stitched.

The officer removed the spectacles and looked up, revealing a handsome, authoritative face. The hair was full and off the forehead, the dark eyes steady in gaze, the strong brows quizzically arched. A half-smile lingered on the lips. Jojo was unsure as to whether he sensed humour or arrogance.

The overweight escort handed the lieutenant a sheet. After a brief inspection it was contemptuously dropped and allowed to float to the desk on which lay open folders containing reports and an assortment of black and white photographs.

"And what was that?" the officer said with slow deliberation.

"I," the escort hesitated, "don't understand, sir."

"This badly typed sheet? Not even an address."

"Sir?"

"Here, look for yourself."

"We're having a busy night sir."

"Yes, fishing for small fry and God knows what else."

"I'll take it back sir and this—." He searched for a word to describe his charge. The lieutenant was not interested.

"We've wasted enough time. I'll fill in the details. You can go."

43

The escort left, glad to leave the office of a man who was, everybody knew, a rising star with all the right connections but a pain in the ass to work for.

The officer retrieved the fallen sheet with an, "I'm Lieutenant Cesar Felipe. Let's check a few details."

Jojo shifted on his seat watching as the man frowned and then thrust forward the object of his irritation.

"Is that how you spell your name? Igorot, isn't it?"

Jojo leaned forward and as he did saw the top photograph. He momentarily froze. With an effort he took the sheet and, forcing himself to blot out what he had seen, looked for his name. It was misspelt, as was usual in the lowlands, but he whispered, "That's correct."

The officer frowned anew. "There's no need to be afraid. I'm not going to shoot you."

"The spelling is correct," Jojo said a little louder and with more conviction.

"At least something is right," Felipe replied. "Now, tell me your address."

The Igorot looked at the poised pen of the lieutenant and said, "Forty-four B Dimasalang, Quezon City," the address of a pension he had once briefly lived in, far, far away from Singalong.

"And where do you work?" he was asked.

"Cubao, the markets at Cubao." Also far, far away.

"Good," said the lieutenant. "Such a simple little task. An idiot could get it right." He put the pen down on the desk and gave his full attention to the man opposite. "You've been picked up for loitering, suspicious behaviour and possible vagrancy. What do you have to say?"

The Igorot replied, "I was not loitering. I was walking home. And I have job. How can I be a vagrant?"

"Do you have any proof of that?"

"I have money," Jojo said, getting a wallet from his back pocket and emptying it of notes.

"That's not proof but it tends to substantiate—" The lieutenant broke off and looked at the wallet. "What's that photograph?"

Jojo took it out. It was creased and becoming tatty but the picture was clear. "I used to be in the army, sir. That's me with some others."

"Where was this taken?" Felipe said, reaching for the print.

"Camp Aguinaldo."

"Oh, yes. I recognise the background. You were a corporal I see."

"Yes, sir, till my discharge for this." The Igorot held up his mutilated hand. "A shooting accident."

Felipe was silent as he returned the photograph. Then pushing the sheet aside he said," I know you'll understand that we have to be careful. But sometimes this sort of thing happens. We don't mean it to happen but it does. It's the price we all must be prepared to pay for vigilance."

The other nodded.

"I knew you would understand, corporal. You're one of ours." The lieutenant picked up the pen and scribbled a note on a handy pad. He tore it free and, giving it to Jojo, instructed, "If you're bothered on the way out just show this."

"Thank you sir."

"Goodbye corporal."

"Goodbye sir," he replied and left the room, gently closing the office door.

Ace saw Jojo pushing through the charge room which somehow had absorbed more van loads in the Igorot's absence.

"What happened?" the callboy asked.

"I can go. What about you?"

"I still haven't been processed."

Jojo looked around, wondering about Tommy. He could not see him. "So your name hasn't been recorded in the log yet."

"No. At this rate I'll be here for the rest of my life."

A youth eased past towards the precinct's front door. No one was attempting to stop him or had seemed to notice. He passed through the doorway to the dark driveway beyond.

"Let's go," Jojo whispered.

"Huh," responded the other.

"Let's both go."

"Oh, I don't know," Ace protested weakly. "I might get caught."

"No, you won't," the Igorot urged, calmly edging towards the glass doors and towing Ace. "Just keep talking normally in case someone is looking. Don't appear to be doing anything wrong."

They reached the doors. A little outside, Jojo stopped and casually put an unlit cigarette between his lips. He searched his pockets for a box of matches and, finding one, lit up.

"What are you doing?" hissed Ace.

"Calmly now," said Jojo, throwing a frazzled match to the ground and stepping to the driveway. "Don't rush."

In unseasonal drizzle they strolled to a deserted United Nations Avenue. There they turned right and quickened stride. The concrete skeleton of an incomplete elevated tramway loomed ahead. Unable to hold back any longer, they sprinted to the structure's shadows and protection. An approaching jeepney decked in coloured lights turned the drizzle into a technicoloured mist.

Speeding towards Singalong on a wet Taft Avenue, Ace confided, "I don't want to go through that again."

In the dark the Igorot smiled.

* * *

With the exception of Efren, all the callboys who lived on the upper floor of Singalong pension had a story that night of how they had evaded the round-up. However, Ace held centre stage, Jojo making light of his release. The rooms adjacent to Jojo's were abuzz with chatter. Food had been bought at nearby all-night eateries and the occasion became a running party, one moment a room crowded, next almost empty. When Tommy made a re-appearance there were shrieks of surprise. "*How* did you escape?" was on everyone's lips. It was simple, he said. They forgot about his confinement in a back office so he slipped out a window. Howls of laughter filled the hallways. Then a boarder complained to the boys of too much noise, Perla being a heavy sleeper. But the boarder need not have bothered because just after he had returned to bed, slamming his door, a blackout began. Matches were struck and candles lit. Minutes later the party had finished.

* * *

In the blackness of his room Jojo allowed the mask to drop. Up till this night only grandfather's final stillness had brought tears to his eyes. Now he felt moisture for Laya. He fell back to the bed, fully clothed, an arm across his forehead. He closed his eyes and thought of the man he had known for less than a month, the man who in that time had been like the father he never had, the man who had given him new eyes. Laya had been right. "It can't go on like this Jojo," he had said only days ago. "Help us make the change. Don't just remain a spectator. We're all travelling in the same leaky boat." And now he was dead. But why? What had happened? Had Laya been caught by them? And would they be after him next even though he wasn't one . . . Not till tonight. Yes, Laya was right. It couldn't go on like this. It had to change. Laya had said it was a revolutionary situation that could only be resolved one way. The New People's Army needed men like Jojo. It was not a time for dallying. So why not, Jojo? What are you waiting for?

Jojo shifted on the bed. He heard the mosquito's faint song but ignored the warning of the stings to come. He was remembering

Laya's first approach in a quiet moment at the market stall and the words, "We've had an eye on you for some time . . ." and later at Laya's boarding house, "I'm putting my fate, my life in your hands by talking this way." Maybe he'd put his life in one pair of hands too many. The air was thick with informers. Anything for a peso. Laya had laughed at his resentment at being thought of as a possible informer and said, "If we really suspected it you'd be dead before you blinked." But now Laya was dead. Riddled with bullets. A death in a gutter. Why? What had happened? What should he do now? And that park prank? After that first talk in Laya's room he had been too embarrassed to mention it. He had been going to tell Zac to forget the whole thing. He had already thought out an excuse. It wouldn't have mattered. Zac seemed to have a different mood every day now. Not like when he got back. Not like the old days. And what had happened to them? Dead, like Laya, like El Torro. Full of dead people. He'd been about to tell Zac when that Martin came up. He'd wanted to finish the thing there. But he had lost the chance. It could wait a few more days. Yet should he drop the idea? Couldn't he turn it a little, in memory of Laya? Only the smallest change. It would be easy. And he could make Laya's death mean something. Maybe Zac wouldn't like it. No, he wouldn't. But he needn't know till it was over. It would do him good. More than that foreign boyfriend. It was safe too. There would be thousands of people. He and Zac would be out of the park before anyone realised what had happened. Thousands of people. And after, he would quit Manila. He would go back to the mountains, not to his village but the guerrillas on its slopes. Yes, it was not a time for dallying . . . he knew that now . . .

The mosquitoes went to work on a sleeping man.

* * *

Fortunato O. Fortunato was unable to sleep but did not mind. Even the snores of that lump of a wife occupying the other half of the big double bed, failed to irritate him as they usually did. Nothing could peeve the *barangay* captain at this moment! He wriggled his toes and savoured the memory of the busy night just ended. Only one little thing nagged . . . Why hadn't the lieutenant personally thanked him and the *tanods* for their work? He'd left it to a sergeant he had not seen before. Well, probably he was busy. Or something. The sergeant had told them that one hundred and seventy four in all had been taken to the station. Fortunato and his *tanods* were responsible for apprehending a third of them! He couldn't wait till he told Crispina in the morning. Should he wake her now? Better not. She probably wouldn't remember in the morning that she'd been told. The woman was getting quite silly. He wanted to share his triumphs and had to put up with this sort of thing. And what a triumph it was! Just at the right time! Just when he needed it to confound his rivals. The ones who wanted his job. He had heard their talk. All behind his back, of course. He had heard the whispers, "Too old for the job" and "Should be retired, senile old fool" and "How long is he going to hang on?" Too old for the job! Huh! He would be around for many more years yet. He looked after himself. He ate his papaya every day. The doctor told him to do that. Why, he might even outlive His Excellency who hadn't looked too well on television lately. Much older and lined. His voice not the same . . . Somehow different . . .

Fortunato pummelled his pillow and thought again of the sergeant's speech of appreciation. Sometime during his fifth recollection he drifted to slumber. He was next aware of tugging Crispina through the palace gates where a crowd had gathered. And they were cheering *him*! He seemed suddenly to be on a lawn besides the palace. A guard of honour was awaiting his inspection. The foreign diplomatic corps was assembled nearby. Under a marquee were tables laden with papaya. Plates and plates of it. He could see the First Lady on an upper floor balcony looking down on him. Why was she scowling? And why were the Manila street sweepers comforting her and throwing bits of paper at him? Then His Excellency was by his side and calling for silence from an excited gathering which now filled the lawn. He heard His Excellency's deep voice, ". . . and as you know I have these many years searched everywhere for a successor capable of shouldering the immense burdens of this high office. Today before you, at last, is such a man." And His Excellency stepped aside and with a flourish, pointed in *his* direction and announced, "Fortunato O. Fortunato."

It was exactly at that moment that a cat fight awoke a suddenly disappointed *barangay* captain.

*   *   *

Lieutenant Felipe tidied the desk, a seed of suspicion germinating in his mind. The officer picked up the photographs and an accompanying report. He weighed them thoughtfully in his hand before putting the lot in a drawer. He locked it slowly, puzzling why the man had stared so at the desk. He'd put the behaviour down to nerves at the time but now . . . he wasn't so sure. Could the Igorot have known Laya? Known a communist?

48

Felipe checked his watch, deciding the matter would have to wait till the morning. If he had no more interruptions. His first night on the assignment and instead he'd spent four hours helping out. Why didn't the precinct have more men? Or cut down on those ridiculous round-ups? He wondered who'd organised this one. The order never came from him. Still, but for the round up . . .

As a last action he scribbled himself a note and put it under a weight on the desk. Then, still unable to shake off the feeling that the Igorot had made him a fool, Felipe grimly headed for the door.

CHAPTER THREE

It was not yet dawn, that morning before Christmas, when worshippers began arriving for mass at a church near the Milky Way disco. In ones and twos and family groups they made their way down aisles, some to kneel before flickering candles and nativity scenes. One white-haired figure who normally would have been seated in a pew three rows from the back, as had become his custom, was not there. That person was Simeon Xavier Santos, truly a man of God, though that state had not preserved him from being placed under house arrest three days earlier. It was his position in secular life as editor of *Maharlika*, a newspaper that dared to criticise, which had been responsible. Along with his enemies' tag of being a radical and therefore subversive. This description, however, revealed more their conservativeness than the true position of Santos on the political spectrum. But these were not normal times, a fact Santos was very much aware of that morning.

Being a devout man he had, after rising at dawn, observed fifteen minutes of prayers and meditation, a rosary bead between gnarled fingers, before preparing for the day ahead. He had eaten breakfast with the others of the household—his son Ricardo, a lecturer at the University of Santo Tomas, his daughter-in-law Fermina, and the grandchildren, Hilaria and Sabina. Melinda the maid, almost irritatingly cheerful, had served breakfast. Then Ricardo had mysteriously left the house soon after the arrival of attorneys who were all first searched by the soldiers in the front courtyard. The meeting in the *sala* behind closed doors had lasted two hours. Not long after, Fermina had gathered up the children and with Melinda gone out for last-minute Christmas shopping, thus giving him a welcome respite from chatter and what he felt was Melinda's incredible insensitivity, as exemplified by her continual humming.

Santos had retired to his bedroom upstairs and caught forty winks till woken by crackers in the immediate neighbourhood. That had put an end to further sleep. He donned soft shoes and shuffled out to the bedroom balcony. He had no sooner put his hands on the metal railing when a soldier below called, "Good morning sir."

Santos looked in mild surprise at the upturned face. "Good morning," he replied evenly, wondering just what other oddities the day would bring. Here he was greeting a man, supposed to be a foe, as though he were the next door neighbour. Probably Melinda had incurred a less civil response. But what on earth possessed her to go around the house in that manner? It was like the way his countrymen got into an elevator without bothering to wait for those trying to get out. Or drove. Inconsiderate to the extreme. Only thought of themselves.

"We'll be changing guards at midday sir," the soldier was saying. "It's my last chance to wish you a happy Christmas."

"I thank you. And a happy and Holy Christmas to you."

The other soldiers joined in and Santos repeated the words, thinking Fermina had probably been responsible for this. Ah, Fermina! Whatever would he do without her? And especially *now*. Ricardo was a fortunate man, as he, too, had been during those brief years after the war with dear Ofelia.

Santos surveyed the courtyard. The soldiers had returned to a shaded corner bench, their backs and rifles resting against a concrete brick wall which was on all its sides topped with broken glass. Only the green metal gate, just large enough to admit Ricardo's Toyota, interrupted the glass spears of security, now a necessity in the thief-plagued neighbourhood. And even the gate was topped with three strands of barbed wire. It had certainly given protection. Equally as certain he knew it was now his prison.

Santos sighed, recalling a time long ago . . . when the house had miraculously survived the battle for Manila, unlike his noble parents Apolinario and Isabela . . . when his brother Pio had died in the pointless defence of Bataan . . . when Pio's wife had lost their only child through a lack of proper medicine . . . when his father's printing works was partly destroyed in the air raids towards the end of the occupation.

God had asked much of his family, he reflected, looking beyond the courtyard to a drab street that had once been magnificently green till it had been dug up for vegetable plots with all the neighbours suddenly planting *camote*, *kangkong* and *talinum* on all available spaces, even by footpaths. And those compulsory garden sessions one day a week, for all between sixteen and sixty . . . he had never forgotten them. How proud he had been of his parents, too. Unlike everyone else in the street, his father had declined to pay a levy or send a servant as a substitute. Hand in hand the couple and the family had walked to the specified field where they bent their backs and soiled their hands. He could still recall some of the words of a song that poor folk used to sing as they worked:

> All day you're bent
> You can't stand
> You can't sit
> Come, come friends, let's go
> Let's renew our strength
> For tomorrow

And how they had worked that field! Half the produce had gone to a neighbourhood association and the rest to authority. They had all thanked God when that merciless sun sank low over Manila Bay! After that experience he had looked anew on the lot of the *provinciano*. He had vowed never to forget. He had also never forgotten the lessons of those terrible days, the collapse of public morals and social cohesion. Terrible days for the individual and the country! Days in which the cursed weed of corruption flourished anew, watered daily by starvation, poverty and that instinct even greater than sex, the will to survive. Theft, swindling and even murder became commonplace. Few had cared for anyone but themselves and family. The enemy had been surrounded and isolated by deceit and hypocrisy that, like a vine, spread till the country was itself the victim. Overnight it had become patriotic for government employees to steal or destroy records, for police to look the other way when confronted by crime. All services, of course, were for a payment. *Everyone had to live*! so the argument went. Looking back to those days he sometimes wondered what had really changed. And the answer had depressed him. Nothing! *Nothing at all*! Those same strangling, suffocating vines were still there!

The sound of children's laughter reached his balcony from one end of the street where a burst water main had flooded the road. A group of young children were dancing and laughing knee-deep in water, scattering with squeals of delight when a jeepney or car surged through the flooded section, creating wavelets. Some of the children were soaked already, their cheap cotton clothes clinging to satin brown limbs; their wet, black hair stuck to foreheads and necks. Screams of pleasure broke out at the sight of more nearing jeepneys. Santos saw on the footpath a middle-aged couple who, by their fair skins, were obviously foreigners. The man, wearing a black baseball cap, was positioning his camera for a snapshot of

52

the happy scene. As a newspaperman, Santos knew it would make a good picture, maybe page one on a quiet day. As a veteran of the media he knew also that it was a deception. The tourists would take home their picture, with others, and in time show them to their friends. They would um and ahh at the almond-eyed children, carefree faces glistening with the spray. They would probably nod appreciatively at a flashlight scene of a park concert or a guest choir of angelic girls halfway through a rendition of "The Lord's Prayer." In all likelihood they would tut-tut or raise their eyebrows at a street scene of friends holding hands or arm in arm, regardless of the partner's sex. He thought it was one of the finer customs but conceded that as he grew older and more disillusioned with people, he cared less and less for any physical contact.

But was he being too hard? he wondered. How could they know what was really happening? How could you photograph a dictatorship, corruption, cynicism, opportunism? God knows, there were enough squatters' shacks and substandard houses to fill a million albums! But these visitors were here to holiday. To forget their own problems, the big mortgages, car repayments, college fees, health expenses, pollution, the financial crisis, unemployment at a level unheard-of for generations, and drug addiction among their children. All the problems of affluent societies. Why should they care? There were worse places on the face of the earth. Wasn't it worse in Russia? So he had once been scolded by a visiting Boston matron whose knowledge of politics was akin to his understanding of Sanskrit.

One of the soldiers had got up and walked to the gate, which he opened before glancing to the street.

"No sign yet," Santos heard him say to the others in apparent reference to the replacements.

The old man checked his watch and estimated another seventeen minutes to the change.

The soldier half closed the gate then kneeled to tie a loose bootlace and as he did so, looked up and smiled. He'd *actually* smiled, Santos marvelled. From the first there had been something apologetic about his attitude. Ricardo hadn't seen this though. He had wanted to refuse the man a requested glass of water but Fermina had allowed Melinda to fetch one. Ricardo had seemed more upset than anyone in the house. Praise the good Lord for Fermina, he thought. Her calm had helped him weather the turmoil. And the grandchildren, what effect would this have on them? Hilaria, though only seven, seemed to know what was happening. Often these past days she had silently wrapped her arms around his shoulders as he sat in a favourite chair in the *sala*. Little Sabina couldn't be expected to fully understand the sudden change in routine, but she was learning.

"Why hasn't Uncle Ralph come with our Christmas presents," she had asked him while looking at wrapped gifts under a green paper tree in the *sala*.

"He could be busy at his office, Sabina. He's a very active man."

And after a petulant pause, "Is he really our uncle?"

"No, it's an honorary title."

"A what grandpapa?"

"Honorary."

"Oh," she said, not really understanding and concerned with only one thing. "Do you think he'll be here in time."

"We'll have to wait and see, Sabina."

But he had known the truth instinctively. Ralph was like all the rest out there. *Cowards!* That and opportunists with fingers ever to the wind.

From the direction of the burst main a yellow and white taxi approached. The vehicle pulled up outside the house. Hilaria and Sabina jumped out followed by a more sedate Fermina. Melinda emerged with parcels.

"Hello, grandpapa," Sabina called, being first in the courtyard. "What have you been doing?"

The old man pointed skyward. "Sending signals to the Martians."

As he plodded downstairs to the *sala* and front door beyond to let them in he wondered if that remark would be produced as evidence at the coming trial.

"Anything could happen here," he told the ginger house cat mindlessly sleeping at the foot of the stairs. "Anything."

*　　*　　*

The slip-slop of Perla's plastic slippers announced her approach in the hall. Santiago, who was in the midst of washing his clothes in a hallway sink, quickly bundled the soggy mass into an old plastic bucket. Covering the damning evidence with an ill-fitting lid, he ambled towards his room.

"Morning Perla," he cheerfully said, wondering if there was enough room in the narrow hallway to decently squeeze past the matronly figure.

"You're up early," she replied, fluffing bobbed hair and regarding the bucket suspiciously with sharp, lively eyes.

"I have a lot of things to do."

"You've forgotten one thing, Santiago. You haven't paid your levy. Remember, non-payers can't go to the party."

Perla was collecting the annual levy from roomers for the Christmas party and all were expected to attend. The manageress had instituted the fixture in her very first year on the job at Singalong and had now held seven reasonably successful functions. She liked to tell new roomers that the party was to promote togetherness at the pension. That was broadly true but not the sole reason for its existence. This year, however, she was having trouble collecting, especially from the boys. She was being sympathetic but firm. After all, payment was practically a house rule.

Most of the many rules were not of Perla's making. She ran the pension on behalf of a Mrs Prospera Chy whom she had not seen in seven years but had regularly spoken to on the office phone.

"Perla," the reedy voice of the widow would command long distance from a mountain residence in cool Baguio, "take this down. Beginning next month all new rentals are to be increased twenty per cent. Yes, twenty per cent. What do they think I am? Mother Christmas? Tell me, has that family gone yet? They have? Good. From now on definitely no more kids. That's right. The little wretches are too destructive for me to afford their presence. I still haven't got over the bill for that broken window. And do try to get rid of the long-time roomers this time. Their fixed rents are making life very difficult for me. I'm finding it quite hard to manage. Get them for a violation of rules or something. Now, Perla, don't tell me about the law or I'll come down and do it myself . . . Oh, have a merry Christmas. Goodbye."

Thankfully for Perla, Mrs Chy had never come yet. The manageress had heard with some relief that the widow was now confined to a wheelchair.

Perhaps the rule that Perla had to be strictest about was the ban on cooking because of the risk of fire and the general lack of ventilation in the pension. Long-time roomers were the single exception and only if they had a window to the outside and fitted in it, at their own cost, an exhaust fan. Perla's sensitive nose had been responsible for the ejection of several violators at Singalong.

One long-time roomer was Reggie. He would help his less-fortunate neighbours by cooking the odd dish of rice and vegetables. Reggie did not mind the chore. He had been jobless for longer than he cared to remember and was ashamed of being supported by his wife. Reggie had been a reporter all his adult life till the day his newspaper was closed on presidential orders. Lately Reggie had been making strange noises in the hall and decamping before doors opened. As his door never had, not even in neighbourly curiosity, all soon guessed who it was. Remembering his charity, they overlooked the behaviour.

Perla ignored Reggie's oddity too. It was the least of her worries. She used a downstairs room as an office and by no accident it was strategically situated right alongside the front entrance. No one left or entered without her knowing. She also had a good view of stairway traffic inside the pension, which gave her clues as to what might be going on. The office was a modest affair having in its confined space a desk, a few chairs and two wall signs. One was intended for everyone in the pension. It read, "Those of us who think they know everything are annoying to those of us who do." The other was directed more at the younger fraternity. It read, "May you be in heaven a half-hour before the Devil finds out you're gone." It was her only comment on their lifestyle.

In her slip-slop round of the halls Perla was always on the look-out for secret roomers. She did not mind Filipinos who stayed the odd night with a relative or friend. It was the foreigners who raised her ire. It never ceased to amaze her that they tried to get away with it. She ignored the ones who came to be with the boys a few hours but not those who stayed a few days. She did not object to the boys' business. They had to make a living somehow. But she did object to non-paying house guests who could easily afford it. Nevertheless, she never made a scene if she could help it. She quietly had a word to the boy concerned and relied on the message being passed on, "Pay up or get out."

Perla did not have a lot of success in detecting violations of a no-washing rule which was imposed to cut down on water bills. She had, on her own initiative, relaxed the owner's rule a little and allowed roomers to wash a few small items each day. All the same, she correctly suspected that somehow they were getting around the ban instead of using a nearby laundry. If Perla had managed to stay awake after midnight she might have learned how. Doors would cautiously open. Roomers would silently emerge laden with buckets of dirty washing and tiptoe to communal sinks in bays off halls. There, taps would run for an hour and, in almost every window of the pension, makeshift clothes lines would appear, Hong Kong style. At dawn the weary washers would rise briefly to whip the semi-wet evidence out of sight.

Perla did allow herself one privilege of office, if it could be called that. She was looking for a man and, like a jealous lioness, regarded the pension as her exclusive territory. Though men had always brought trouble to her life she could not do without them.

She had tried to escape again and again. The hunger in her body always drove her back. So, with mature acceptance of her nature, anything in pants that strayed in her direction was surveyed from head to foot, pocket to paunch. If she detected the smell of money, so much the better. For a while she had even considered a Briton who came upon Singalong by chance and stayed for six months. Tim had proved accommodating in bed and Perla had thought that just maybe, at long last, she had found her man. But Tim's appetite had not been limited to one sex and after his dalliances with some of the boys down the hall Perla had resigned herself once again to a continuance of spinsterhood, at least for a while.

Men aside, Perla's big problem at the moment was the Christmas party.

"Can I pay later?" Santiago asked.

"As long as it's before the party."

"When's it on?"

"This evening."

"I'm not sure I'll have the money by then," he said feeling the weight of the bucket.

"I can't allow credit."

"Then I don't think I'll be there."

Perla had suspected that would be his answer. It seemed to be everyone's. Her cousin wouldn't like it one little bit. Pinkie would be mad. "I'm sorry to hear that, Santiago. I was hoping you could make it."

"Me too," he responded unenthusiastically.

"I'd better tell Pinkie," she thought aloud, not looking forward to the phone call. Pinkie had a flash temper where money was involved. And the party involved quite a bit.

"Pinkie?"

"Er, Mrs Aranzanso," Perla replied hastily, immediately annoyed at her indiscretion. "She's the one who caters for the food."

"You mean the party's off?"

"I haven't much choice. Only four boarders have paid."

Santiago was surprised. "I'm sorry if we let you down. We know what this means to you."

Perla wondered if he really did. If he *suspected*. "Don't apologise. It's not your fault."

"I feel sort of bad. Is this the first cancellation—" he trailed off, feeling the bucket handle give way.

"Santiago," Perla exclaimed at the evidence scattered on the floor. "What have you got there?"

"Uhh," he stalled while he searched for a pausible excuse. "Just a few rags. I'm cleaning my room."

"With your clothes?" she queried, helping him put the washing back in the handleless bucket.

"They're old."

"Like your excuse," Perla observed caustically but suddenly remembering her indiscretion. "Because it's Christmas I'll forget the matter. See that it doesn't happen again."

"Oh, it won't," he assured the manageress, backing away towards his room and vowing silently to wash in future with the midnight brigade.

*   *   *

Perla did not manage Singalong without help, though it was doubtful if Gilbert contributed much to the welfare of its inhabitants. Gilbert was a security guard whose job it was to keep the peace in the pension between nine at night and six in the morning. Gilbert and Perla had few encounters.

If the manageress had known of Gilbert's work habits she might have had second thoughts about the necessity for his presence. Gilbert was probably the oldest guard in the metropolis. Because of his age and a life-long tradition of doing as little as possible, he had made a couch in an upper floor hall his unofficial office. All the midnight washers, callboys and insomniacs knew of his practice. In the spirit of live and let live, they shrugged it off. It was no secret, either, that Gilbert was a coward of the first order. The gun that was a part of a security guard's uniform made no difference. At the slightest hint of any trouble the man would vanish. As it was common knowledge that security guards were always accidentally shooting people, no one particularly objected to this failing. It actually made them feel safer.

If Gilbert was living a good life, young Felix the cleaner was not, though he was secretly working on his lowly status with the help of one boarder to whom he was distantly related. The teenager was, for the while, following a family tradition. His father had been a cleaner at a high school and his grandpa had had the honour of being one at the American Governor's mansion in Baguio in the years before the Pacific war.

Felix had wanted to be a rock star or, if that was not immediately possible, one of those men who rode around all day in cars with the decal, "Presidential Security Command." They could crash red lights or do *anything*. But Felix had been undersized and, in any case, grandpa's connections decidedly obsolete. So, the youth had begun at Singalong through grandpa having also once been a reliable servant with Mrs Chy. Felix had objected but no other job had been available. "No argument," his father had said. "It's all arranged." For a year now his routine had been to mop the halls, clean the sinks and toilet cubicles and empty trash cans before the Singalong cats scattered the contents in their continual search for scraps. Knowing of the Baguio connections, Perla kept a watchful eye on the youth's welfare. As events were shaping up on that day before Christmas, it could be said she was not being watchful enough.

The manageress was wondering if she had correctly handled Santiago's violation of the washing ban when down another hall she saw Felix slipping out of Lito's room.

"What are you doing in a boarder's room?" she asked sternly.

"Just returning a cassette tape to Lito," the teenager said, cheerfully seizing the chance to practice his lying.

"Your hair's looking neater today," she observed, satisfied with the explanation. "I hope this means you'll be taking more pride in your appearance."

"Oh yes," Felix replied as he accompanied Perla down the stairs toward her office.

"I can see this place is beginning to have a good effect on you," Perla said and, dismissing the boy at the base of the steps, added, "On your way. There are halls to be cleaned and cans to be emptied."

Perla would have had a sudden vacancy had she witnessed what went on in Lito's room. Actually, it was more of a schoolroom. Felix was training to be a callboy and was having his very first lesson. The teenager had decided on the career when he realised the boys got more in one good night at El Torro than he earned in a month of mopping floors at the pension. Of course, Felix was only seeing a part of the picture. The boys never spoke to uninitiates of the rest: the vicious competition, unmentionable nights when they lay with the darker side of human nature, fear of age and eventual rejection. Such things were only for the confessional of their Singalong rooms in those spent, spiritless hours before the faint greyness of pre-dawn. In fact, feeling the star with Felix's near adulation, cousin Lito had condescended to become his tutor, time permitting. That morning the youth had been granted his first lesson.

"You're a quick learner," Lito had observed of Felix just before he left the room. "How would you like a trial run at El Torro?"

"D'you mean it?" Felix had said almost breathlessly.

"Sure kid," Lito had grandly replied. "But half your earnings go to me for training and expenses. Okay?"

"Okay," said the novice callboy shaking hands with a novice pimp.

*   *   *

Zac was a part of the great exodus from Manila that day. He rode a jeepney from Singalong, past Rizal Park and across the Pasig to Santa Cruz where he got off and threaded his way through the footpath throng to a bus depot.

Inside the cavernous structure men, women and children pushed and squeezed their way into big, dusty buses that might have been maroon or dark brown. Engines revved, horns honked in warnings of imminent departures. "Beware, beware," he heard a gravel voice boom from a loudspeaker fixed to high rafters. "Pickpockets are everywhere. Guard your wallets and valuables. Report to security police if anything is missing."

Zac got on an already crowded and stuffy bus in which an image of Christ maintained vigil above the driver's head. All aboard knew Divine Intercession would be needed at least once on their journey! The driver revved the engine, this time edging forward. Vendors of eggs, sweets, papers and comics got out. Hastily, so did a family group who had discovered with shouts of alarm that they were on the wrong bus. Zac slipped into one of the vacated seats as the driver bullied a path through footpath pedestrians to the roadway and crawling traffic beyond. Then they were slowly negotiating backstreets, all the time bouncing and pitching on the cratered surfaces. Eventually the drabness that was at every window gave way to green fields and the rice bowl of central Luzon. But Zac, like many aboard who had seen it all countless times, had begun to doze uncomfortably.

He awoke with a start when the bus suddenly braked to a standstill. A stationary queue stretched ahead. They had stopped on a highway that cut across a vast expanse of rice fields. In the distance he could see farm labourers bent at work in the morning sun. The bus conductor got out and walked ahead, soon being obscured by a long line of trucks, buses and cars. At length, he returned.

"What's happening?" the driver asked, his passengers all ears.

"The highway's closed," the conductor reported. "An army helicopter is going to land there with a new general who came from a town near here. His buddies are waiting down the road in a motorcade."

The bus driver slapped his steering wheel in exasperation. "How long are we meant to sit here waiting?"

"I don't know," replied the other. "The drivers up ahead say the highway was blocked an hour ago."

"What next?" exploded the driver as a buzz of conversation filled the bus.

The woman next to Zac looked concerned. "My family is meeting me at the bus depot," she confided to him. "I hope they don't worry." Another woman told a travelling companion, "I'm carrying fresh meat. It might spoil."

Zac got out of the bus and joined a line of men urinating beside the road. He was about to re-board when he became aware of a distant throb. The farm hands had stopped working and were looking skyward. Zac searched above the green fields and saw an approaching helicopter, little more than a speck in size. A confusion of horns and sirens erupted from the direction of the motorcade. Several bus passengers were now excitedly gesturing skyward. The helicopter's khaki panelling became visible and the throb more of a vicious, repetitive thump. It rapidly overwhelmed the noisy reception on the ground. As the machine dropped towards the highway an unseen hand of turbulence advanced across the green carpet of grain. Then the helicopter was almost over Zac's head. Dust from the roadside swirled around his narrowed eyes. A metallic mayhem penetrated his hand-muffed ears. He saw the machine drop out of sight behind the outlines of trucks. He looked for a sign of the reception but saw nothing. Suddenly, the helicopter was airborne again and swiftly shrinking into the obscurity from where it had come. Car and truck motors started ahead. In the green fields the grain basked undisturbed in the morning sun and the workers were again bent earthward. The men drifted slowly back to the waiting bus.

*　　*　　*

Through Zac's window the Cordilleras of northern Luzon appeared as a distant and immobile herd of great elephants on a plain. Then they were gone, the bus turning to approach a bridge over a wide, dry riverbed that allowed only a trickle of water on the far side. Zac heard the swish, swish of metal framework as they sped by and, looking down to the dry bed, saw the makeshift shacks of the landless who eked a living salvaging anything of value the river would yield. In the water were glistening and unconsciously naked, skinny bodies. Zac remembered those of summer-time Villablanca. The nourished shapes, tall, tanned, in skimpy costume and neck jewellery, never unaware of their appearance, parading themselves as they shopped in narrow lanes and broad boulevards behind the beaches. Even fully clothed they never forgot themselves. Never. It all now seemed so artificial, so pointless. Yet, he knew he was tempted to take the easy way out of his present difficulties and go back. But did he really fit in? Did he belong there? What should he do? He just didn't know or, at that moment, care.

The questions drifted from his mind as the bus entered a new terrain of low foothills and colourful foliage obscuring settlements nestling by the highway. He noticed also the first suggestion of cooler air coming off the heightening mountains. Others had too and slid shut their windows. The driver changed to a lower gear to cope with steeper inclines and bends ahead. Higher and higher they went, cliffs now one side, chasms the other. Then they would cross a bridge and reverse the view. Zac caught glimpses among crevices and foliage of slender waterfalls that had lost their wet-season rage. But more obvious were the scarred paths of rock falls and denuded slopes, testimony of man's appetite for the wood of trees. Up and up the bus endlessly crawled till it got to a zig-zag ascent so great it seemed to threaten the life of the straining engine. Hands clenched in fear at the thought of a backward plunge. But the driver would snatch yet another, lower, gear and gravity continued to be defied. And quite suddenly the gradients eased, bends unravelled and houses appeared here and there. Patches of fog were in evidence, too, with the air noticeably chilly and passengers, as if at that moment reminded of the height, took jackets from bags and struggled into twisted sleeves. The bus picked up speed as it passed makeshift housing and abandoned quarries, obviously the ugly edge of city sprawl. Gradually the City of Pines asserted itself through parkland and a curious mixture of architecture embracing Swiss chalets, turn-of-the-century Americana and Oriental edifices.

Zac reached for his shoulder bag and, seeing a familiar city street, rapped on the ceiling. The driver steered to the kerb and stopped. Zac stepped out and the bus was away.

The spine of Baguio was steep, busy Session Road. With swift steps through narrow side-streets Zac was soon at the low end of the thoroughfare. On the overcast skyline the red spires of a cathedral rose above a commercial jumble thronged in the late morning with a chop-suey blend of humanity, changed forever since the days of pagan rule by head-hunting Igorots.

Zac approached the city markets, its frontage of many stands displaying, first, countless tiny baskets of strawberries, bottles of jams and honey. Next came hats, matting, clothing, shoes and souvenirs. Then it was masses of fruit. Bananas big and small, individually or in clumps, green, yellow, or black-streaked; mangoes, green and sour or amber and sweet; pineapples, whole or in slices enclosed in plastic wrap; papayas lumpy and yellow striped. And finally bins and bins of rice. Off the long frontage were numerous entrances, some mere slits between stands, and others wide and framing a view of the market proper. But Zac had no time to dawdle and, spotting a jeepney that would deliver him to the judge's house, got aboard.

*　　*　　*

He found Judge Enrico Garcia reading Don Quixote in a *sala*. The room overlooked a patio bedecked with various plants. Below the patio the land fell sharply away to a boulder-strewn brook, at first glance attractive but on acquaintance a gutter for garbage from surrounding houses. On the opposite bank the ground rose steeply, supporting leggy houses amid twisting pathways and tall trees. The judge's wife, who first greeted him, absented herself from the room in the manner of those *provinciana* who rarely joined the conversation of their menfolk. The judge extended a hand and fixing his piercing eyes on Zac said, "Ah, you kept your promise. It's good to see you again. Tell me all about Spain."

They sat down in separate armchairs, a timber coffee table between them, the Cervantes' novel and an ashtray on its surface. The judge listened to the younger man, nodding now and then and, when the conversation switched to their homeland, smiling faintly as if what he was hearing had a familiar ring. Knowing his host's fondness of holding court, Zac lapsed into a diplomatic silence allowing him to begin in his precise and often didactic manner of speech.

"Zacarias," the older man said, adjusting an armchair cushion, "do what you think right. I cannot advise which path you must take. But remember these words: nothing has really changed. You speak of corruption, political opportunism, election fraud, national division and the plight of the people. I can add another you have forgotten to mention—foreign meddling in the affairs of this poor land of ours."

The judge paused, apparently considering carefully his next words. "You should always remember that many of our ills originated in the days of the Spanish colonisers. That is said not to absolve us of responsibility but to state a historical fact. The Spanish governors,

63

officials and friars were often too busy making money instead of governing or attending to spiritual matters. The officials wanted security for their retirement in Spain. The friars wanted power on earth as well as heaven. With this state of affairs it was inevitable that in time, awe of the Spanish would be replaced by dislike and even hatred. Conversely, the Spaniards would know fear. And so it came to be. The Spanish rulers chose to remain inside their Walled City which you know as the Intramuros in Manila. And what is different today? Our new masters live behind walls in the capital. And for much the same reasons! As you know from your history books the Spaniards, despite their walls and guns, were challenged with increasing frequency by the people, especially towards the end of their rule. Their twilight years saw agitation from abroad by exiles and armed resistance at home by patriots. The Spanish resorted to trials by court martial and other forms of repression, again a not dissimilar scene to today. You know that the Americans replaced the Spanish rule eventually and new Filipino leaders arose but did you know of some of the election practices carried out under the guise of democracy? I know of these things because I, too, was a young man worried about my country's future at the time and wanted to see an end to shames of the past."

A maid carrying a tray came into the *sala* and set down two glasses of coconut juice and a plate of *sapin-sapin*, layered sticky rice cake.

Zac looked hungrily at the offering but did not make a move.

Judge Garcia shooed a fly away and proceeded, "Let me give you one example. And remember this was a practice of our brother Filipinos, not the Americans. The object was to get the vote of the masses. That means the *provinciano* was the main target. At election eve—and this was only a few years before the Japanese invasion—the *barrio* captains would carry out the orders of the political bosses and march the usually illiterate voters down a track to a community hall. There they would be harangued on how to vote. The *barrio* captains would reward with a few pesos every smiling face happy to carry out their instructions. Those who weren't, and they were few, would have to stay there all night if necessary till they changed their minds. We virtually had one-party rule as a result, not unlike the situation today. Do you see what I mean?"

"I suppose so," the younger man said, a little surprised at the direction the judge was taking, "but didn't we have a two-party system after the war?"

"Yes, we did. We had that but it was more the result of foreign interference than our natural tendencies." And, noticing the food was still untouched, hastily diverged, "Oh, please, do have something to eat."

Zac complied gratefully as the judge continued. "Understand that from the moment MacArthur waded ashore he played politics in the style of a Caesar. The American commander was supreme with his only superior—President Roosevelt—worn-out and dying half a world away. The general had his own favourite whom he wanted to lead our nation but to get him into power a new, second party had to be created, there being no vacancy for the leadership of the other. When the Americans went home we had as our first leader that man. So those years were an aberration and now we have reverted to normality."

The judge took his first sip of juice.

Zac said, "So you don't think things will change?"

He put down the glass. "There will be changes of face but, I believe, it will not alter the direction we are taking. Whichever group gains power by whatever means, even the hand of God, there will be an intolerance of rivals by those in power. Just look at some of the evidence since the war. In forty-eight the peasant masses represented by the Hukbalahap and associated unions were isolated from the political process when their movement was outlawed even though they took part peacefully in the previous election. Since then the Huk's descendants—The New People's Army—have been similarly outlawed. How many voices do they represent? Some say millions! I do not know but it is many. Now that *intolerance* is being paid for in blood. It's a high price. Massacres have occurred but can we always be sure whose finger is on the trigger? Thousands of guerrillas have supposedly surrendered in publicised ceremonies but are they all what they seem, or men selling their identities like the poor selling their blood?"

Judge Garcia paused, sadly shaking his head. "So, think about my words, Zacarias. And think about those who fill our history pages. You will see that our tradition is for strong men, as in the rest of Asia, and the past dictates our future course."

Later the two had lunch together in an elegant dining room, the judge's wife alternating between supervising kitchen help and promptly attending to her husband's needs. But when Zac resumed the broken journey that afternoon he still had not resolved on which path his future lay.

*   *   *

65

Ricardo Santos shifted uncomfortably on a rickety wooden stool, his back to a dirty wall. A spotlight directed at his goateed face almost blinded him with tears. He looked aside. He guessed the place was a warehouse basement. Of that he was fairly certain. Everything else was a confusion of impressions.

Earlier that night, by arrangement, he had waited in a poorly-lit back street of the university belt on the north side of the Pasig. Then a blackout had struck, leaving him in pitch darkness. Minutes later a vehicle on high beam had pulled up short of him and, before he fully realised it was his contact, several burly figures manhandled him into the back, unceremoniously shoving him to the cramped floor. As the vehicle lurched forward, a bag was put over his head. He was aware the driver was deliberately confusing him by taking a tortuous route. No one said a word. Just as he was starting to feel he would suffocate, the vehicle stopped. He was roughly pulled out, the bag still in place. He was waiting to be guided to his eventual destination when he heard a muffled horn and for no accountable reason got a vague impression he might be in a Chinatown lane on the north bank. He was shoved forward a few steps, bumping what he thought was a door frame. He had been led along a passage or area that smelt, even through the bag, of salt fish. Hands had held him firmly as he descended a flight of steps. He had become aware of a murmur of voices and had felt himself being gently seated. Retreating footsteps sounded on the stairs. At length, a man's soft voice had said, "You can remove the bag yourself now, Mr Santos."

When Ricardo recovered a little from the glare, the voice continued, "Thank you for coming. I must apologise for the precautions we take but there is no alternative if we are to survive."

Ricardo nodded.

"I am told you want to get your father out of the country in view of his present, uh, difficulties. Is that his wish also?"

"No, but he's open to persuasion. I think if I can convince him that it is feasible he'll go along."

"Oh, so he *is* reluctant."

"He thinks it's better to stand and fight than become another exile in the United States or somewhere else in the world."

"I would agree with that. The more the jails fill and graveyards flower with pressmen, politicians, union leaders and patriots the more inevitable becomes the downfall of the oppressors."

"There'll be enough names without adding my father to the roll. In any case, he knows a lot of influential people in the United States and will probably be more effective there."

The voice hardened. "The exiles over there don't seem to have made a great deal of difference, Mr Santos. Could it be that our enemies have more influential ears to whisper into?"

"Well, perhaps my father will help change th—"

"Could it be," the voice continued in cold disregard, "that they are bleating in considerable comfort—steak commandos I believe they are called—and in the wrong country? Bleating, in the very same country which stole this land! A country that pretended to be our friend and ally, ruled us for forty years and after wresting it back from the Japanese, who tried the same colonial trick, gave us a phoney independence that guaranteed us the perpetual rule of their friends, the elite. Oh, the oligarchy were only too happy to carry on a puppet role learned so well under both the Stars and Stripes and the Rising Sun. They didn't want to lose their position at the pinnacle of society. What better way then as conduits of neo-colonialism? Even the Usurper came to realise that. Let us give him his due. He had to establish a new order, a new power structure. So he threw out the old rules and promised the masses what they had never had in our recorded history: equality and justice, land reforms, and freedom from want. But in reality what did we get? What do we have instead? Why, the creation of *another* elite! This one with the military as henchmen, with licence to plunder and kill our fellow countrymen, to stuff their bellies and bank accounts, keep mistresses or pretty boys. Oh dear, how sad! How *disappointing*! The new order is not so new after all. And what of the old elite, the old order thrust aside to make way for the Usurper? A man they and their children will forever regard as a poacher of the power that is only theirs by birthright. I'll tell you! They left their poolsides and hurriedly dressed in immaculate *barong tagalogs* washed and ironed by their many slaves. They sped cool behind black windows through endless steamy slums. They glided past manicured lawns to the palace portico, their peace scripts rehearsed, their dry tongues ready to do the brain's bidding. They had reasoned there was no choice, no other way to keep what was theirs. So, they delivered the spiels and also, right on cue, laughed, joked, grovelled. Anything necessary to stay in the game to get their time-honoured slice of the cream cake. And they went away having mostly got their fill, but more importantly, surviving yet again to plot for the day when they would reassume power and get their revenge. Not like their proud, noble brothers, too squeamish to contemplate the thought of a little blood on their hands and who preach non-violence and faith in the Roman church and its God Almighty to restore a world that should never have been in the first place. A rotten world of serfdom under the blinding sun of Jesus love. A world smothered with comforting words and ideals serving only the perpetuation of bondage. Of bent backs in muddy fields forever belonging to others. Of exploitation in the workplace, of the jobless and idle living out existences in backstreets and squatter shacks. But no! no! protest the proud ones. Pray, persevere. Have faith in a better future. A place in the blinding sun; these nobles, of course, having the highest earthly elevations so that they can with the holy hierarchy continue to bestow upon those lower the high ideals, the God-given guidance. Middlemen for the manna from heaven! All of which, you may have deduced, Mr Santos, brings me to your father. He *is* one of those, isn't he."

Irritated, Ricardo waited to hear if the speaker had really finished. Or was he going to ask yet another rhetorical question? He had come to get help for his father and instead was captive to a political harangue.

"Well?" said the voice impatiently. "What do you have to say?"

"I didn't come here to listen to insults. I don't have to defend the record of my father. His contributions to this country and democracy are well—"

"Pah!" scoffed the voice. "Ask the poor downtrodden masses what democracy is. They don't know! They've never had it!"

"You've had your say," Ricardo snapped. "Let me have mine. Or is this your idea of equality where *I* must sit silent and only listen to *you*?"

A brief silence followed. Then the voice commanded, "Continue, Mr Santos."

"Thank you," he said. "If my father was born into privilege then that was fate and nothing else. Individuals have no control over that. But they are responsible for the conduct of their adult lives and I think, in that respect, my father can be truly proud. He has devoted his life to opposing oppression of any kind. At the same time he believes in non-violence, even if all around him don't. If you choose to regard him as simply one of the old elite that is your decision. He knows differently. He would never accept your view. He is one of the people but not for a people's dictatorship. There's a big difference."

"Mr Santos," a second voice interrupted. "Surely you will agree it is better than a dictatorship of the new elite which we have now. Do you know that the overwhelming majority of the wealth of this country is owned and controlled by a few per cent? That most of the people live in abject poverty? That most of the children are malnourished? That half the people in this metropolis are anaemic? I could go on and on."

"Of course I know. I have eyes."

"But not the will to fight for justice? Not the conviction to take up weapons and do something about it?"

"There are other ways to fight, though I admit to having doubts at times."

"Words are no match for guns," a gruff third voice said. "Guns keep our enemies in power and only days ago, not five minutes from your comfortable house, ended the life of a valued comrade. You would not know him but he had even surveyed your place the night before his death in a gutter, we anticipating an approach for help. He had reported it would not be easy. He never mentioned words as weapons. But we will hear no more from him. The enemy commanded too many triggers. That's the power of guns. We mourn him but know our day will come when our guns outnumber theirs. As for your father, see where he is now. Under house arrest and about to be tried for sedition. His newspaper is gathering cobwebs and you are begging us to risk our lives to save this man of words from jail."

"Asking not begging," Ricardo said tersely.

"Ah," the gruff voice responded. "The pride of the elite is coming out."

"You and your prejudice," Ricardo scoffed. "I suppose you would regard Rizal as one of the old elite."

"Rizal? Huh! A powder-puff. He was a faint-hearted revolutionary at best. He didn't stay with the people. He wrote stories in Spain. And when he came back he didn't think the people were ready for a revolution. He didn't support the people's greatest hero yet — Bonifacio. He didn't think the Spanish would arrest Rizal. He was a thinker who couldn't really think. No, give me a militant like Bonifacio every time! He was a true man of the people! We might not have been still fighting this struggle today if Bonifacio had got his way."

"Oh, forgive me," Ricardo said in mock apology. "I didn't know revolutions existed without writers. I didn't know words were so unimportant."

"Maybe they are necessary in the early stages. But the real power is the gun. You have a lot to learn, young man. Your father never will if he hasn't by now."

Ricardo shook his head in frustration. "Obviously I'm in the wrong place. If you feel that way about my father why bother with this sham?"

"Because Mr Santos," the first voice answered, "we do intend to help him get away."

"But I thought—"

"Yes, of course. We just wanted you to know what we thought. That's all. Pardon our manners. We don't get much opportunity to *socialise* with anyone these days."

Ricardo ignored the sarcasm.

"But why would you want to help?"

"We have our reasons, Mr Santos. And it suits us to demonstrate solidarity with others in the cause of combating the ruling reactionaries. Now, as for your father, this is what we have in mind . . ."

· CHAPTER FOUR ·

Midnight mass in the old adobe church was over. Worshippers spilled into the dark streets of tiny Baza, shouts of "Merry Christmas, *Maligayang Pasko*," rising above the chatter and laughter. Zac and his brother Arturo separated from the excited cluster. The older Arturo disliked crowds. He had never ventured far from the family farmlet just outside the township. Arturo feared the uncertainties of the world beyond and had told Zac once, "I'll be a farmer till I die."

They walked slowly away and towards the town's park. Alongside its boundary they stopped.

"Can you ever forget?" Zac asked softly.

Arturo shook his head of thinning hair. "Never."

In the moonlight the brothers looked at the dim outlines of shrubbery and an elevated concrete lookout that the townsfolk called a tree house. At length, Zac broke the silence and said, "The place looks better now than it did then."

"That was eighteen years ago," Arturo said. "Sometimes it seems like yesterday."

"It was all so meaningless."

"It usually is."

"What did happen to the man who fired the first shot? I've often wondered about that lately."

Arturo rubbed his forehead. "I think he was killed too. But I'm not sure. It was so long ago."

The moon had disappeared behind high cloud drifting towards the South China Sea. A strengthened darkness enveloped the park. The brothers stood motionless, yet drifting like the cloud towards a time past. They did not see anymore the dim outlines of shrubbery and swings. They did not even hear the last faint goodbyes of distant worshippers departing the churchyard. Their thoughts were instead locked in unison on a night embedded in memory, a night that began as one of festive revelry . . . a night in which two small boys at the back of a crowd strained precariously for height on an unharnessed *carabao* cart.

71

"I still can't see," Zac complained to his brother. "Hold me up Arty."

Arturo was tired of Zac's complaints and crossly replied, "No! If I do that I can't see. And the cart's too wobbly." But feeling that perhaps he had been too harsh, Arturo softened his tone. "I'll tell you what's happening instead."

And much was happening that night in Baza. It was the annual festival and almost everyone in the farming community was there. In the showground, little more than a large plot, a charity queen contest was reaching a climax. All the twenty-two *barrios* of Baza had put forward their candidates — always young unmarried women — whose task it had been to raise money that would eventually go to a fund for the town's benefit. *Barrio* residents had enthusiastically supported their choices with dances and charity auctions. All the same, most in Baza expected the young lady representing *Barrio* Mabusag to win because its inhabitants could always rely on relatives from Hawaii to considerably boost contributions. And yes, a cheer went up from a section of the crowd in front of a stage. Voices buzzed. *Barrio* Mabusag had won again! Fireworks were readied nearby for the crowning ceremony.

The charity benefit was not the only attraction. Over the road on another open allotment, behind the two boys, a ferris wheel did brisk business, stalls sold pink cotton candy and coloured movies filled a screen in a big tent. Outside another tent a magician on a wooden platform demonstrated his skills in an endeavour to entice a crowd inside.

At the back of an audience watching the magician was a uniformed policeman, an automatic rifle held loosely in the crook of his right arm and pointed earthward. The officer was completely engrossed and failed to notice a man approaching with a revolver. A little girl did, though. She tried to tell her parents but her voice was lost in the audience's *oohs* and *ahhs* and applause. The man continued his advance, stopping a few strides short to aim unsteadily at the capped head.

A spurt of flame erupted. The patrolman swayed in shock, his lower jaw a bloody pulp, the rifle dangling from a limp arm. From where his tongue had once functioned came inarticulate gurgles. The horrified crowd wheeled and stared, the magician now forgotten. A woman screamed, then others. The policeman saw the horrified faces and his mind became a mirror. His eyes bulged in fear at the knowledge of imminent doom. Death! Death! Death! the crazed brain screamed. Oh, horror! Sweet Jesus! Merciful God! Why me? Why not them? Why not . . . He slowly raised the

72

rifle with both arms. Screams of terror erupted anew. The dying man squeezed the trigger. Figures before him collapsed as the rapid-fire began to take its toll. Aghast, the crowd stampeded away from the spray of death, away from the still and bloodied bodies of Pablo and Josefina Campora and others sprawled on red splotched earth.

Then the crazed man began to stagger onward . . .

On the opposite ground fireworks erupted noisily as Baza's newest charity queen was crowned. Cheers and clapping accompanied her moment of triumph. As they subsided, other noises began to dominate: confused shouts and sharp, rapid cracks that turned heads away from the bright stage to their source. Those at the back of the audience, including the boys, were first to see a mob spilling to the roadway. The sight was met with stares of incomprehension till screams of "Massacre, massacre, Man amok," registered. In seconds the carnival was a nightmare, the cart an island in a sea of panic. Arturo and Zac looked into the blur, seeking the faces of their parents. As cracks broke out again they instinctively crouched low inside the cart, arms covering their heads. They felt a bump and heard a moan, "Dear God. Mercy. Mercy." Trembling, they remained huddled for what seemed ages. Only when an eerie silence enveloped their refuge did the boys dare raise their heads and peep out. The road and dark surrounds were strangely empty of life except for still figures seemingly asleep on the ground. Arturo pulled Zac's sleeve and hoarsely whispered, "Come on Zac. Quickly." The two scrambled out and ran and ran. The outlines of the Town Hall loomed ahead. Figures silhouetted by dim lights within shouted, "In here boys. It's safe."

. . . It's safe, it's safe. The words spanned the years.

"How many did die Arturo?"

"Sixty-two," he said, shivering in the oddly cool night air.

As moonlight returned the two linked arms and began the walk home.

*   *   *

The farm faced the rising sun. It was reached from the town by a narrow earth road that wound its way around patches of jungle and fields of rice, garlic, vegetables and tobacco. Farm houses were grouped by the road in threes and fours with short stretches of thick foliage between. Aunt Maria's house was on stilts, a traditional design and consequently one of the oldest structures in the community. Oblong in shape and made of weathered wood and bamboo, it had a crude volcano-style roof and wooden window

73

covers patterned with whitish shell inserts. At dawn, when the insect swarms that filled the night had finally vanished, the covers were slid open. Midway at the front of the elevated house was a verandah entrance reached by sturdy bamboo ladder steps. At the rear was a stone well amid greenery and coconut palms, a collection of makeshift shelters for a variety of animals, and a thatched-roofed hut with a drainage hole in its earth floor for defecation.

Roosters crowing from tree branches by the house awoke Zac just before dawn, stirring memories of childhood. His parents had always been superstitious about them, fervently believing that if one crowed from its perch only hours after sunset it meant bad luck. His mother had also believed that the clicking of a wall lizard meant she would receive a letter soon. Quite often that had happened. When she had gone to the town market and post-office, as she always did twice a week, a letter would be waiting and she would say, "There, I told you." Everyone pretended not to remember the lizard's warning if no mail had been received. Once, however, the post-master, who knew her belief, said, "None today. Lizard's annual picnic."

The parents' superstitions had continued almost to the day of their death. A week before the festival Pablo and Josefina had begun a journey to town by cart to sell some produce. Zac had accompanied them, riding on top of big bundles of garlic and watching the farm recede into the distance. Then, he heard his parent's concerned voices and felt the cart come to a stop. "We're going home. We saw a girl," his mother had said. How disappointed young Zac had been to miss a market day! He had voiced his feelings but his parents would not waver. They *knew* there would be no sale if the first person one met on the way to the markets was a girl and that was that.

Some of their beliefs had concerned food. While the rice seed was sprouting prior to its transfer to the field, no one was allowed to eat soft bamboo shoots otherwise the germinating seed would fail to grow. Another superstition had been about young bachelors who sat at the dinner table after others had started their meal. All the plates had to be washed at once or the young man would never find a wife. And so on it went.

Zac rose for breakfast, his feet touching a floor of smooth, slatted bamboo strips that allowed in air and a view underneath the house of stored grain in bags. A fowl and her brood had begun the daily round, pecking among the bags for spilt seed. Zac's aunt was busy in the kitchen, squatting by a mud-brick platform on which pots steamed over burning wood and glowing ash. He knew it was useless to protest at her activity though he was an accomplished cook and always welcomed the opportunity.

"Happy Christmas, Aunt Maria," he said and gently chided, "I could have done the cooking. You shouldn't work so hard."

"Uh," she grunted in a response that could have meant anything but Zac took to represent her oft-repeated words of earlier days, "I like work, my boys. I will always work while God gives me strength."

"Where's Arturo?" Zac asked, as if they were having a normal conversation.

"Ah," she gasped, pointing a weathered arm towards the fields beyond coconut palms.

"I suppose Ramon is sleeping in as usual," Zac commented of his elder brother.

"Umm."

"Nothing really changes, does it, Aunt Maria," he said, suddenly remembering the judge's verdict on the nation.

His aunt pointed to a heavy urn of cold water and then to an empty bowl. Zac poured water into the vessel and watched the old woman wash soot from her hands. A fowl flapped up to a window sill and surveyed the scene with jerky motions of its head. Zac waved it away and helped his aunt carry food to the table. Arturo came in and they ate breakfast together.

Towards the end of the meal Ramon appeared and, as usual, sat down to eat in silence. He had little in common with the others, his interests being gambling, cockfights and wine. And he did not care what anyone thought of his behaviour now because he was staying only till the day he got a letter from the American Embassy in Manila clearing his departure for Honolulu. In fact, he had already bought a big blue suitcase in preparation.

Ramon had married a widowed Filipina who had American citizenship and lived in Hawaii. The widow had a job as a sales assistant in Honolulu's vast Ala Moana commercial centre. Ramon had a picture postcard of the complex atop of which was a revolving restaurant. He had pinned it to his bedroom wall as a reminder of his future in a land likened, by the Baza townsfolk who had been there, to a paradise. A photo of Louisa was pinned beneath. Louisa returned to her family home in Baza every year. It was on her last visit that she had wed Ramon. Louisa's savings made her a wealthy woman by the standards of Baza. She had bankrolled her new husband before returning to Hawaii so that he could speculate in garlic while waiting for his papers to come through, a lengthy process which someone had told Ramon could take years. In any case, the garlic business was keeping him occupied in the day and he had enjoyed some success at the markets after he correctly anticipated rising prices. Subsequently he had made the rounds of surrounding farms, buying up more stocks. Unfortunately, prices were now falling and scores of bundles lay unsold under the farm house. However, win or lose at the markets or the cockpit, he ignored the family plight beyond a token few pesos for housekeeping. Aunt Maria had long stopped holding her hand out to Ramon for more money. But one thing she had not stopped doing: praying to God nightly that Ramon would soon be gone.

Arturo was the first to leave the breakfast table, returning to the field. It did not matter to him that it was Christmas Day. The ploughing would not wait. Ramon was soon on his way, too, for a possible sale, at cost, of the garlic to a group of Chinese businessmen up from Manila. Zac drifted to the front entrance and rummaged through a pile of old shoes. He found a pair that fitted and called to his aunt, "I'm going to the field for a while."

The ground that Arturo worked was a distance from the house and beyond a line of trees. As Zac approached he could see his brother in a battered straw hat wrestling with a wooden plough harnessed to a *carabao*. Arturo was too engrossed to notice he had company. Zac stood apart as he watched the plough rip another jagged furrow of exposed dark earth giving the partly worked plot an increasingly striped appearance.

Then Arturo reversed direction and saw his brother.

"Come to give a hand?" he called.

"Would you like one?"

Arturo did not reply, but when he got close reined in the big, gentle animal and said, "You'd better wear my boots."

They exchanged footwear. Zac felt dampness inside the boots.

He took the reins and plough handle, it all bringing back dusty memories. Suddenly the *carabao* was lumbering forward, Zac having to almost run lest he be left behind. At the same time he was wrestling with a twisting plough and wishing he had Arturo's experienced arms to cope with its vindictiveness. He glanced back and saw a snaking furrow. Did he also see a grin under that hat? He swore as the plough seemed to want to veer this way and that. Then they were at the end of the plot and turning for another furrow. Zac was conscious of sweat trickling down his shirted back. He had meant to wear the hat too. Perhaps he would get it on the way back. He noticed his brother now sitting and chewing a stalk and surmised that he was probably having his first rest by a field for months. Or years. Ramon was never available. He hadn't been, either, but at least had not depended on the others. Zac changed direction again and saw with satisfaction the completion of a straighter furrow. Not as good as it should be, but reasonable.

"Much better," Arturo said as Zac passed the second time.

"See what you say next time."

Zac gripped the plough anew, determined to achieve what had been usual once. Then he could match Arturo, furrow for furrow. At the end of a day they would go, towels around waists, to the well behind the bamboo stand at the back. For added privacy from the elevated glimpses of others in the house at their revealed nakedness, they would squat on a smooth, wide stepping stone while each in turn operated a weighted bamboo pole beside the well and brought up cool buckets of water. After dressing they would briefly watch the western sun sink behind the trees, darkness never far away. They would wander back to the house above, its interior lit by kerosene lamps. Steaming rice, vegetables and meat always awaited them on the kitchen table. Zac knew those had been good, simple days.

Arturo was by his side once again.

"Very good, brother," he said.

"I haven't finished."

Arturo glanced around, measuring the shrunken strip of smooth earth. "About twelve more furrows."

"And then?"

The other smiled. "Why not a dip in the river?"

"Why not? It is Christmas," Zac laughed, urging the *carabao* forward again.

A little way down the plot Arturo called, "With you home it is," and quite suddenly Zac knew where he *should* be.

* * *

At the Singalong pension the boys were playing their usual game of hide and seek with Luz. The manageress had left the building for a Christmas lunch at her relatives, unaware the vendor was roaming the hallways to confront those in debt. The boys did not deliberately defraud Luz when they promised to repay her for meals bought on credit. They intended to honour their word the next day, or if things went wrong—meaning a shortage of clients— payment would be at the end of the week. Or, at least that is what they hoped would happen.

The boys had other ways of getting money aside from the hours spent at El Torro, the Milky Way, shopping centres and Rizal

Park. It only required the investment of a few pesos, an often difficult task, and a bit of imagination to yield quite spectacular results. The boys called it drama. Most of it took place in letters written to former clients or current boyfriends who had given their addresses before flying away till the next visit.

Typhoons were a favourite dramatic prop. In a typical year about twenty-five swirled across the archipelago, the sky a canvas for Nature's violent temper. Most struck between June and November and caused loss of life and considerable damage to property and crops. The boys cashed in on the international coverage that the calamities often attracted. "The damage was terrible in my home province," they would write. "The iron roof of my parent's house was ripped off. Luckily no one was hurt. Now they are living with neighbours. They don't have enough money to get a new one. I'm doing my best to help." A month later cheques would arrive from soft touches in Perth, Auckland, Seattle, Berne, Salzburg and Nice.

Student fees ranked a close second. "Fees have gone up again," concerned lovers in Australia and Hawaii would be told. "I'm giving up the course. What a waste of eight months." Urgent, registered letters from Ipswich, Queensland, St Kilda, Victoria, and Hawaii Kai, Oahu, would be sent with the advice, "Don't give up . . . Education pays dividends . . . Nothing good comes easy . . . Sending another draft around Easter."

In letters, the mortality rate of the boys' parents was alarming, too. Mothers died regularly of breast cancer, heart failure and even childbirth caused by inconsiderate fathers. For their part, fathers died from lung cancer, brain tumours or blood feuds with drunken neighbours. Frenchmen seemed particularly affected by the passing of mothers. "I very sorry to hear your mother's death," they would lament. "You must miss her. With money you buy some flowers for the grave and try be happy."

Post-office theft was a good standby. "I got your letter today, my darling, but not the money," one boy wrote sadly to Ilford, Essex. "The envelope was torn. Registered mail is the only way." A second letter, this time registered, would arrive in due course. And for good measure a bank cheque had been sent instead.

The other form of drama involved live encounters. Many award-winning performances were given in the privacy of hotel suites. "God," gasped a callboy arriving a little late for an assignation and collapsing on a handy couch. "I've just been robbed. I took a short cut through a dark alley and," pausing to catch his breath, "two men with knives took my wallet and watch." If the performance went well—and the callboys were troupers—the startled client made up some of the imaginary difference.

Several in the colony would arrive at hotel assignations carrying books, though the comics and porno magazines strewn about their Singalong rooms belied true preferences. The books were props for assumed identities that hopefully would boost their incomes. The most commonly adopted role was that of struggling student and so the weightier the title the better. A "Student's Introduction to Engineering" or "Principles of Chemistry" were considered perfect for the job. The impressed client, who had arranged the hotel rendezvous earlier in the day when he first met the boy in Rizal Park, would say, "You never told me you were a student." The boy would shrug and reply, "First year science. This helps pay the fees." Feeling somehow pleased at his choice, the client's reward would be a little larger.

Every so often the book ploy would backfire, especially with more classic works. The client would peer at the cover of "Sons and Lovers" and ask, "How do you find D. H. Lawrence?" Pleased that the prop had been noticed, the callboy would confide, "He's my favourite author. I always get his latest book."

The deceptions were not all on one side. Quite a few clients evaded paying for their pleasure. "I'm fresh out of money, old chap," an English bank manager based in Bangladesh said as he got under a shower. "I tell you what. Come around tomorrow at noon after I've been to the bank. I'll fix you up then." Early next morning the Englishman checked out for a flight to Cebu. His deception was more subtle than the doctor from Tasmania. As the man dressed after a session with two boys he snapped, "I bought you both lunch. That's enough."

Young foreign customers had to be watched too. They were prone to hang on to their money but more for reasons of pride than thrift. Afterwards, they would sometimes say in surprised, hurt voices, "I never pay for sex. I thought you liked me." Or, shocked, "I didn't know you were a callboy."

If drama failed to get results the boys would resort to selling their possessions or pawning them. Lito had pawned his yellow camera to Jessie, rich overnight again after meeting a grateful old Austrian. Poor again, Jessie had pawned it to a married couple in the next room. Private pawning, however, was limited as few boarders had much money to spare. So the boys would visit the pawnshops scattered throughout Manila. If the boys unwittingly went to unscrupulous ones they risked not seeing their possessions again. These pawnshops deliberately posted maturity notices with incorrect addresses to their hopefully forgetful customers to prevent them redeeming the articles or renewing the contract. Complaints had swamped officialdom and the Bureau of Post had exposed the racket but the practice continued.

Loan sharks were the last resort. The illegal business flourished in Manila with interest rates reading like a balloonist's altimeter. In any case, callboys were considered poor risks.

Whatever the excuses for unpaid debts, Luz had grown weary of hearing sad tales and the boys embarrassed at telling them. With the vendor's bellows sounding through the hallways it was simpler to remain quiet in their locked rooms or if caught elsewhere in the pension, the darkness of a toilet cubicle.

In the process the pension sometimes became a ghost house.

"I know you're all here. Come out and pay up," she yelled to an unseen audience. Silence.

"No more credit then," she threatened.

A curious cat peeped at the fat figure from a hallway corner.

"And no more food." More silence.

The war of words began to escalate.

"I'll tell the constabulary!" she bellowed as crackers erupted in the dry canal outside.

"They'll put you all in jail!"

A door slammed in another hallway.

"And they won't let you out!"

Jojo was in his room and could hear the performance. It was beginning to greatly irritate him. The word constabulary had stirred him to action. He opened his door and said, "I think they've gone out."

The vendor waddled up to the Igorot.

"Gone out? They didn't pass me and I was outside."

"Early, Luz. Before you got there."

The vendor's eyes narrowed. Was he telling the truth? Or covering up for those good-for-nothings?

"I'll come back," she said, deciding the Igorot was in league with the other side. "They'll be sorry. I'll teach them. You tell those boys."

Outside the pension, Luz puzzled at what she had glimpsed in the Igorot's room. Why did he have on the floor an open paint tin? And black too. What was he painting? Not the room. That wasn't allowed. One of the boarders told her that. Along with all the other don'ts. That bitchy manageress was a tyrant with her rules. No, the paint was for something else. And it was something odd. Her beady eyes came alight. Why not sell the information? Maybe this time the *barangay* captain would listen to her suspicions. He had been uppity of late. Just because of that other business. Anyone could make a mistake though she still didn't think she had. Yes, she would tell Fortunato. This time he should listen.

*   *   *

Jojo was partly correct when he told Luz the boys had gone out. Only Efren, Santiago and Carlo, all in debt, remained. Efren had been in a hallway when he heard the vendor's bellowing and fled to a smelly toilet cubicle. Santiago and Carlo locked their doors and turned off radios. Ace was on his way to Jakarta with money in his pocket, having sold his treasured cassette to a callboy from another colony. Martin had gone to the popular Christmas Day movies where in the dark he hoped to forget about Roderick for a few hours. Lito had got up early and was cruising Rizal Park because it had been lucky for him last Christmas. He had got a trip to Hong Kong out of his client. Tommy had been out all night and had not come back. Jessie was visiting his big family in their squatter's shack in the suburbs. Aussie Max slept exhausted on the sixth floor of a luxury hotel near Rizal Park, in the arms of an Australian macho from Dubbo. And Bongbong was, once again, on his way to Mindoro, this time with a young German as a client.

The trip was Bongbong's fourth this year. The unusually-tall callboy with merry, dancing eyes had instantly attracted the blond youth. Bongbong had been cruising the park without success for nearly an hour. Competition was heavy with boys hovering around prospects. About to leave, Bongbong saw the European smile at him. After that signal they had spent the night together and, in the small hours, Klaus said, "Can you take me to a place called Mindoro." Now they were about to sail on the morning ferry from Batangas, having risen at dawn and journeyed by bus to the port city. Throbbing engines announced an imminent departure. Bongbong had chosen the upper deck because of the better view. Crewmen were about to cast off.

"Wait!" yelled a deckhand at the sight of two approaching figures running along the wooden pier, bags in hand. "Late arrivals," he called to the skipper.

The first to reach the gangplank was a woman in her twenties dressed skimpily in bright colours which announced her trade.

"Jee-zus," gasped her pot-bellied foreign companion in a nasal accent as he finally caught up. "Thought we'd never make it luv. Ran like a bloody Bondi tram."

Bongbong stuck his head out the port-side window and recognised

Rizal Rita clambering aboard. As the ferry got under way the latecomers made their way to the upper deck, bags in hand. The woman's eyes met Bongbong's in mutual hostility.

"Hoy! *Bakla*!" she boomed in Tagalog, letting all on the top deck know Bongbong's sexual orientation if they had not already guessed. "Having a paid holiday in Mindoro?"

"Hoy! Ugly!" he called back. "Are you paying the fat man to go with you?"

Not speaking Tagalog, the fat man happily found a seat opposite Rita's apparent Filipino friend and said, "This'll do nice luv," and sat down.

Once settled, Rita opened Round Two.

"Oh, a yellow banana this time," she observed of Bongbong's youthful companion now reading a German novel.

"Tastier than pumpkins," Bongbong replied as the pumpkin dipped a hand into a canvas bag and got out a can of beer.

"Pumpkins are better for you," she retorted.

"Bananas are sweeter," he countered.

Titters came from behind. The banana turned a page. The pumpkin pulled a tab off the can with a pssst! and took a swig.

Round Three saw Bongbong take the offensive.

"You look so different with your new false teeth, Rita."

"Better than your crooked ones."

"I hardly recognised you. Have you dyed your hair as well?"

"Perhaps you need glasses."

"And those clothes, Rita. Where did you get them? From a trash can?"

"Can't you tell fashion when you see it?"

"There's not much to see."

"More to show off."

"So I see. Are you expecting again?"

"You really do need glasses."

"Who's the man this time?"

"My grandmother has a spare pair."

"Or don't you know?"

"Probably you need two."

"Is it that park cop?"

"I don't go with Filipinos anymore."

"Or won't they go with you?"

Rita hit back in Round Four.

"Your banana likes books. Maybe more than you."

"Your pumpkin sucks cans. Maybe they smell nicer."

"Your banana was picked too early."

"Your pumpkin is rotten."

"*Baklas* eat bananas like monkeys."

"Whores eat pumpkin like pigs."

"*Baklas* like sewers as playgrounds."

"Whores have playgrounds in sewers."

Gasps broke out among Filipino passengers. The banana looked up momentarily, then resumed reading. The pumpkin pulled the tab off a second can of beer.

Bongbong went for a technical knock-out in the Fifth.

"Where did you pick up your pumpkin? Rizal Park?"

"Probably the same place as you."

"Did you show him your old workplace in the park toilets?"

"Shhh! Not so loud."

"Do you miss cleaning the bowls?"

"Someone had to do it."

"But you gave it up in a hurry?"

"An opportunity came by."

"You mean an Arab."

"Stop it, stop it, big mouth," she hissed. "Everyone can hear."

"You started it Rita."

"I don't care. Just stop it."

"Next time don't start what you can't stop."

"All right! Just leave me alone."

Klaus looked up from his book again and saw the Filipina seemed upset about something. "What's wrong with her?"

"Gut ache," Bongbong confided in an ear. "Too many pumpkin seeds."

*   *   *

Klaus was not particularly impressed with his first sighting of Mindoro's Puerto Galera. There were tall yachts riding at anchor in a tranquil harbour and distant mountain tops shrouded in cloud, but it all seemed marred by an ugly waterfront and ramshackle structure behind. Ashore the impression firmed as he trailed Bongbong, filling in time till a motorised outrigger became available for the final leg of the journey. To the European the commercial hub was a TV rerun of Main Street in a horseless Wild West, housing the other side of a rise unremarkable and on the dreary outskirts a market, a cemetery of overripe, blackened fruit. Only the sight of clucking fowls patrolling the hot, dusty streets brought a smile to his thin lips.

"Don't take much notice of the town," the Filipino advised. "The scenery gets better."

Klaus came upon a wooden sign nailed to a tree trunk. The youth spoke English well but was still puzzled to read, "We enjoy the parade of finery. Please respect our enjoyment."

"What does it mean?"

The other said, "Oh, *that*. Culture clash I guess. Too many Manila bikinis. We're in the provinces now. That isn't liked here."

Returning to the waterfront, the pair were about to board an outrigger piloted by a gap-toothed man when they saw military police hurrying towards the craft.

"Open your bags!" a captain loudly commanded Bongbong, ignoring the European.

"Why? What do you want?" the callboy asked.

"Just open the bags. We'll put the questions."

Bongbong unzipped the bag and set it down.

"Where are you going?" the officer asked as his men emptied its contents on the wharf.

"To an outer island," Bongbong replied, not taking his eyes off the hands rummaging his belongings.

"To an outer island *sir*!" the captain barked.

Bongbong was silent.

"Why don't you address me correctly?" the officer asked.

Bongbong remained mute.

"Anything there?" the captain queried without diverting his curious gaze from the Filipino youth.

"Nothing sir," one replied.

The captain narrowed his eyes. "You are lucky you have company," he said softly, menacingly. "You may go but next time, I warn you, watch your manner."

As the boatman impassively looked on, Klaus helped Bongbong gather the scattered contents of the bag and asked quietly, "What was that for?"

Bongbong shrugged. "Probably they were searching for drugs."

"But they can't treat you like that," said Klaus who had not understood a word, only that he was witness to an ugly scene.

Bongbong smiled at his companion. "Forget it," he advised, zipping his bag and stepping carefully into the narrow hull of the waiting craft.

Underway at last, they skimmed glassy waters, jagged coral passing beneath. Vegetation was thick on all shores. Klaus, whose youth had been partly spent in Brazil with his parents, thought he was on an Asian delta of Amazonian proportions. Actually, it was an illusion created by a confusion of islands and shoreline. The craft beached in a sandy cove. Bongbong paid the boatman, rejoining Klaus already ashore. He led his companion up a rise through coconut palms. Then Klaus saw their destination through a clearing: a line of elevated, native-style huts of bamboo and grass weave. All had criss-cross verandahs. At a glance the European knew he had arrived at a place as close to paradise as he would ever get in this world. Klaus mounted steps for a view while Bongbong negotiated with the owner. From a verandah, he saw the sweep of blue bays and thin lines of yellow, behind which green palms rose in waves to mountain peaks. He marvelled at Nature's grand design. Bongbong returned, a bargain struck, and the pair moved into their new home. Here, for a short span of their lives the two would find a peace that they would always remember as long as they drew breath. There would be days of sun and sparkling water; nights of conversations under kerosene lanterns and bed matting under mosquito nets. They would forget air-conditioning, television, hot showers, cinemas, icecream, tele-phones, newspapers and all the paraphernalia of civilisation. For they were in a time warp where mankind had left his gadgets and taken a giant leap backward into a slow and isolated world.

*   *   *

Jessie trudged a dusty path between ragged rows of shacks. He was tempted to take the handkerchief from his back pocket and press it firmly to his nose. He did not. He knew it would be the action of an outsider, though that was what he really was. He had lived here for seven years, yet had no bond with Balut, Tondo. Only revulsion. And maybe fear. That was his other reason for staying his hand. He was carrying money and knew that strangers were the first to be rolled in Balut. He had seen it happen before. The money had come from a client the previous night and he wanted to give it to his parents before it slipped from his hands, as it always was seeming to do. Maybe it would get his family into a better part of the slum away from the stench, he thought, recognising a familiar alley distinguished from all the others only by a neighbour's frontage of board and orange plastic sheeting, just then being urinated on by a little boy without pants.

Jessie reached a door and pushed. He was adjusting his eyes to the gloom when he heard a voice say wearily, "Hullo son."

"Hullo mama," he said cheerfully. "Merry Christmas."

His mother sighed. "How long are you staying with us this time?"

Jessie had intended going after an hour but instinct warned him otherwise. "I thought I'd spend the day with you all."

"That's a welcome change," she said, a little brighter.

Jessie glanced around. "Where's pa and the others?"

"Oh, they'll be back soon. They've been at the dump all morning. Something was tipped last night and they're seeing what they can get."

"Business as usual even on Christmas Day, huh?" he said, looking into the sad eyes of his mother.

"I guess so, Jessie," she replied, putting a bony hand on a cheek. "Nothing ever seems to get better."

Jessie sat on a wobbly chair and began unlacing his shoes.

"I've got something for you mama. It might help."

"Oh," she said, curious at his actions.

"I saved it. Maybe it might get you away from this stink."

"I stopped smelling that years ago," she said, watching him pull the shoes off and take out something compressed.

Jessie thrust a wad of notes into her hands. "You know best what to do with this," he said.

"Blessed saints," she gasped. "Where did you get it all?"

"I just saved it from my job," he said casually.

"But there's so much. How can a kitchen hand save all this?"

"We get our share of tips from customers."

His mother looked at Jessie doubtfully. "How can people have so much money?"

"I ask myself the same question everyday," he replied, putting his shoes back on. "I guess they're born in the right place at the right time, not like us."

"We should never have left the provinces," she said bitterly.

"Why did we, mama?"

"For a better life. Or so your papa and I thought."

"Perhaps things mightn't be as bad now."

She put the money inside a rusty tin on a shelf and faced her son. "Just how bad are they, Jessie?"

"Well," he shrugged, puzzled. "You should know."

"Do I, son?"

"What do you mean, mama," he reluctantly asked, suspecting a scene he had often dreaded.

"There's been talk around here about what you do for a living."

"Talk?" he asked, feigning innocence. "What's being said?"

"Teresita next door says her son saw you talking to men in Rizal Park."

"So what?" he said with a wave of hand. "Everyone talks to everyone in the park. It's a friendly place."

"These men were foreigners."

86

"Them too, mama. They come to the park to enjoy the music and scenery."

"Then you were seen going off with one."

"Probably going the same way," he replied, growing increasingly disturbed.

"And Roque followed you."

"Yes?" he asked weakly.

"You went to a big hotel near the park. Roque tried to go in too but a security guard at the door stopped him."

"Yeah. They don't let spies in," he said savagely.

"Son, what were you doing?" his mother asked anxiously.

Jessie scratched his forehead. "When did the little snoop see all this?"

"Teresita says two weeks ago."

"Oh, yeah," Jessie pretended to remember. "An American asked me to his hotel for a friendly drink. His first visit to Manila. I couldn't be unfriendly and say no. I wasn't even going to mention it because I know you don't like drink."

"Are you sure that's all there is to it son?" she asked, her face still concerned.

"Of course mama!" he lied. "What else could there be?"

She evaded the question. "Are you sure you're all right?"

"Sure," Jessie said giving his mama the first hug in months. "I'm a big boy now."

Jessie felt a wetness on his shoulder sleeve. "Don't cry," he said softly.

"I thought we were losing you," a muffled voice said. "I've been so worried."

"No chance of that mama," the Superstar replied, mentally crossing Rizal Park off his day-time schedule.

*   *   *

Lito was having a frustrating morning at Rizal Park. Ever since he spotted his first prospect minutes after walking in the southern entrance, he had been dogged by bad luck.

He had no sooner sat down by a pale man wearing dark glasses and said, "Hullo, my name's— ", when the prospect got up with an "Excuse me" and strolled over to a boy reading a book on the grass.

Lito had then moved to the other side of the park and sat down next to a middle-aged man in a floral shirt.

"Hullo, my name's Lito," he said. "What's yours?"

"You'll have to speak up," the stranger replied. "That's my deaf ear."

Lito had risen to change sides when a rival sat down by the floral shirt's good ear. He watched them walk off together.

Lito had been sure of the third man when he saw him winking in his direction. Lito had checked around and could see no one else. The man had to be winking at him. The callboy had almost run to the bench seat and sat down.

"Hullo," he said breathlessly, "My name's Lito. What's yours?"

"Heindrick," the man said, in an accent which Lito assumed to be German but was Dutch.

"Have you been in Manila long?" the callboy asked, slipping into a well-practised conversation.

"Three days," Heindrick said, winking at Lito.

"And do you like it here," the callboy queried, pleased at the rapid progress.

"It's a bit hot for me."

"Does your hotel have air-conditioning?"

"Certainly," Heindrick replied, winking twice.

Taking the plunge, Lito ventured, "Would you like me to come to your hotel?"

"What do you mean?" the man responded, winking again.

"Er, to see your room," the callboy said, puzzled.

"Why do you want to do that?"

"I thought *you* did."

"It never entered my mind," Heindrick said, equally puzzled.

"But you—"

"But what?" Heindrick demanded with countless winks.

"Forget it," Lito said and walked off.

That had happened half an hour ago and he had not seen anything resembling a prospect since. On another bench Lito debated whether he should try once more or quit the park and go and eat something for lunch. He was feeling famished. His stomach had just decided in favour of food when a ginger-haired man approached and sat down besides him. Lito rejoiced. It was a small bench and a third person would have difficulty joining them.

"Do you have the time, mate?" the foreigner asked.

"Nearly midday," Lito said, happily showing his watch.

"Thanks," the man said, resetting his own.

The callboy took a breath. "My name's Lito. What's yours?"

"Frank," the man replied, wiping his nose with the back of his hand.

"Is this your first visit here?"

"Yeah. Just got here yesterday mate."

"Then you don't know your way around?"

"Reckon I do mate," Frank said, with a sly dig of his elbow in Lito's ribs.

Puzzled, the callboy pressed on. "Do you need a guide?"

"Oh, no. Not me," Frank said. "That'd cramp me style."

"I know all the places," Lito persisted, deciding to drop a hint. "The good restaurants, the best places to get bargains and," he paused, "the gay discos."

Frank stared at his bench companion. "I know what you are. One of those bloody pooftas, aren't you?"

"A what?"

"A dirty little poofta," Frank exclaimed, turning heads in the park.

"Oh, *bakla*, you mean," Lito said, recognising the enemy.

"I'd give you a whack in the balls if you had any," Frank said, disgustedly getting up.

"Don't be so superior, carrot head," Lito replied, rising too.

"Piss off and don't bother me or I'll get the cops on to you quick."

"They'd arrest you first."

"Yeah? What for?" Frank challenged.

The callboy looked around at passing figures. Suddenly he backed away from Frank, his hands raised. "Don't touch me!" Lito yelled. "Get away you homosexual!"

"Shut up," hissed Frank. "Everyone's looking."

"Homosexual! Homosexual!" Lito shouted, backing further away.

"Shhh! for Christsakes be quiet," the foreigner shushed.

Lito took a handkerchief out of his pocket.

Frank watched, amazed. "Don't make a bloody scene."

The callboy dabbed his dry eyes.

"It's not *me*. It's *him*," Frank protested to staring faces.

"A homosexual," Lito sobbed, backing towards a park exit.

"Hey," called Frank. "Come back and tell 'em the truth. Tell 'em what you really are."

But Lito had gone.

* * *

Aussie Max opened his eyes. He was in a big double bed on the sixth floor of a hotel minutes away from Rizal Park.

"Ah, awake at last, sleepy head," the naked man with muscular hairy legs and a bushy moustache observed, from the other half of the bed.

"What's the time?" yawned the callboy, throwing back a sheet.

"About midday."

"Oh," Max said apologetically. "You should have wakened me, Dave. I could always go back to Singalong and sleep the night off there."

"David," he corrected. "Dave was last night when I didn't really know you." And after leaning forward and tenderly kissing Max on the lips, "Now I do."

"Is that my Christmas present?" Max asked, thinking of the money to come.

"A down payment," David teased and, as the naked Filipino got up to go to the bathroom, added, "You were my present."

"I hope you liked it," Max called back.

"I like everything here," his companion sighed. "It's not like Dubbo, thank God, you can't get away with it there. They'd laugh you out of town."

"For being a *bakla*?"

"For being a poofta."

"I didn't think it was like that," Max replied, flushing the bowl and returning to the bed.

"You've only been to Sydney not—"

"And the Snowy Mountains."

"And there," David smiled. "You didn't stay elsewhere. If you had, you might have noticed a difference."

"I thought it was great," Max said, not at all convinced. "I might even live there one day."

The Australian frowned. "How can you do that? It's a pretty hard place to get into. Your skin doesn't help either."

"It's simple. Just marry a girl. That's what my friend there wants me to do. He knows a girl who's willing."

"Don't do it," David advised. "It's been tried before. If they find out it's a bogus marriage they'll kick you out quicker than you can count ten."

"My friend knows that. He says after I marry I should live with her for at least a year. It sounds okay to me. There'll be no sex. The girl's only interested in the money."

"It'll cost your friend a bit."

"He's got plenty," Max shrugged.

"I don't like it," David said. "It's risky and could land you in the soup if it goes wrong. Your friend too."

"Why? That's the way we do it here."

"What d'you mean?"

"Take a trip down to the Intramuros and renew your visa if you want to stay here longer, David. Then you'll see what it costs in bribes to get your passport back in time. The Chinese from Hong Kong and Taiwan who want to live here pay bribes too. It happens all the time. Don't tell me it's different in your country?"

"Maybe your government employees are underpaid," David suggested, ignoring the question. "Maybe they need a bit of extra money."

"Huh!" Max retorted, quite unimpressed. "At least they have jobs."

"I still think it'd be a mistake if you changed countries." David insisted. "You have so much here."

"Like what?" Max asked incredulously.

"It's the way of life," David replied, groping for the right words. "You're free to show your feelings. There's no shame here."

"No? Just giggles and calls behind your back. When you walk down a street the newsboys call out, '*Bakla*, *Bakla*.' Or someone waves a limp wrist. And you should go to the provinces. Just do anything and everyone around knows by sunset."

"It's worse back home," David said. "Being a man means never showing your feelings towards other men. Not if you don't want to be an outcast. It means being interested in beer and cars and sport and sheilas or chicks. It means going with your missus to a barbie on Sunday arvo and drinking tinnies and yakking about bloody footie with so-called mates while some poor sap cooks steaks and sausages. Shit, I hate it."

"I went to one of those backyard parties," Max said brightly. "It was great. You don't get food like that here."

"And I'm not yet twenty-five and already everyone at home is asking, 'When's Dave getting married?' and 'Has he met Mrs Right yet.' Christ, why don't they mind their own bloody business! You'd think we all came out of a sausage machine."

"I had some of those too," Max said. "They tasted much better than ours. You can't trust meat here. My cousin works in an abattoir and he says it's filthy. Sometimes they cut up the animals on the floor."

"Better a bit of dirty meat than sausage brains," David retorted.

"It's not just dirty meat," Max explained. "Sometimes the rice is old and the fruit and chocolates wormy."

"It's a small price to pay."

"No, no. They're expensive and always going up."

"That's called inflation. We have the same thing too."

"It's much better in Australia," Max said, still unconvinced. "Everyone has a car and TV and nice homes. I know because I often went with my friend to other people's places. Some even had swimming pools. We had a great time."

"Maybe you did," the Australian replied. "But you have beaches. And if you don't own an idiot box there are plenty of movies to see."

"If you can get into one," Max said indignantly. "They're so overcrowded. And I lit a match in one once and found roaches crawling on my clothes."

David shook his head. "A small price, Max. A small price." And remembering he had not paid the callboy, got up and took some notes out of his wallet.

"Something from Santa," a smiling David announced, throwing the money to the bed.

As the Australian stood naked before a tinted window and gazed down at a street crowd milling around an assembling brass band, he was already anticipating his next Christmas present.

*   *   *

Tommy was undressing two floors higher though neither he nor Max was aware they were in the same hotel. Tommy had been in a coffee shop in del Pilar about half an hour earlier when he was approached by a middle-aged man called Heikal who said he was from Tripoli. Sure enough, within minutes the foreigner suggested they walk to his nearby hotel. "Would you like a nice hot bath?" Heikal asked as he shut the door of the suite. "Sure," the youth replied, always happy to enjoy what the pension and its miserable trickle of cold water could not provide. Tommy filled a bath and got in, a little surprised that Heikal did not follow. Most of Tommy's clients liked to bath or shower with him. Also, by the sound coming from the bedroom, the Libyan was strangely busy on the telephone. Tommy thought it a peculiar time for such business but he had known weirder things about foreigners than a few telephone calls. The youth dismissed it and lay back in the soapy water, playing submarine periscopes with a semi-erection. After a while he began to wonder why he had not yet been summoned to the bed. For him a patient customer was a rarity. Tommy got out of the bath and, wrapped in a towel, padded into the bedroom. Heikal was undressed but seemed to be nervous as though expecting something to happen.

Tommy announced airily, "I'm ready" and flung the towel aside

92

on to a handy chair. Heikal, standing in the middle of the room, did not move towards the youth or the bed. Instead he looked at his watch and said, "Good, good." Tommy frowned in puzzlement and asked, "What are we waiting for?" Just then he got his answer. The door buzzer sounded. Heikal moved quickly in its direction. He opened the door enough to let in three men who could have been the Libyan's brothers. Tommy paled when he saw their leers. He had good reason to feel fear. He was about to be brutally and repeatedly raped.

*　　*　　*

As Martin sat in the crowded dark of a Makati cinema watching Charles Bronson rush a phone his thoughts strayed to Roderick's call earlier in the day. There hadn't even been a "Merry Christmas" from the man, he recalled with disgust. And why was that insulting question asked? It was almost as if Roderick wanted to hurt him, to drive him away. "Roderick here," a curt voice had greeted him. "Do you want a present or the money?" The abruptness had stunned him and he hadn't been able to reply. Roderick had been impatient and crossly said, "Well, what's your answer?" What could he say? He had wanted to know why Roderick had asked such a question but had thought better. Roderick might know about his money problems despite the allowance. And there would be no point in discussing the matter. It would only end in argument. Or a final break, he thought watching a beautiful, naked man stab a woman.

Martin searched for another reason for Roderick's manner. Was it jealousy? When the man had called in unexpectedly last month he'd been in Baguio with a German. Jessie had met Roderick in a hall and, not knowing all the rules of the game, told the American, "Martin's gone north." That would be enough for Roderick. The man was no fool. Yet Roderick had told him many times in the past, "I don't get jealous." So, what was the reason? Why did Roderick bother to see him at all if a hostility existed.

The naked man chased another woman along an empty, dark street.

Was it the lack of a job? Surely Roderick knew how hard that was now, especially without a skill. He'd sought jobs but was always being told by some interviewer, "We'll let you know," and they hadn't even bothered to get an address.

Charles Bronson was running along the street too.

And once he'd seen an ad for a bus conductor and hadn't been able to apply. The company had wanted applicants to have a driving licence in case of emergency. None of the boys could drive. What was the point? None of them would ever own cars. Or anything.

Police were holding the naked man who was shouting at Charles Bronson. Shouting like a madman. Charles Bronson raised his gun and shot the man in the head . . .

Some of the audience made for exits. Martin followed, pushing through a crowded foyer. Outside, he wandered windy canyons past closed banks and offices and then into avenues and avenues of tall, modern condominiums. He saw his reflection on plate glass doors. He drifted into back streets all depressingly devoid of people but lined with sleek sedans, their windows menacingly black. He came to a small, triangular park and dejectedly sat on the grass, wondering just how long he could go on like this.

*　　*　　*

In Reggie's room, a Christmas lunch of chicken, vegetables and rice was not quite cooked. Irritated at his presence, Yolanda told him to take a walk. So Reggie roamed the halls. Passing a half-open door, he saw a new boarder and decided to introduce himself.

"Hullo," he said. "I'm Reggie, one of your neighbours."

"Ismael," the man replied, extending a hand.

Reggie inclined a head of thinning hair and looked over Ismael's shoulder. "Still unpacking, I see."

"Just some books."

"Ah, a reader like me," Reggie observed, inviting himself in and taking a chair. And after a pause he instructed the new roomer, "Go right ahead. Finish your unpacking. Don't mind me."

Ismael went ahead.

"What do you do?" Reggie asked, always interested in other people.

"I'm a compositor."

"Is that so?" Reggie said surprised. "I used to be in newspapers too, some years ago."

"I don't work for a newspaper."

"My mistake," the ex-reporter apologised. "I must be getting out of touch. As a young man I was first taught never to assume."

"When did you get out of the industry?"

"When the newspaper I worked for was closed," Reggie replied. "That was an age ago." And after a pause that Ismael noticed and took to be some sad, private reflection, "I do other things now."

"What was your field?" Ismael asked with interest, his curiosity now matching that of his fellow boarder.

"I was one of the Malacañang pressmen," Reggie said proudly. "In those days it was a lively scene. Not the stenographer's job that it is now. We saw the President every day. It was pretty lively, I can tell you. We were true newspaper men with real questions and we expected real answers. 'Mr President,' we would say, 'Can you tell us what is being done about corruption at high levels in the government?' And if we didn't think much of the answer, and we usually didn't, we would say so to our readers the next morning. And to hell with what the palace liked or didn't like. Ah, yes. We were the freest press in Asia."

Reggie fell silent again.

"You miss it, don't you," Ismael observed.

Reggie nodded and fished in his back pocket for a wallet as he had a thousand times before. He unfolded it and pointed to a photograph behind perspex. "That's me and the Malacañang press corps," he told Ismael, adding needlessly, "and that's the President . . . We all looked younger then."

"And what of your friends?" Ismael asked quietly.

"Oh, most of them are out of the industry too."

An impatient call reached the room.

"I'd better go," Reggie said, rising from his seat. Ambling down the hall, he returned the memento to the darkness of his back pocket where it would remain till Singalong got its next new boarder.

*   *   *

Ever since the night of the round-up, Jojo had been discreetly trying to find out how and why Laya had been shot dead. No one had seemed to know about it at the markets. He had even scanned newspapers he would never normally get and watched the TV news in the room of the married couple down the hallway. All for nothing. Then he had thought of visiting Laya's boarding house on some pretext till he realised the danger involved. Jojo had just about given up.

He was in a street near the pension when fate intervened as he debated where to have lunch. Only two eateries were open for business, others being closed for the holiday. One was a Chinese takeaway, its competitor a nearby *karinderia* where the food was cheaper but cold. He decided in favour of the takeaway. Almost inside, he checked himself in mid-step. A drunken man was arguing with the proprietor. Jojo turned away and walked to the *karinderia* to avoid being involved in an argument. He had seen it happen before, especially in rows involving Chinese. He had nothing against them but it was not his concern.

Jojo fronted a long counter open to the street and waited his turn for service. As usual, the eatery was busy. He spied a stack of used office paper on the counter. He leaned forward and began reading the top sheet of the wrapping which paper merchants recycled to *karinderias* all over the city.

"To whom it may concern: This is to certify that the above named subject whose right thumb print appears below has requested a record clearance from this office. An examination of the National Bureau of Investigation fingerprint records has been made and the results of this investigation are listed above. This certificate is issued in connection with the subject's application for a visa to Japan."

Jojo perused the subject's name, address and record on the Ministry of Justice form. He lifted the sheet and read the next form. It too was from the Ministry of Justice and dealt with a citizen's application for a visa to the United States. Jojo uncovered the next form. It was from the Ministry of Labour and Employment and sub-headed, "Affidavit of undertaking." It stated that Salvador C. Castro was leaving the country to work as an oiler on a ship plying South East Asian ports and had pledged to remit seventy per cent of his salary for twelve months to his family. Names, addresses and salary details were listed. He was about to read a fourth form on the stack of hundreds when an aproned man interrupted with a cheery, "Merry Christmas. Sorry to keep you waiting."

Jojo placed his order and watched the man at work.

"We had a bit of excitement the other night," the man said in the course of conversation, scooping cold noodles into a plastic bag.

"Oh, what happened?" the Igorot said casually, but suddenly alert.

"A shooting at a boarding house near the markets," came the reply, a little muffled as the man stuck his head in a large cupboard at the other end of the counter looking for something.

"What did he do to deserve that?" Jojo asked when the figure returned.

"I didn't see it but my brother who was in the street at the time said the man came out of the house with a gun in his hand. He was trying to run away when police shot him. Dozens of them were swarming all over the place."

"The papers had nothing about it."

"No . . . Now that you mention it, they didn't," the man replied frowning. "I wonder why?"

The shop owner wrapped the plastic bag of food in the Ministry of Justice forms and handed it to Jojo.

"I guess they don't have room for everything, do they?" he said, taking the money.

"No," said the departing Igorot, "they don't."

*   *   *

The moon-faced proprietor of the Chinese takeaway gritted his teeth. Normally he wore a broad smile for his customers. In fact, he had been told by an old aunt that it was unwise for him to be in business with such a countenance, she believing an old Chinese maxim that a man with a smiling face should not run a shop. This day, however, she would have been proud of her nephew whose smile had evaporated the moment the drunken man staggered to the counter.

Roberto Lopez could have called the police but did not because he had seen ugly results from this course. He grimly recollected having this scene before with the same lout, though then the man had been sober.

"Ha!" the unkempt drunk was saying, shaking an unsteady finger at the proprietor's flat nose. "We don't need you Chinese. You lot are no good for us. We can do without you."

"Just try it for a day," Roberto muttered, unheard by the other.

"You're parasites," the man continued, "growing rich on our blood. We're going to throw you out. Back where you came from."

An angry clatter of pots and pans erupted from the direction of a half-open kitchen door. Roberto knew his wife could hear the abuse and was signalling her ire.

"Hoy," said the drunk, suddenly remembering his reason for being in the takeaway. "What about my order. When's it coming?"

Roberto called to Corazon in Fukien, "The order, fast." It was an unnecessary command. The little woman was working like a demented ant in a thunder storm.

"Don't even give good service," the drunk rambled on. "You take our money and give us nothing. You're thieves in our country. Ha! we'll get rid of you Chinese. Every single one!"

Roberto moved impatiently towards the kitchen door. Just as he got there, a cardboard box was thrust into his hands.

"About time," the drunk mumbled, taking possession from the fuming proprietor. Box in hand, he swayed by the entrance as if trying to remember something. Apparently unable to do so, the drunk drifted away.

"He's gone," Roberto called to the kitchen.

"Till the next time," came his wife's sharp reply. "Why do you put up with him? Isn't once enough?"

Why indeed? he thought. He would liked to have told the lout he was abusing a seventh generation citizen. He wanted to say he loved the land but not loafers like him; that he had adopted the name Lopez in the cause of racial harmony; that in his body flowed some Filipino blood; that his wife and children had even more; that Rizal had the same mix though no one talked much about it. Yet, what was the use of arguing with ignorance and hate?

"What else can I do?" he belatedly asked with a gesture of helplessness. But she did not hear him above the Chop! Chop! Chop! of steel hacking chicken flesh and bone with more than the usual vigour.

*   *   *

Ricardo Santos was exasperated. He always tugged his goatee in such situations and his father's stubbornness had subconsciously prompted the action again.

"It's your best chance papa," he implored. "We can have the passport within a day. A few hours later you can be on your way to the States. We'll join you there."

"Huh," Santos said gruffly. "And if you're arrested too?"

Ricardo ignored the question. "Your trial doesn't begin for another four days. Your absence can be concealed till then. We'll have time to get out. No one will suspect. We can give Melinda time off to see her family in the province. Believe me, it has all been thought out."

"Where's the passport coming from?" the old man asked suspiciously.

Ricardo sighed. "It's better you don't know." And, seeing his father about to voice doubts, continued, "But these people are reliable. Be sure of that."

Carol-singing from the *sala* below penetrated the upstairs room where the two had gone for privacy after finishing Christmas dinner with the family and friends. The soldiers outside had been given, and had accepted, slices of cake and soft drink.

Santos frowned in concentration. At length, he said. "I pray to God you're right, Ricardo. Something like this is an informer's dream. All the same, what would I do when I got to the States? The place is full of snow half the year." He shook his head at the memory of a week spent at a boring convention in wintry Minneapolis. He'd never seen so much snow.

"Better than a prison here," Ricardo wearily countered.

"Maybe that won't happen, son."

"Papa!" Ricardo exploded. "They're after you. They want to silence you and they will. Already a man who might have helped us is dead."

The other stared. *Who* in the name of heaven—or hell!—was Roberto involved with? Abhorrent thoughts materialised but he elected not to probe as he had with the passport. Instead, he replied mildly, "There's no evidence to convict me of anything but telling the truth."

"An irrelevance. Perjury and sham are courtroom fixtures."

"A lot of newsmen are privately behind me."

"And behind quite a few in prison too."

The widower looked at a sepia photograph on a cabinet of a young Ofelia and said softly, "I don't have much to live for now. But I do have my honour and running away will help my accusers more than me."

Ricardo heard Fermina call and moved towards the door.

Before leaving he looked back and said, "I had to try papa but if you do change your mind—and I hope to God you do—let me know fast. Time's running out."

*   *   *

Yolanda was fed up with sharing everything with Reggie. She figured it was enough that he was provided with three meals a day, bed and sex without her having to endure the rest. She had no savings, the sewing machine wasn't working again, her wardrobe was the same as last year and the year before, the room was driving her mad and the wretched man's snores kept her awake half the night. Only her determination to seek out life's little compensations had kept in check a regular urge to scream.

Romance paperbacks were her main escape along with the late, late snack, the latter a secret indulgence being silently betrayed by an expanding waistline.

Her favourite food was banana cake. On the way home from work she would call at the Yum Yum Bakery and after a quick chat with a friend behind the counter buy a roll. The banana cake was a popular line. Often it sold out long before late afternoon and Yolanda would have to settle for something else, usually a jam roll or pineapple pie. However, as Yolanda tip-toed out of bed to her corner kitchen in the last hour of Christmas Day she anticipated an entirely new treat. The day being a holiday she had not worked or called at the bakery. Unknown to Reggie she had put aside a small tin of Danish biscuits sent to her by a younger sister now living in San Francisco. Holding a plate under her chin to catch crumbs and leave no clue, she munched away in the dark to an accompaniment of snores. She finished off with a packet of chocolate milk.

It was Yolanda's routine to fastidiously clean up after a snack, however small. The reason was that she had a horror of cockroaches. Consequently she washed everything the moment it was used. Her corner kitchen did not have the luxury of a sink. It was a hardship she cursed nightly, along with all her other burdens, but there was no alternative in the seemingly endless war with the reviled creatures.

Yolanda silently opened the door and checked for the presence of midnight washers. Seeing only Gilbert's feet protruding from the end of a couch in a branch hall she flitted to a bay of communal sinks. She was washing the plate and her hands when a voice startled her.

"Hullo, Y-Y-Yolanda," it stammered.

"Oh, Lito," she gasped at the familiar face now at her side. "Don't creep up like that. I nearly died."

Lito closed his eyes. "You're dying?" he whispered, as if about to swoon.

"Don't be silly," Yolanda said, returning to her task in a feeble flow of water. "I just meant you scared me."

Lito still did not understand. "Why—" he started to say and stopped to swallow. "Why do I scare you?"

Yolanda turned to the callboy and stared at his flushed face. "You're drunk," she accused, adding after a pause, "or *drugged*."

Lito smirked.

And, as her horrified gaze fell to his naked lower half, gasped, "How revolting."

Lito's smirk widened.

"I've had enough," she muttered and directing a louder voice around corners, "Gilbert! Gilbert! Come here!"

Santiago appeared in the hall and saw trouble.

"I-I'm talking to Y-Yolanda," Lito explained to his friend.

"He doesn't mean to be offensive," Santiago half apologised. "He's had too much to drink."

"It's disgusting," she said, turning off the tap and wondering why the security guard had not appeared.

"I'll take him back to his room," Santiago said quietly.

"I'm not sleepy," Lito protested, puzzled at the fuss. "I just want to talk."

"Not to me," Yolanda retorted. And looking around a corner at the now-empty couch, "Where is that man?"

"*Please*, forget it Yolanda," Santiago asked. "Lito will apologise later when he's sobered up. He wouldn't do this normally. He's just had a bad Christmas."

"He's not the only one," she snapped. "That doesn't give him the right to strut around naked."

"Lito doesn't know what he doing," Santiago pleaded, catching his swaying friend by the shoulder and preparing to take him back to his room before he fell asleep on his feet.

"I still think I should report this to Gilbert so that Perla can do something about it in the morning."

"Why make a big fuss, Yolanda? Everyone will talk about it and you know how people twist the truth."

Yolanda thought of Reggie and his reporter's nose. The first question Reggie would probably ask was, "What were you doing at the sink?"

"Oh, all right," she said reluctantly. "But see it doesn't happen again." And plate in hand, the secret snacker returned to her snoring husband.

* * *

Torrential rain was falling as Ian awoke in his Villablanca apartment. Donning slippers as protection from cold, vinyl floor tiles, he wandered over to the big windows and looked out at a blurred greyness. Remembering that he had not put on his spectacles, he returned to a bedside table. Back at the window again the view was not much better. Some Christmas Day, he thought. Buckets of rain. The noisy brat above. That letter and no invitation to Christmas dinner. What next? he asked himself.

Above, Ian heard the scrapings of something being dragged across a floor. He cursed and being cranky thought again of the somehow *irritating* letter. It had come from his mother two days before. He had read it countless times since. As the rain lashed the apartment's windows he decided he would tear it up. Then, he amended his decision. He would read it one last time. He fetched it from a drawer.

Dear Son, (his mother began)
I have been meaning to write for some weeks on a matter of
importance, however, for once I have simply not had the time.
Since the passing of my Donald I have been very lonely. I

101

thought perhaps you would be of some comfort. As events have turned out I have hardly seen anything of you in past years. I have no wish to scold you Ian—you have your own life—but you are not the best of correspondents either. So be it. Do you remember Georgie Ferguson? He was a friend of your father. He used to drive up on visits from Newcastle in his green and black Riley when you were a wee bairn, but perhaps you don't remember. Well, I don't quite know how to break this news (any clot would have known what was coming, Ian thought once again) but Uncle Georgie is now your step-father. We were married quietly in Newcastle a few days ago. We have decided to make the city our home. Georgie has now retired from his job at the plant—which has since closed—and has a lovely cottage by the seat at Whitley Bay. I'm selling the old house—too many sad memories. I'm sad in a way to leave Edinburgh but you really wouldn't know the Tyneside now. Those awful slums have been replaced with gardens and big blocks of apartments. The city itself has one of the biggest covered shopping centres in Europe. The Norwegians have been over here snapping up Christmas bargains and going back home on the ferry. Best of all is the metro—such lovely yellow and white electric trams which whisk us from Whitley Bay to the city and back in no time. Georgie has no car and with such good transport there is no need. Ian, the beaches here are just lovely too, some of them so unspoilt. You would like them, though of course most of the year it is perhaps a wee bit cold! All the same Ian, I do hope to see you, even if I have to wait for your arrival in warmer weather. I'm getting a bit old for travelling now, so it's up to you. Georgie says you are most welcome anytime. You are to regard Newcastle as your home too. You have my love and I hope I have understanding . . .

Ian carefully tore the letter up and dropped the pieces into a waste paper basket. A sudden gust of wind rattled the windows. He thought of the Tyneside.

"Wee bit cool," he scoffed. "More like bloody freezing."

Ian shuffled to a gas stove in the kitchen. From a cupboard above the sink he got out a pot. In another cupboard he found the last of his supply of oats. He emptied the contents into the pot and after adding water put the lot on the stove. He lit the gas and adjusted the flame.

Ian did not really enjoy Spanish porridge. It was cheap enough but annoyingly peppered with little bits of inedible husk. He spotted a few tell-tale dark pieces floating on the surface of the mixture and removed them with a spoon. He had tried several brands but they were all much the same. He stirred the liquid which was beginning to assume a gluey appearance. The wind howled outside again and he shivered.

"Well, I'm not going up there," he told the porridge.

The thump! thump! thump! of a bouncing ball broke out overhead. Ian turned off the gas. He poured the steaming contents of the pot into a white bowl on the bench and added sugar and milk. He took the lot to a table and sat down.

On his second sip he wondered what the Australian couple next door might be eating. Now that sounded like an interesting country to visit one day, he thought, finding with irritation another piece of husk. The couple hadn't stopped talking about the place though they had been in Spain for months. Talk, talk, talk and especially of food. According to Gwen, they had tropical fruit from the north, crisp apples from the south, seafood all around and everything under a glorious sun in between. According to Bob the place was much better than Spain. In fact a beery Bob had announced to him one night, "Best place in the world, mate. And Townsville's the best little spot to live in for sure."

Well, thought Ian, if they liked it so much why the dickens didn't they stay there? Very strange indeed! Like their behaviour, too. He had always thought Australians a friendly lot. He wasn't so sure now. He'd enjoyed his regular chats . . . so when he got the letter from his mother he naturally decided to pass on the news. And that Gwen had opened the door and said, "Thought it was you. Always know what time lunch is, don't you." The *cheek* of the woman! After that he didn't bother to pass on the tidings. And they didn't ask him to Christmas dinner. Well, he'd arranged his own Christmas even if it was to be a late one! He'd gone out, bought a ticket and sent a telegram to Zac. Yes, they could all go to blazes! Uncle Georgie, Gwen and Bob! Why should he care? Tomorrow he would be on his way.

Ian took the empty bowl and spoon to the sink, leaving it with the pot to be washed later. From above, a toy whistle shrilled. The Scot moved towards a bedside radio. He switched it on, tuned into the BBC and turned up the volume.

· CHAPTER FIVE ·

Luz found Fortunato conducting an inventory in the windowless backroom of a grocery he managed on behalf of a higher authority which operated three hundred such outlets in the metropolis.

The *barangay* captain was balanced on a step ladder. A fluorescent light illuminated the room but he had an unlit kerosene lantern handy in case of another blackout that morning.

"And what's so unusual about a tin of paint?" he asked pompously after she had told him of her suspicions. "Don't you know about the national beautification programme? It's one of our highest priorities. Those rooms could do with a fresh coat of paint. There should be more of it."

Luz stared increduously and said, "With black paint?"

"That's a bit strange," he admitted, wondering suddenly where all the tinned tuna flakes had gone since his last inventory.

"More like suspicious," she insisted.

"That's what you said last time and look what happened."

"The police were too slow."

"The same day," brusquely asserted the *barangay* captain in defence of his official brethren. "The *very* same day."

"Well?" said the vendor ignoring the last retort but pressing Fortunato for a decision. "Are you interested or not?"

"I'll think about it," he said, beginning a count of another line.

"You'll think about it," echoed an unimpressed Luz.

"I'll look into it," the official said absently, now wondering about a sudden depletion of sardines.

A waste of time, the vendor thought with disgust, waddling out to the hot street beyond.

*   *   *

When Jojo returned to Singalong pension from work at the markets that day he began to clean out his cupboard in preparation for a quick departure from the city. Less than thirty minutes later he had almost completed the task. Aside from a half-filled shoulder bag, a few clothes, some string and a folded piece of canvas shaped in the fashion of a curtain, it was bare. He was leaving nothing behind. He would take only what was essential.

However, two items remained untouched on the shelf above the bed. Both were links with the past. One was a *baliing*, a bamboo flute. It had been given to him by his grandfather when he was still a young boy in the village. The flute could be played with a single nostril and it was frequently used for ceremonial dances as was the *gansa*, a gong. His grandfather had told him that the flute was special. It had been used to entertain General Emilio Aguinaldo, President of the nation's First Republic. The general had slept at the village for a night. In the morning he had continued his flight from the pursuing Americans.

The villagers had known of the general's coming for days. Word of the party's progress, along mountain trails, over rivers and through ravines, had preceded them. The tired, slight man and his party had walked into the village at sunset. The villagers had given them *camote* and *tapuy*, the wine of the gods. After the party had eaten their fill, villagers danced the *chunno* but the visitors were tired and asked to be allowed to sleep. At dawn they were gone. A day later, hundreds of American soldiers had passed by. The villagers heard no more of the general for about a year, then word finally came that he had been captured and taken to Manila.

The second item was a small carving of an Igorot warrior. The varnished surface had dulled somewhat and a corner of its square base had been chipped for some years, as evidenced by the colour of the exposed wood. Hidden from sight on the base was a yellowed sticker which bore the faded words, "To Jojo of whom I expect much. G.S." The carving was from Miss Silang. She had taught Jojo for the two years before her death. At first the youth had been afraid of the old spinster, as were most of her other charges. However, that had soon changed and Jojo had become a favourite pupil.

Miss Silang was a marvellous teacher and enthralled the class with her accounts of history. She never hesitated in taking sides with historical figures or denouncing those whom she believed to be the villains. To Jojo's surprise, she was critical of General Aguinaldo, judging him to have been too trusting of the Americans in accepting them as allies against the Spanish colonisers. But she had reserved her strongest criticism for the general's role in ordering the execution by firing squad of his rival for the leadership of the revolutionary forces, Andres Bonifacio. Jojo had been so disillusioned with the general that he had thought of giving away his flute. But time had passed and so had the thought.

105

The year after she died, Jojo and a friend decided to run away to the brighter lights of Baguio of which they had heard so much from others. With their few possessions in a shared sack, they hitched a ride on the back of a truck. The journey was longer than they had ever imagined. For most of the day the truck had bumped along a twisting, dusty road that hugged the mountain sides. It was a revelation to the youths that the world was so huge. Towards evening they entered the mountain city.

The driver had dropped them by a big park near the centre of Baguio. They saw a festival under way in its grounds and many people. They had wandered over and were surprised to come upon huts similar to those in their village. Then they realised it was a *cañao* put on by Benguet Igorots so that the townspeople and lowlanders could witness the celebration. But it was different to the *cañao* he and his friend knew. As the tribesmen squatted by the huts and chanted to the god Kabunian, the lowlanders milled around and gawked. The foreign tourists jostled for a better view, their cameras clicking and flashing all the time. Jojo had felt no sanctity in the ritual. This had never happened in the village and he knew such behaviour was forbidden in the Christian church. They had left the park feeling almost embarrassed to be Igorots.

After a few hours in the city they realised their money would not last the next day. Jojo's friend had relatives living near the markets and they went to stay with them. Jojo had sensed he was not really welcome and so looked for work in order that he could live elsewhere. It was at that time he considered selling the flute for a few pesos.

He saw a store off the main street in which books and native crafts were for sale. He went in the door, a tingling bell announcing his presence. A man behind a counter seemed busy so the youth pretended to browse. Jojo was also nervous and wanted more time in which to pluck up courage to offer the flute for sale. It was with surprise that the youth saw a poster on the wall, calling for an end of "military abuses." He had never heard such criticism of the army before and did not believe it to be true. He was about to show his flute to the man whom he assumed to be the shop owner when a tall, balding foreigner with a whitish blind eye entered the store. The foreigner talked with the owner for a while and then said, "Why don't you have a poster on nepotism as well?" Jojo did not know then what nepotism meant but he knew it was a criticism of something. The owner said to the foreigner, "I don't think you understand my country. That is our tradition. When we win power we shall do the same." The foreigner had laughed and said, "Then what's the point of elections?" The owner had noticed Jojo and said abruptly, "What do you want?" Jojo had produced the flute and replied, "I want to sell this." The man had glanced at it and turned away rudely with the words, "Not interested." Jojo had found work at the market that day so he had not felt the need again of selling his grandfather's gift. However, he did sometimes think about the bookshop conversation. It was years before he realised its significance. He had even mentioned it to Laya who had commented. "Yes, politicians are all the same."

Jojo reached for the flute which he took to the cupboard and put inside the bag, knowing the old man would never have understood if he did otherwise. But that was not his reason. He would need music on those lonely slopes.

He regarded the carving, alone on its perch. Miss Silang would have approved of what he was going to do. He would just leave it there, like a signature. She would appreciate that, he thought with a faint smile. For now, *he* would be the warrior.

*   *   *

Zac got on the big, dusty bus. As it moved off he waved to Arturo standing on the side of the highway. Zac made for the back and sat down. Not many people were aboard. It was always like that when he got on at Baza but by the time the bus had reached the half-way point in the nine-hour journey it would be packed. Already the outside roof rack was covered in market produce and the last row of seats stacked with sealed cardboard boxes.

With Baza behind, the bus was passing through flat, open country. To the right Zac could see a horizon of blue sea, with fields and clumps of vegetation in the foreground. On the other side were more fields, then low hills rising sharply to a rugged mountain range. He knew it was guerrilla country and wondered at the hardship that such a life ensured.

The bus braked and pulled to the side, letting on a man and a woman. They were apparently from an old dwelling by a tree a little back from the highway. Some figures standing at the front of the structure waved goodbye. The pair stooped to a window and responded. The man was about Zac's age, yet somehow seemed worn. His face was sun-darkened and with a tightness of skin that often partnered hardship or illness in the tropics, his hair now unkempt from the window draught. His companion had a perky air about her, a face of rounded cheeks and quick, mischievous eyes. They sat several rows ahead. At the next town the bus took on

107

more passengers and the two moved to empty seats immediately in front of Zac. Gradually the bus began to fill, with numerous, brief stops along a holiday highway clogged with tooting, impatient queues of brother buses, cabin motorcycles, the odd Mercedes, trucks bearing bamboo poles or sugar cane, and sometimes led by a *carabao* cart on which rode an indifferent, deaf farmer.

At Agoo, a pleasantly leafy township, the few remaining seats went, including one next to Zac. His companion was a foreigner wearing a white top which had on it a scarlet maple leaf emblem. When settled the man introduced himself with an, "I'm Scott. Mind if I smoke?" Conversation between the two soon followed, Scott revealing an interest in flags. Did the Philippine flag have a story behind it?

Zac admitted his ignorance. The woman in front turned and said it did. Introducing herself as Esmeralda and her companion as Mario she said she would be happy to explain. She was a librarian and had often been asked the same question.

"School's in," said a delighted Scott.

Esmeralda began with a mischievous laugh. "Our flag was made in Hong Kong."

"Really," gasped Scott.

"Yes, really," she said.

"Well, that's amazing," he said a little doubtfully, as if he did not quite accept the truth of the statement.

"Perhaps I should hasten to add that it was made in Hong Kong by the wife of a Filipino diplomat," she said.

"Ah, that does make a difference."

"To begin with," Esmeralda continued, "our flag was red with white lettering in the centre. That was at the time of the Philippine Revolution against the Spanish, from 1896 to 1898. The K.K.K. lettering represented the revolutionary movement founded by the patriot, later to become a general, Andres Bonifacio. The society's full name was *Kataastaasan Kagalanggalang Na Katipunan Ng Mga Anak Ng Bayan*."

Esmeralda, Mario and Zac laughed at Scott's grimace.

"I've recovered," Scott said. "Please go on."

Esmeralda resumed. "Later the lettering was replaced by a single K with eight rays. In Malay K meant *kalayaan* or liberty and the eight rays represented the first eight provinces which revolted against the Spanish. Then, another few months later the K was replaced by a big sun with—and no laughing please—two eyes, a nose and a mouth. This was retained a little longer till General Aguinaldo designed and the diplomat's wife, with others, sewed the flag we use today. You have of course seen that flag in your travels?"

Scott nodded.

"The white triangle at the left symbolises equality. The sunburst in its centre those eight provinces. The stars at each angle of the triangle represent Luzon, the Visayas and Mindanao. The upper stripe of blue extending back from the triangle stands for peace, truth and justice and the lower stripe of red for patriotism and valour."

"That's most interesting," the visitor said. And after a pause, "Can you tell me anything more about the K.K.K."

"*Katipunan*," Mario said.

"That does sound better," Scott replied. "The K.K.K. means something else in North America and not very nice."

"I can tell you a little," Mario volunteered, making Zac feel the odd one out.

"The *Katipunan* was more than a secret movement. It was an alternative government of the people. It had a Supreme Council and a structure to govern the country. Most of its members, including Bonifacio, were the poor labourers, artisans, lowly clerks and peasants. They held house meetings at night. While the revolutionaries deliberated in a back room their womenfolk would dance and sing in the *sala* so that patrolling soldiers would think it merely a social gathering in progress."

Zac was surprised at Mario's knowledge. Just what did he do? He looked with renewed interest at the man.

"I don't know all their beliefs," Mario went on, "but one I haven't forgotten. It is: 'To do good for personal motive is no virtue.'"

"That's interesting," Scott said again. "And not bad for someone who doesn't know a lot about the subject."

Much conversation later the bus neared the metropolis, an endless queue now heralding its approach. A dying sun hung low in a hazy western sky and the green that had been their view suddenly changed to a monotony of shabbiness. A contemplative quietness enveloped the passengers, the spirit of travel finally dissolved in weariness. At length the bus pulled into the depot and Scott said his farewells.

"I've had a marvellous time and met some truly hospitable folk," his road companions were told with obvious sincerity. "All the same, I'll be glad to be winging my way home tomorrow. There's no place like your own."

*   *   *

At Singalong pension Zac groaned when he read the telegram. In Jojo's room a few minutes later, he announced, "We have a complication. Ian's arriving tomorrow around lunch. I'll have to go to the airport and meet him."

The other registered no particular expression. Instead, he quietly asked, "How long is he staying in Manila?"

"I've no idea."

"Can you find something for him to do that day?"

"Yes," Zac replied slowly. "I'll think of some diversion."

"There should be no problem then?"

"No, I guess not. Except, when will I get time to help you with the paintwork?"

"It's already finished," the Igorot answered. "Don't worry about that."

"Good," Zac said without enthusiasm.

Downstairs, as a fusillade of explosives erupted somewhere outside, Zac read the telegram again before crumpling it up and throwing it on the floor.

"Oh, God. What a *mess*," he groaned.

*   *   *

In a room above, Martin undressed in the cooling air of an electric fan. He carefully hung his brown slacks and best shirt in the small cupboard and slid his shoes and socks under the bed. Clad only in briefs, he sunk to the sheeted mattress, his back to a wall. Martin ignored the news as well as the exploding crackers outside. He turned straight to a big entertainment section quickly finding his favourite columnist.

Martin had not intended staying in the pension that night. In fact, he should have been at dinner with Roderick. He had even waited outside for the American's arrival in the familiar red car. Just as he began to suspect that something had gone wrong with the arrangement, Efren had come out and told him of the phone call. Martin had gone back in and picking up the phone heard Roderick say at the other end of the line, "I can't make it tonight, Martin. Perhaps later." And that was the end of the phone call. Martin had been so angry that he had thought of going straight to El Torro and taking the first ugly, old face leering in his direction. Then, on reflection, he had admitted that ugly, old faces were leering at younger bodies than his. And Roderick must have good reason to call off the date even if he did not explain.

Martin began reading.

The producer of a movie presently being shot in Cebu is

110

considering the sale of his casting couch after getting word the other day that a certain irate señorita has broadcast plans to sue him for breach of promise. Apparently he figures it will not only save him from future troubles but will also get rid of supporting evidence.

Ah, promises, Martin reflected. He knew all about *them*. Roderick had promised to love him forever, Pierre had waved goodbye to a tearful Ace at the airport and promised faithfully to return soon. That was two years ago! But best of all was Barry. He'd promised Lito a fortune if he could find him a wife. "She must be tall," Barry had written from Geelong. "If you find one I like by the time I get to Manila, a thousand dollars is yours." And what had happened? Lito had searched everywhere for weeks. He'd even visited young cousins in the province and when Barry finally came and saw Lito's selections the Australian hadn't been satisfied. Probably he never would be, Martin mused, looking for the next item. Barry liked the boys too much.

Many in the industry are finding that, despite the financial crisis all about, clouds certainly can have silver linings. The scarcity of the Almighty Dollar in the national purse has led to a sharp drop-off of film imports from the States. Local producers are falling over each other to fill the yawning gap. Top talents on Manila screens are not missing out either. They are reportedly demanding—and getting—million-peso contracts. Seems like some linings are of gold.

Martin put a pillow behind his sweaty back and resumed reading.

Red faces over the accidental interruption of a leading lady's dressing room act. If only her companion had been a man . . .

He laughed loudly, thoughts of Roderick quite forgotten.

And, lest it be said this column shops only one side of the street . . . Is that young Adonis lately being seen in the company of a director a forthcoming talent or something a little more, ahem, private?

The room light flickered. Martin looked up expecting a blackout. It would be the third in the pension that day. Nothing happened. He read the next item.

A visiting and nameless celebrity is pleading jet lag as the reason for the faux pas at his opening show the other night. Between numbers, the poor man told his capacity audience, "It's wonderful to be with you folks once again. My only regret is that Mrs Franco was unable to make it."

Martin frowned. Mrs Franco? Who was she? And what was it all about?

111

Just then he heard shouting outside.

* * *

In a hallway, Perla folded her arms and announced triumphantly, "Ha! You didn't know I was back did you?"

The vendor turned and looked into a pair of lively eyes and flushed cheeks set off by a bright red dress the manageress had chosen for an outing with a man friend that evening.

"I'm just seeing some of the boys," Luz explained.

"You know my policy."

"This is social, not business."

"Rubbish! You're collecting debts. You were here yesterday doing the same thing while I was out. The boys told me."

"They owe me money," Luz spat, hatred rising at their protector.

"This is a pension. And you will kindly observe the rules of the house."

"You and your rules," taunted Luz. "It doesn't stop you from flouting them."

Perla stared hard at her accuser. "What do you mean by that?"

"You know."

"No, I don't. Explain yourself!"

"Don't be so high and mighty with me. You sleep with your boarders. Everyone knows you can't keep out of their beds."

"How dare you speak to me like that!"

"Oh, getting upset now, are we?" the vendor sneered with glee.

"Get out this moment!" Perla ordered as doors opened in the hall.

"With pleasure! I never did like brothels."

"And don't ever come back!"

"Oh, I won't. I wouldn't want to be seen coming in or out of the place."

"Get out now!"

"I'm going, I'm going," said the vendor, labouring down the stairs. And at the bottom, the jeer. "A sex den with a whore as house mother."

"Out!" screamed Perla and Luz was gone.

Clapping broke out in the hall.

"Thanks Perla," called Efren. "She was giving us a hard time."

"Yes, she sure was," Martin said.

"She had no right," the manageress replied, mindful of unpaid rent.

"Perla," Efren began hesitantly. "About the rent at the end of the month."

112

"Yes, Efren?" she said sternly.

"Uh, can I owe it?"

"You're already a month behind."

"Yes, I know. But next month my friend from Adelaide is arriving and I can fix all debts then."

Perla looked at the curly headed youth and felt a wave of compassion for all the Efrens of Manila.

"Very well," she said firmly. "Next month when your friend gets here. But no later."

Efren smiled broadly. "Thanks Perla. We all think you're great."

"Yes," said Martin in agreement.

Perla felt a glow inside.

"One more thing Perla," Efren said.

"Yes?"

"That business about your friend downstairs."

"What about it?" she asked frostily.

"Just this," Efren said and gave her a broad wink.

*   *   *

Roberto was upset. He disgustedly threw the newspaper aside.

"They've done it again," he told his wife, who was cleaning benches now that trading had finished for the night.

"Done what?" Corazon asked wearily.

"Called us Chinese."

"They have to blame someone, don't they?"

"I mean it's almost every day," he complained, disregarding her cynicism. "It doesn't matter that they are writing about people who are Filipino citizens, not Chinese. Sure, some have all Chinese blood but some have Filipino blood as well."

"Help me lift the batter mixer," his wife interrupted.

"So far," he said, taking hold of one side of the heavy machine, "we've been branded the top swindlers, dollar blackmarketeers, smugglers and corruptors of public officials."

"What about drug runners?" she said as they manoeuvred it to a new position.

"That too."

"Huh! I didn't think they'd forget that one."

"Almost every day a story," he grumbled.

"Why not? It sells papers, doesn't it?"

"I guess you're right."

"No guess about it. I *am* right."

Roberto shrugged. "You usually are."

Corazon put down a tray she had been wiping and moved closer to her husband. She regarded him as a good man, a hard worker and a wonderful father. Corazon considered herself lucky. In a softer voice, she said, "Forget about it, Roberto. You alone can't change it."

"I should know that by now, shouldn't I?"

"That's right. It's going to take a long time, if ever."

"A long time," he said taking her in an embrace.

"In the meantime you have me and the children. And we have you."

They continued to embrace.

"Oh," Corazon said, breaking apart a little. "I told the children about that drunk yesterday."

"What did they say?"

"They're coming with you this year to Rizal Park."

"Are they? Because of yesterday?"

"Yes. They feel very strongly about it."

"I'll take the car then," Roberto said.

"I thought you would like to hear of the children's decision."

"The more of us the better," Roberto said, resuming the embrace. A certain look came into his eyes. "It makes me feel like having another one."

"Not without *my* say-so," she murmured.

In the midst of the half-cleaned kitchen the pair kissed tenderly.

* * *

The kicking began somewhere over Switzerland. Ian frowned and half turned in his cramped economy seat. He peered between a gap. A Filipino child of kindergarten age was excitedly swinging his shod feet back and forth, more often than not coming into contact with Ian's backrest. The child's mother appeared not to notice.

Ian resumed his normal position but after some thought, remained silent. He consoled himself that in this case it was his contribution to international harmony. For diversion he thumbed through an in-flight magazine, all too soon becoming bored with that. Thankfully, the cabin crew began distributing meals and, as he was seated near the tail, was among the first to be served, along with the mother and child. Ian enjoyed the meal but more so the respite from kicking, the boy being apparently incapable of activity at both ends of his active body. However, over Italy kicking resumed. The Scot gritted his teeth, sustained only by the thought that the Italians were enduring more with the Mafia, corruption and earthquakes. Over Yugoslavia his tolerance diminished as the tempo of kicks increased. He did not know or care what was happening below. He was wishing to God that the little boy's legs would fall off. As he was about to erupt, nature intervened and the mother rushed the child down the aisle towards the toilets fortunately lit with the Vacant sign. In their absence he entertained the possibility of a deity and acts that must be considered miracles. When his ordeal resumed over the Holy Land he returned to atheism and prepared himself for the inevitable confrontation.

Ian disliked scenes and usually did anything he could to avoid them. When Zac had been at Villablanca, Ian had decided to get a second-hand TV set. While on his morning patrol of restaurant menus the Scot had spotted the set in the dusty window of Manuel's repair shop. It was going at a bargain price. He had bought it the next day even though his Spanish remained, at best, scratchy and he could only partly understand programmes. The middle-aged proprietor had assisted Ian and Zac to the street and waved them farewell, his neat little moustache twitching in secret delight at the departure of the wretched contraption. At home Ian had plugged the set into a power switch, turned it on and waited. A picture resembling a crazy mirror at a fun park appeared.

"Needs an outdoor aerial," the Scot authoritatively told his companion seconds before a loud "Plop" came from the set's innards.

"It needs more than that," Zac said, looking at a blank screen.

Ian scowled and twiddled knobs.

"Did you give it a test run at the shop?" Zac asked.

"You were there. Why didn't you suggest it then?"

"It was your idea. I was more interested in the toaster. We need one."

Ian ignored the remark. "I suppose we'll have to see the man about it."

"Oh, no," Zac corrected. "That's your job. You see him, not me."

"Very well," the Scot said stiffly.

At the repair shop Manuel was utterly surprised by the news. He gave a sad shake of his head and said, "Tomorrow I come."

Three days later at the apartment Zac brought up the matter of Manuel's continued absence. Ian appeared unconcerned and instead scanned the local paper for property prices.

"It's about time Manuel got here, isn't it?"

"Oh, he'll be here eventually. Spanish tradesmen are always slow to arrive," the Scot said, secretly preferring to forget the whole unfortunate business rather than have a scene with the tardy Spaniard.

"He sold you a defective set," Zac reminded.

"Yes, I know that," the other replied, mildly irritated at Zac's persistence.

A few days later Zac said, "Are you going to see him or not?"

Ian sighed. "I suppose so."

"Don't let him get away with it."

At the shop Manuel was horrified with his memory lapse. Palm on cheek, he exclaimed, "So sorry señor. So busy. Too many customers."

"Very well," said the mollified Scot. "Come as soon as you can."

"Oh, thank you, señor. So understanding." And steepling his grimy fingers. "Enjoying your little *holiday*, eh?"

"Oh, no old chap," Ian corrected proudly. "I'm no tourist. I live here."

"Oh, so sorry," Manuel said flatly. "My mistake."

At home Ian told Zac the proprietor had been full of apologies. "It really was quite touching, you know. I almost felt sorry for the poor, overworked man."

Zac was unimpressed. "When's he coming to fix the set?"

"As soon as he can," the Scot assured.

Zac went with Ian to the shop three weeks later.

"Well," Zac asked the agitated man, "just when are you coming?"

"Tomorrow, señor," the Spaniard promised, rushing with gratitude to serve a startled customer who had just wandered in from the street.

Back home, Ian was indignant. "It really is quite disgusting," he told Zac. "Nearly a month. I really should give the blighter a piece of my mind."

"Why didn't you do that in the shop?"

"There was a customer," he said weakly. "But I will when he gets here."

Early next morning the door bell rang.

"That'll be Manuel," Ian announced with part accuracy.

The proprietor came in, pushing a coy little girl before him like a shield.

"My daughter," he said, taking a quick look at the set and immediately pronouncing it a workshop job.

Since that day Ian had never seen Manuel, his daughter, or the set again. And that had suited Ian too.

But thoughts of the television set were not on the Scot's mind as the aircraft began its descent to Dubai. He was wondering instead whether he could make the terminal. The kicks suddenly intensified and he knew the moment had come. The Scot unbuckled his restraining seat belt. He half stood and turning in the offending direction stared down into the dark and suddenly apprehensive eyes of the child.

"Little boy," he boomed in his most regal tone. "Stop kicking my seat."

If the Scot had slapped the child the effect could not have been more complete. The boy's jaw dropped. The eyes enlarged in fear. The offending legs froze. The startled mother was confronted with a choice of loyalty or justice. "Yes," she agreed with the angry man, "stop kicking his seat."

As the aircraft taxied to the terminal the kicking briefly resumed. Ian groaned and began to regret that he had hastily decided to return to Manila on this particular flight.

· CHAPTER SIX ·

The morning after Luz's banishment from the pension she failed to appear at her usual spot in the street outside. Efren was an immediate beneficiary. He was now able to stand under the fern baskets and intercept visiting tourists. The boy barely had time to pick his nose when a toothy Belgian got out of a battered taxi looking for Jessie. Within minutes they were in Efren's room waiting for Jessie's return "from shopping". Actually, Jessie was a few rooms away sleeping off a hectic night and would not have cared if the Usher had a roomful of his regulars, particularly ones who came to the pension before midday.

As Efren locked the door of his room and turned on the music, Santiago and Carlo got up and drifted to the hall mirror where they compared notes on the previous night. Both were relieved that for once it had been free of Antiques.

All the boys at Singalong used shorthand slang when together. Their speech was peppered with Antiques, TYs, Hungry Wolves, Butterflies and so on. Butterflies were unfaithful foreigners who flitted from Filipino to Filipino. It did not matter that the boys themselves flitted. After all, that was their job. Hungry Wolves were unattached gays with voracious sexual appetites. Their presence was a plus factor in the callboy market. The more Hungry Wolves the better for business. However, Antiques were in the main a hated breed.

"Don't bother about him. He's just an Antique," the younger callboys at El Torro were often told.

The name had been given to long-term foreign residents of the metropolis. Antiques were generally known for their nasty habits, the chief one of which was underpayment for services rendered. Glass in hand, an Antique would move around the potential clients at a gay bar and say in hushed voice, "Now don't pay the boys too much. It gives them silly ideas about their worth. Here's what I suggest . . ."

This would enrage the boys because they knew Antiques did not really care about tourist pockets, only their own. If a tourist paid a higher rate Antiques would have to match it. Or quit the bar alone.

118

As most Antiques operated on more modest incomes this sometimes happened. The boys had no fixed price and were willing to let a client name a fee but felt Antiques had tried to depress the market too much. Already room rents were taking most of their earnings. And they had been told by tourists that they were a welcome relief to the excessive demands of their counterparts in London, Sydney, Los Angeles and Vancouver.

Some persistent Antiques so upset the Singalong boys over their activities that an informal meeting had recently taken place at the pension. Other colonies had been represented. The boys decided to blacklist a particularly active one called Hank who, oddly enough, ran an antique shop. The word was spread. But from the start the boycott was doomed as Manila had a massive oversupply of callboys. Nevertheless, feeling remained high at Singalong about Hank.

Not all Antiques were necessarily stingy though. And certainly not old Jan. He was a fixture in the gay scene and had been a welcome one for quite a number of boys. Jan was the general manager of a large European company which had its eastern headquarters in Manila. Jan would be seen almost nightly at discos, usually wearing a pair of loud pants. Red seemed to be his favourite colour and, with his silvery swept-back hair, gave him a Santa Claus touch. Unlike Santa Claus, however, his figure was not rotund and was even mildly athletic for a man nudging seventy.

Jan played Santa to many of the boys from time to time. Some had even had trips to Europe in his company. The hospital bills of others had been paid. One boy had spent four weeks in a bed at the prestigious Makati Medical Centre with second-stage syphilis and owed his restored health to the man's considerable generosity. Not surprisingly, boys came in droves to his Makati penthouse. There they cooked fancy meals and played party games with cash as prizes. The games were Jan's way of assembling talent. The boys knew that and hoped they would be the one. After all, living with Jan certainly had its advantages even if the man was nearly fifty years their senior. The penthouse was air conditioned, the fridge full of goodies, the bathroom four walls of tiled elegance. There were no rent worries, colour television and a home video were at hand, a four-channel stereo played heavenly music.

That was the credit side. Disillusioned lovers had spread the word that Jan was possessive, yet reserved for himself the right to wander wherever his passions took him. Jan was dictatorial too, saying, "I want you to wear this tonight." Or, "You are to stay here in the apartment and not go out while I'm away for a few days." Or,

"When we are out together you are not to talk to anyone but me."
Or, "Say only what I tell you to say." And at the end of a few
weeks, months or maybe even a year came the "you'd-better-leave-
if-you-can't-fit-in" scene. Even if a boy accepted a favour from Jan
but did not live in the penthouse there was a price to pay. The
youth cured of secondary syphilis, who let Jan pay the considerable
medical bills, paid later in bed at the apartment. Next came the
public account. The youth was dancing at a disco one night when
Jan approached him and said loudly, "I think you left something at
my place." Then Jan raised a hand and, fingers arched delicately,
dropped a very brief pair of briefs into the embarrassed youth's
hand. Everyone on the dance floor knew what it meant. And they
also knew that was exactly Jan's intention.

A close second on the hate list were TYs, clients who deliberately
evaded their obligations through excuses or disappearing tricks, in
effect paying with a "Thank you." Such clients were able to
operate that way because the boys rarely asked for money in
advance. Many a Singalong boy had spent a restless night in the
arms of a foreigner wondering what the morning would bring. If it
brought a TY there was nothing they could do except warn others.

Commercials were callboys who had lost *all* illusions. They
thought of nothing but money. They were the antithesis of the so-
called Innocents. The two groups were separated by only a few
years but, more importantly, by a thousand hotel bedrooms. All
the boys at Singalong remembered the El Torro Innocent who was
taught an expensive lesson with a pair of golden earrings. The
youth had seen them in a shop window. Imagining himself a
twentieth century pirate he impulsively bought and wore them at
the bar. For three nights he had no customers. When he gave the
earrings away the very next day he knew that the appearance of
youthful innocence was precisely what the customers were
seeking.

OA was associated with callboy drama. The initials stood for
Over Acting. To OA while trying to extract money from a client
with a tale of woe was to invite added financial hardship. But it did
not happen often, experience being a speedy teacher. In fact,
many of Singalong's colony were certain they could teach their
brothers and sisters on the screen a thing or two.

Afams were foreign clients. The expression was something of a
mystery at Singalong. It was not a Tagalog word and many spare
moments were spent arguing about its origin. Bongbong had,
his eyes raised, suggested it stood for All Foreigners And Monkeys.
That was howled down as most boys actually had a physical

120

preference for foreign men. The discussion never got anywhere but the description lived on, unlike most of the Singalong short-hand which would change as inevitably as faces in the colony.

The slang was not confined to the pension halls. It was common for the boys to talk so in crowded streets, in a packed jeepney or, of course, at discos and gay bars. Outsiders were never any the wiser. However, the same could not be said of their habit of feminizing names. About half of the Singalong tribe had been allocated one. Carlo was Carla. Lito answered to Lita. Martin did not care much to be called Martina but endured it philosophically. Aussie Max laughed at Maxina, though not so loudly if another callboy yelled out across a street, "Your slip is showing Maxina." But in deference to public sensibilities, such names were usually used only in the pension. Thus Santiago, having heard Efren lock his door and turn on a radio, was able to say to Carlo, standing before the mirror, "I think Efrenita is back in business."

"Oh, who with?" Carlo asked, flexing his muscles.

"An Afam, I think."

"How d'you know?"

"I heard voices in the hall. One sounded European."

"Hmmm," Carlo said, studying his biceps, "maybe the Usher has struck again." And then scowling, he voiced the thought, "He'd better not be with one of *my* regulars."

Martin poked his head into the hall.

"Did I hear the Usher's back in business?"

"We think so," Santiago replied.

"That means Luz isn't around," Martin surmised.

"I guess not," Santiago said. "What's keeping Luz from her stand? Only a typhoon can do that."

"Perla had a screaming session with Luz last night and kicked her out," Martin told the boys. "Look's like she's taking her trade somewhere else."

Dumbell's jaw sagged. The Bird whistled.

"Tell us all about it," they said with unconcealed joy and promptly invaded Martin's room, shutting the door.

Martin was right about Luz. The vendor had abandoned her regular spot. Already she was at work on the other side of the canal and seven blocks away. In less than an hour she had had twenty-three customers and was satisfied with her new site. Besides, she exulted, there had been some very peculiar activity in a nearby church. And maybe some other *barangay* captain would be interested this time.

*   *   *

Tommy had a friend called Danilo who, because of his large, attractive eyes, looked like an owl. The pair had roomed together at the pension for a time. Unfortunately, Danilo had twice fallen foul of the house rule prohibiting ironing. Then Perla had entered his unlocked room unannounced one evening and discovered a third violation. The young man had to go. Danilo thought his privacy had been violated more than the house rule but being a three-time loser could not argue.

Moving house had posed a few problems. The first was where to put his toy owls while he looked for another place to stay. He had started collecting them as a hobby after friends had continually reminded him of the likeness. The collection had grown quite large. There were cloth owls, plastic owls, knitted owls, wooden owls, cardboard owls and plaster owls. His married sister had solved the problem when she offered them a temporary home, though there was no room at the time for Danilo. That had been his second concern: where could he afford to live? He had not been able to find a job and had hardly any funds, in the absence of public welfare. After a string of awkward, overnight visits to various friends he reluctantly drifted to old Jan's penthouse in Makati. Danilo found himself very welcome. Jan was then between affairs and open to a casual relationship, especially with a Filipino who was something of a star in the kitchen. Danilo knew his new home was probably even more temporary than that of the owls but, as he confided to Tommy, "Beggars can't be choosy."

Besides providing tasty meals, Danilo could talk to Jan with some authority about the outside world. The Filipino had spent a year working in a hotel in Bahrain as a junior administrator and had done well. In fact, such was management satisfaction that he was offered a contract for a further year. To their surprise Danilo politely declined. He did not say why but in his heart knew he could not bear another day in Bahrain. Quite simply he had come to dislike Arabs and, as a close second, the extraordinary heat of the place. Even in the airconditioned hotel it was only just bearable and at times he felt he was suffocating. His homeland too was hot, but it had its days of relief. How the Filipino had yearned for a typhoon! Danilo's dislike of Arabs had no discernible origin. Rather it was a trickle of little things that seeped into his consciousness like sand into a shoe. After a while he began to play games with his hosts in an endeavour to keep his sanity as he worked out his contract. Baiting Arab taxi drivers became a regular sport.

"Where are you from?" a driver would ask, eyeing him curiously in the rear vision mirror.

"Brazil," he would say nonchalantly.

"Oh! I thought you were from the Philippines or somewhere like that."

"No, Sao Paulo in Brazil."

"I tell you something," the driver would confide as they waited for a green light. "I don't like those Filipinos. We have too many of them working here." And probably mindful of a big tip, he would add, "You Brazilians are nice people."

On his next taxi trip Danilo would try a different tack.

"And where's your home?" the driver would eventually say after talking about the price of oil and gold.

"Manila in the Philippines."

"Ah, yes, we have a lot of guest workers from there."

"You certainly do."

"And between you and me," the driver would predictably say, "they're the best too. Not like those lazy Pakistanis."

No matter how many times Danilo changed nationality he was never on the losing side.

It was inevitable, therefore, that when Tommy rode the elevator to the Makati penthouse at midday, two days after his traumatic Christmas Day, Danilo did not give his friend a sympathetic reception.

"Why do you go out with Arabs at all?" he snapped. "They're stupid people. And you can't trust them."

"I didn't know they were like that," Tommy pleaded in defence.

"Well, they are, all of them," Danilo said uncharitably.

"It was horrible," Tommy said, again close to tears in yet another recollection of the event. "They said they were sorry after but I couldn't forgive them. I just lay there crying. And then one of them threw some money on the bed. After a while the others did too."

"Did you take it?" Danilo asked quietly.

"I wasn't going to. I said, 'Keep your money. What do you think I am?' And they said, 'No. We're sorry. We want you to accept it.' So I thought, why not? I need it. So I took it."

"What did you do then?"

"I came around here but you weren't home."

"I was at my sister's for Christmas and I stayed overnight. Jan's in Hong Kong for a few days."

Tommy looked vacantly at an aquarium of tropical fish before turning to his friend. "Oh, Danilo," he cried. "What will become of us?"

Danilo was unable to reply. The very same question had troubled him of late.

"I have such bad luck with foreigners," Tommy continued. "Something is always happening to me because of them."

"Then give them up," Danilo said, somewhat recovered from Tommy's haunting question. "Don't have anything to do with them."

"But some of them are my friends. I like them." And after a pause he said without spirit, "I don't know what to do. Maybe I should go and live with Khalid. He wants me to come. He wrote to me last month and said he has a big house in Morocco now."

"You'd hate it," Danilo said with a little shudder. "It would be hot and just like Bahrain and much worse than the worse slums here."

"Do you really think so?"

"And what if he abandoned you?" Danilo said, ignoring such a silly, silly question. "What would you do then? All that distance from home."

"He wouldn't do that!" the other exclaimed. "He loves me. And he's a prince. He's related to the King of Egypt."

"What are you saying? Egypt doesn't have kings any more. That was a long time ago."

"Well, he's a prince. And he's living in Morocco," Tommy said defensively.

"Did you reply to him? Did you give him an answer?"

"No, I wasn't sure. I didn't know what to say."

"I'll tell you why. Because you don't know your mind," Danilo scolded. "So stay here. You're better off. At least you have friends."

Tommy smiled weakly at Danilo. He knew his friend was being bossy but with good intentions. It was always like that. Danilo had given the same advice about Yussef.

"I still think about him," Tommy said, thinking aloud.

"Who? Khalid?"

"No, Yussef."

"Oh, him. I thought that was all forgotten."

"He didn't want to go back to Beirut. He knew he'd get killed in the war. But he went back. And after three letters I heard nothing more till Ahmed saw me in the street and told me what had happened."

Danilo had always been suspicious of Yussef's purported departure from the world and said caustically, "Yes, and his cheques stopped coming too."

"He was so young," Tommy lamented. "Only twenty-four."

Danilo moved to the kitchen to prepare some coffee. He called back, "We are alive. We have to think of the future. So forget about them."

Tommy returned to the aquarium and studied the fish.

* * *

Ian's aircraft was on its descent to Manila. He had snatched little sleep on the overnight leg to Hong Kong and had been thankful when early that morning the Crown Colony had appeared below through broken cloud, its headlands like dragon's feet on slate. He had stayed on board at Kai Tak with the airport cleaners to avoid what he considered weak-willed travellers milling around the terminal's duty free shops. He was not so sure now that he had been wise in passing up the chance to stretch his legs. As the aircraft touched down at Manila with a bump he looked forward to a rest in his favourite hotel near Rizal Park. They finally came to a stop. He gathered his hand luggage and joined the stream up an aisle.

To his surprise he entered an air-conditioned terminal, unlike the last occasion when he had been processed in a stifling, rabbit-warren of a place, its dingy walls lined with curious onlookers who, he considered, undoubtedly had no right to be in the restricted area. This time a green carpet led the way past walls of glass and what appeared to be, in the absence of his spectacles, transit lounges. Following the stream of arrivals he moved down a long passageway with big windows each side overlooking the busy tarmac. He came to a large hall where he was speedily processed by a passport officer. After collecting a suitcase he was waved through customs. As Ian headed for the terminal exit he was most impressed and felt it augured well for his mission with Zac.

Then he stepped outside into another world. Instant sweat bathed his body. A blur of brown shapes jostled him on all sides. Strange voices competed for his ears. Shrill whistle blasts and revving motors came from beyond. Sensing his salvation lay in the direction of the traffic he grimly pressed forward. As he did a hand wrestled the suitcase from his grasp with a command of, "This way." Obediently he followed, pushing aside all till he reached a stationary taxi and clambered in. To shut out the chaos he slammed the door. He heard the suitcase being dropped into the boot and the thump of the lid closing. The Scot knew what came next but never tipped anyone. Ignoring the hand rapping at the window, he took command.

"Ermita," he barked to the driver and with a jerk was away.

Had the Scot worn his spectacles he would have witnessed Zac's amazement as the taxi took off. Had he worn them from the onset he might have even seen Zac standing close by the terminal doors reserved for arriving foreigners. Had all the taxi touts, hotel scouts, hustlers and pimps stopped shouting, the traffic whistles and engines been silent, he should have heard Zac's, "Over here Ian." And had Ian not been so vain, Zac would now not be so angry. However, Ian was blissfully unaware of these things as the taxi sped towards its destination. He was anticipating the opulence of the five-star hotel, the colonnaded foyer, the elegant suites and their luxurious bathrooms, the sumptuous food in stunning dining rooms, lazy hours besides a sparkling swimming pool. All this and Zac.

Ian frowned in annoyance at Zac's absence from the airport. It was a bit casual, he thought. He was composing a suitable reprimand when the world seemed to spin. He did not hear the crash or even see it. He only remembered scrambling out of a sagging door onto a raised nature strip in the middle of the road. Once there, in a flower bed, he took stock of his situation.

The taxi's nose was buried in the back of a van, the boot lid half open. The taxi driver and another man, whom he took to be the van driver, were arguing by the wreckage, blurred metal shapes whooshing by their gesticulating arms. On one side of the busy road he could make out a line of high-rise apartments. On the other side he recognised Manila Bay. He knew his task was to get to a footpath and for the first time since Spain thought of his spectacles deliberately packed in his suitcase. He clambered down and retrieved it from the boot, returning to the safety of the garden. He briefly debated whether to get his spectacles while in the flower bed or make a quick dash without their aid during a traffic break. Feeling unlike a public unpacking, he watched for his chance. He waited as the argument below neared the point of blows. He waited as his shirt became saturated. He waited while what seemed to be the entire output of Japan Incorporated streamed past. And then a gap appeared. Gripping his suitcase, the Scot leapt to the road and began a staggered sprint.

"Hoy," the taxi driver called, suddenly losing interest in his argument, "what about my fare?"

Ian stopped and was about to answer when he realised a wall of metal and chrome was advancing on him. To the multiple screeches of brakes and burning rubber he leapt to the footpath. To the sound of impacting car bodies and shattering windscreens he uttered a faint moan. Head down he scuttled quickly away, lugging his suitcase in the hot afternoon sun. The purposeful resolve that

126

had carried him half-way around the globe was, like the Swiss chocolate in his suitcase, beginning to melt.

* * *

Zac got up from a comfortable lounge in the hotel foyer as a red-faced Ian made an entrance.

"What took you so long?" Zac asked, his anger abated.

"A traffic accident," the Scot tersely replied without elaboration.

"Let me carry your bag," Zac offered. "You look worn out. Are you okay?"

"It's a bit late now to carry my bag."

"Oh, really? Good. Carry it yourself then."

"Very well," Ian said stiffly, wondering at Zac's reaction to a mild censure.

They advanced on a reception desk. As they waited for service Zac said, "You can let the bell boy carry it upstairs to your suite."

"I will," Ian replied, miffed at such peculiar behaviour.

"And don't forget to pay porterage too. That's the rule you know."

"There's no need to tell me. I've travelled before."

"Maybe you have forgotten, Ian. You *didn't* pay at the airport."

"I don't remember," Ian lied. And suddenly wary as he filled in a registration card, asked, "How would you know?"

"I was the porter."

"Oh," Ian said, his face a deeper shade of red. "I see."

"No you don't," Zac disagreed. "Not without your specs."

"It wasn't that," the Scot countered in front of a lift button which the bellboy was mercilessly jabbing. "How on earth can I be expected to know if you keep changing your hair style?"

"By not being vain," Zac said.

In a hall on the fourteenth floor Ian muttered, "I'm not vain."

"Then wear them," Zac said as they entered a suite overlooking a corner of Rizal Park and the metropolis beyond.

The bellboy deposited the suitcase on a luggage rack. Ian wandered over to a window with Zac.

"First class," the Scot approved.

"Great view," Zac observed.

The bellboy hovered by the coloured TV.

"Oh, Zac," Ian said with dismay, "I've no change. Can you oblige?"

When the door closed the Scot told Zac, "I quite forgot to get some change in the rush through the airport."

Zac said nothing and wandered back to the window. In the park he could see workmen painting a flagpole near the Rizal monument.

"Did you get my letter from Spain?" Ian asked.

Zac nodded, his thoughts elsewhere.

"We can be on our way back in a few weeks."

The other shook his head. "It's not so simple."

"Surely you don't want to stay in Manila?"

"Not particularly."

"Then how about it? Let's try a restaurant business for starters. We'll make a perfect team with your cooking and my hosting."

"It sounds okay, Ian, but I don't think it's for me."

Ian looked surprised. "Why not? What alternative do you have in mind?"

"There's always home," Zac said, a little resentful of the man's assumptions.

"But I thought you didn't want to stay here?"

"Home in the province, I mean."

Ian frowned. "Don't be too hasty in rejecting the idea."

"I'm not convinced it's best for us," Zac said with a shrug. "Especially after what happened. And besides there's the money problem."

"Money problem? I have no worries now," Ian corrected. "It won't be like last time."

"No? Why shouldn't it happen again?"

"How can it? I've plenty in the bank."

"What if the banks collapse?"

"Don't be so ridiculous Zac. Really!" he exclaimed and laughed.

Zac ignored his mirth. "How safe are your banks these days? They've lent their future away. Or so I read in the newspapers."

"Oh, don't you worry," Ian readily assured. "They'll pull through."

"Only if the borrowers do."

"You really shouldn't concern yourself about this, you know. The financiers will never let it happen. Never."

It was Zac's turn to laugh. "It'll be too big for them. And maybe for their governments too."

"You really are a pessimist," Ian said in amazement as he began to unpack his suitcase on one of the beds. "I still don't see how this affects us."

"It did before when you struck trouble."

"Past history, old chap. Forget it."

"I'm sorry, I can't. Too many things were said."

Ian retrieved his spectacles and put them on a table while trying unsuccessfully to forget the scene of crumpled metal and shattered glass. "Perhaps this is not the best time to discuss it," he said. "I'm tired and hungry and you're still upset about the airport."

"I'm not upset," Zac replied.

"Jolly good," Ian said, putting the limp chocolate in a bar fridge. "I say, why don't we go down the coast first thing tomorrow to a beach resort and stay the night. We can sort matters out there. What do you think?"

Zac considered the suggestion, pleased that it at least got Ian out of Manila. "Okay," he said at length. "But I don't think I'll be changing my mind."

"We'll see," Ian said, putting away the suitcase and considering his next move in the unexpectedly difficult game of placating Zacarias Campora.

*   *   *

Lieutenant Felipe stood in the smelly, dark hallway and knocked loudly on the door of room number nine. The wailing of a child and loud music came from within. Behind him was room number twelve, Laya's old room and the reason for his visit. The door was opened by a woman with sunken, dark eyes.

"Mrs Teresita Cruz?" he shouted above the blaring music.

The woman nodded.

"Can I come in?"

The woman moved away from the doorway and shuffled to a crowded table beside a double bed. There she turned off the radio, next to which was a portable gas cooker, a water jug, a bottle of soy and packets of unopened noodles.

"Go outside Alberto," she wearily told a little boy whose cries had subsided to sniffles at the intrusion of a stranger. Alberto reluctantly left the room.

"I won't be long," Felipe told the woman as he glanced around and wondered how people could endure a life like this. "I've come about your neighbour across the hall."

"Not that again," she said, half-closing the door so her neighbours would not get the wrong idea.

"I'm afraid so."

"I've already told the others all I know."

"Just one more time, please, if you don't mind," he said with more civility than he felt.

"All right," she said flatly. "What do you want to know?"

"Can you tell me anything about his visitors."

129

Mrs Cruz shook her head. "He kept to himself all the time. He hardly had any."

"Can you describe any of them."

"There were only two that I can remember. One I saw going in to number twelve had his back to me. I wouldn't know what he looked like."

"And the other?"

"I did get a look at him. But my memory isn't that good."

"Any description will do," he said, suppressing a desire to shake the woman by the shoulders. "Anything."

"I'll try," Mrs Cruz responded with a sigh. Then after some thought, she said, "He was a little, well, different. It was his hair I think. Very closely cut, almost shaven. I can't remember anything else."

Felipe was aware of a quickening pulse. "How old was he?"

"Oh, not old. Less than thirty, I think."

"Did anyone use names?"

"No, they were saying good night to each other."

"How did he dress?"

"I really don't remember."

"And you're sure there is nothing else you can recall?"

"Not a thing."

Felipe looked around the miserable room. Not enough, he thought. Damn her. Not enough. "Do you live here with your husband and child," he asked, hoping something else would come into the woman's mind. He knew the answer.

"Alberto's not the only child," she said as expected. "I have three other boys. They're selling newspapers. Alberto's too young."

"I suppose it gets pretty crowded when everyone's home," he replied, affecting sympathy.

"Like a madhouse," she smiled weakly. "You need an extra pair of hands to take care of everything."

"I'm sure you do your best," he assured her, knowing he'd done his with the woman. Felipe moved reluctantly towards the door. "Thank you for your co-operation."

But Mrs Cruz did not respond. She was staring ahead as if fixed on a vision of the Madonna.

"There's something else?" he asked.

"Wait," she said with some urgency. "I do remember something. Some of the fingers on the man's hand were missing."

"You're sure?" the officer queried, nevertheless feeling a rising elation.

"Oh, yes. I don't know how I ever forgot something like that."

Felipe reached into his pocket and pulled out a handful of notes.

"For the children," he said, thrusting the money into the surprised woman's hands.

"And for me a breakthrough," he told himself, hurrying in the afternoon shadows to a police car parked outside.

* * *

The Igorot scanned an old newspaper as he lay on his bed at Singalong pension. He had just eaten an evening meal bought at the Chinese takeaway, finishing it with a beer. He was feeling a little bloated. Then a heading caught his eye: "Fugitive Priest Scandalised NPA."

> Myth and fact have been rudely separated with the release by the army of documents pertaining to the character of the late rebel priest, Dominic Tabbang. Far from being a simple cleric forced to take to the hills and lead a life of privation with the outlawed Communist New People's Army, he is now revealed as a shameless womaniser whose exploits disgusted even his hardened comrades. A certain Adong, who was recently captured by elite forces in a new sweep not far from the cave hideout in Abra where Tabbang was trapped and killed five months ago, has testified of the man's constant debauchery.

Jojo paused to identify noises in the hall.

"Well, I can wait," a foreign voice said.

"He might be a while," he heard Efren reply.

"What do you suggest?"

"Why don't you wait in my room down the hall?"

"Are you sure it's no trouble?"

"Oh, no," he heard Efren say. Then footsteps sounded and a door closed.

He resumed reading.

> Tabbang kept two women in his lair, according to Adong, then himself one of the fifteen in the rebel band. When word finally reached NPA superiors about the arrangement, Tabbang was commanded to make his choice and end bickering between the men, many of them womanless. Eventually Tabbang complied but later, when his common-law wife became pregnant, resumed the relationship with the other woman. After disobeying another directive the rebel priest was temporarily relieved of command pending a full inquiry into his conduct. Tabbang's death intervened and whatever his superiors might have decided will probably never be known. However, the testimony of Adong runs counter to the popular belief by misguided sympathisers that Tabbang

131

was a latter-day Friar Tuck forced into the company of a band of reluctant Robin Hoods. In fact, army authorities say, Tabbang was secretly a committed communist wanted for numerous offences including unlawful possession of weapons and subversion. The priest had eluded arrest by disguising himself as a woman worshipper and slipping through an army cordon set up around *barangay* San Juan in Capalonga preparatory to the arrest of Tabbang and several of his kind. In retrospect, the practiced deceptions seem symbolic of the man who— — —

The Igorot contemptuously threw the paper aside. He closed his eyes against the naked bulb and thought of Pricilla. How would he be treated if he ever reached the prominence of a Father Tabbang and had to be knocked off a national pedestal? Would they interview her and extract all the little details? Her tears and words to him, "You don't love me." Maybe she was right. Maybe he could only hate and had never loved her, only her body. Her beautiful, beautiful body. He could see it now, a sight that had always aroused him . . . But what was the point of remembering? He had finished with all that. There was no turning back. Not now.

He got up and reached for a bath towel draped on a chair. Slinging it over a shoulder, he headed for the showers.

* * *

Fortunato had just finished another busy day. As he prepared for bed, where Crispina had retired hours before, he decided that sometimes the job was not worth all the trouble it brought into his life. Fortunato conceded that the position had considerable compensations. He wouldn't be in charge of a *kadiwa* store for one. He wouldn't have access to people of influence and be able to enjoy privileges, for another. And, as it should be, *nobody* in the neighbourhood ignored him! They were always on their best behaviour when he was around. Yes indeed, it had to be admitted, he enjoyed the status. But today had been one of those days when he had his doubts. The missing stock in the store had bothered him all morning. Then there had been that letter from City Hall about the new tax collecting role for the *barangay* captains. Somebody higher up had figured the captains could do the job better because they knew the neighbourhood. But he thought the whole thing sounded a nuisance. He had phoned City Hall immediately to express his doubts. The voice at the other end had instead laughed and said, "Stop complaining and think of the money." And when he had replied, "What money?" the voice confided, "Don't you know? There are cash incentives for the collectors." Well, why didn't they say so in the first place! Perhaps the idea had its merits after all. He had no sooner put the phone down when the residents of A. Luna Street rushed into the store all shouting at once. He could not quieten them till he climbed onto the counter and banged his shoe on a wall. When the din died one of them had complained about a *tanod* being drunk and refusing to pay for a duck egg. Such a piffling trifle! But it had taken the rest of the day to settle. He certainly hoped tomorrow would be better!

Fortunato yawned as he put his false teeth in a glass remembering he had meant to see his friends at the police station about the vendor's tip. Climbing into bed he determined he would attend to the matter in the morning, if he had time.

CHAPTER SEVEN

Zac awoke to a grey dawn and looked at Ian sleeping in the other bed. The Filipino smiled realising what day it was and, quietly picking up the phone on a table between them, called urgently, "Wake up, Ian, wake up. It's your mother."

"Uh," Ian sleepily grunted.

"A long distance call from your mother," Zac said with feigned impatience. "Quickly. You're wasting time and money."

The Scot groped at the receiver, wondering whether to address his mother as he always did in the accent of his homeland, and thereby surprise Zac, or use his preferred gentleman's voice.

"Oh, hell," he said as the cord tangled with an ashtray.

"I'll fix it," Zac volunteered.

Ian held the phone in position. "Hullo, mother," he said in palace tones, dreading her reaction. Perhaps the silence was her reaction, he thought.

"It's Ian speaking," he added, to clear up any confusion on the other end.

"Ask her what the weather's like over there," Zac prompted.

Ian cupped the mouthpiece and hissed, "Be quiet you fool. I can't hear."

"Maybe it's a bad connection."

"There doesn't seem to be any connection now. Damn the phone!"

"Oh, there's a connection all right."

"Well, listen yourself," Ian said crossly, thrusting the phone into Zac's hand.

Zac listened intently. "You're right. It's dead."

Ian rubbed his forehead. "I wonder what she rang about?"

"Probably to wish you a happy New Year," Zac said, hanging up the phone.

"But that's days away. Anyhow my mother could never do that. I hope nothing is wrong."

Zac shrugged and advised, "Don't go back to sleep in case she rings again."

"I suppose not," Ian said irritably.

134

"Your mother has gone to all this trouble," the Filipino scolded. "Don't be so cranky. You should always respect your mother."

"Oh, why don't you shut up!" the Scot exclaimed and then said in puzzlement, "I wonder how she knows I'm—"

The phone rang and interrupted his thoughts.

"Ah, she must be ringing again," Zac said cheerfully. "You answer it this time."

Ian picked up the receiver. "Hullo. Is that you, mother?"

"Pardon sir?" the other end queried.

"What's going on?" Ian muttered and, raising his voice, said impatiently, "This is Ian MacPhe—, er, Essex speaking."

"Yes sir. Can I help?"

"Are you the operator?" Ian asked.

"That's right sir."

"Good. At least we have one thing straight. I'm ready to speak to my mother."

"What is the number sir?"

"Well you should know. She's in Britain."

"Oh, you'll have to book an overseas call for that sir."

"But I thought this was an overseas call," Ian protested as he saw Zac sniggering.

"No sir. This is the hotel operator."

"I don't understand. Why are you phoning me?"

"Didn't you want to place a call sir?"

"No. I'm waiting for one."

"We have nothing for you here sir."

"What about before?"

"When sir?"

"A few minutes ago."

"I don't know anything about that sir."

"Forget it," the Scot said crossly and hung up.

"Having trouble?" Zac asked innocently.

"You bloody fool! What was that about?"

Zac became suddenly serious. "I'll tell you on one condition."

"What's that?" Ian said cautiously.

"Tell me why you have *two* last names."

* * *

Martin sat at a window table in an air-conditioned cafe a few blocks from Rizal Park. He looked beyond a frilly curtain to the busy street, watching for Roderick's approach. The engineer had phoned the pension that morning and hastily arranged a pre-lunch snack, saying, "I have something to tell you."

135

"Can't you say over the phone?" he had asked.

"It's best that we see each other," Roderick had replied.

So Martin had showered and dressed in preparation for the meeting. Now he watched the flow of humanity outside the restaurant. A vendor was having a hard time trying to sell sandals. Everyone hurried by. Then he heard a siren and a military jeep appeared at the head of a convoy of trucks. The procession halted in front of the cafe, its way blocked by an apparently stalled bus. As the jeep's siren died a tall officer got out and began waving his arms in anger at the frightened bus driver. Pedestrians were gathering in watchful knots on the footpath. The soldier strode over to the bus, a hand now resting menacingly on a revolver holstered at his side. The footpath crowd swelled as if expecting something. Martin found his view blocked. Then he glimpsed some people pushing the bus out of the convoy's path. The soldier walked unsmiling back to the jeep. People were drifting away.

"You seem absorbed," he heard Roderick say from behind.

Martin looked around and was surprised to see the engineer casually dressed as though going to a golf course. Roderick sat down at the table and said, "I'm not working today. I have other business."

"Is that what you want to tell me about?" Martin asked.

"Yes. I'm arranging my departure home."

"When?" he asked, feeling sick.

"In two days."

Martin attempted a brave smile. "This is a bit of a shock. You'll have to give me a few minutes to adjust."

"I've talked about it before. It was always my plan."

"But this seems so sudden."

"You must accept it," Roderick said as a waitress came to the table to take their order. After the woman had gone he said, "I'll write to you when I can."

"It's not the same," Martin said quietly.

"I'm sorry. It's the best I can do."

Martin bit his lip. "Why don't you take me along?"

"Why should I?" Roderick asked harshly.

Martin averted the other's eyes. "It doesn't matter. I was just joking."

"No, you weren't. I know you."

Martin's face reddened.

"Don't make it harder than it already is," the engineer said, in suddenly softer tones. It was almost a plea.

"What am I meant to say then?"

136

"Just take things as they come."

"Do I see you again?"

"If you wish."

"I do," Martin said, inwardly cursing his weakness.

"I'm free tomorrow. What do you suggest?"

Martin thought a moment. "Can we get out of the city and go somewhere peaceful?"

"Why not?" Roderick agreed.

"Early? Before the morning rush?"

"Sure. Let's see now," he said, pausing. "How does breakfast at a river-bank restaurant sound?"

Martin nodded with approval.

"Feeling better?" Roderick asked as the order arrived.

"A bit."

"A bit," the engineer repeated, gazing at his downcast companion. "You can't stop caring about me, right?"

"Right."

"I'll tell you something else," Roderick said, putting a hand on his companion's shoulder. "Something that I should have told you long before this."

"What's that?"

"It's mutual," he said.

Martin stared in surprise.

*   *   *

Santos crossed the *sala* floor and cautiously parted floral curtains that Fermina had bought only weeks earlier. He turned to his son and said, "Why can't you take no for an answer?"

"Because you'll go to prison if you don't get away now. We all love you too much to want to see that happen."

"Oh, Ricardo," he sighed. "Does Fermina know of this mad scheme of yours too?"

"Yes. And she also knows you're being stubborn. That's why she took the others out shopping. She agrees with me. She wants me to try once more to convince you before the trial starts tomorrow. It's your last chance and you should take it."

Santos returned to the table where a passport and airline ticket lay. Outside the house, somewhere, fire crackers were exploding.

"Your flight departs four hours before the trial starts," Ricardo explained. "You're leaving the house in a laundry trolley. A van will be waiting in the courtyard. The usual service has been told not to make a collection tomorrow. The man who does come will take you to the airport where a contact will ensure a smooth boarding. We're following on another flight two hours later. There's no need for Fermina, myself and the girls to use false passports. By the time our absence will be noticed we'll all be safe and together."

Santos thumbed through the passport. Everything seemed in order. The photograph was of him but he had a new name and Cebu address. The round-trip ticket indicated a return in fourteen days. A nice touch, he thought.

"How do you know the trolley won't be searched!" Santos asked, putting the documents back on the table.

"Because it hasn't been once in the eight days since this circus began. As guards they're somewhat lax."

The old man drew imaginary lines on the table top. "If I go it will only be for your sakes, not mine."

"Then you'll go," Ricardo said hopefully.

"I'll think about it."

"Papa, you've said that for days. You have no more time."

Santos shrugged. "I've spent almost all my life in this country. If I go, there's no coming back. You're asking me to die in an alien land."

Ricardo shook his head. "We're asking you to live for your country, not rot in a prison."

"Rot or be of service to my country? Maybe prison has its positive side. And I will always have my faith as a companion."

"You've done enough, papa. At least think of the children. Is their suffering really worth it?"

He smiled wistfully. "Perhaps the issue is bigger than all of us." But seeing his son's disappointment added, "I'll let you know tonight after dinner."

"You'll really consider it?"

Santos thought of Hilaria and Sabina. "I will. That's a promise."

*   *   *

At San Andres market the morning crowd was beginning to thin and Jojo took the opportunity to restock shelves. He could see a woman eyeing the strawberries but knew from experience she had not made up her mind.

"I think they're too dear for me," she told him after moving closer to the stall.

"Fixed prices, lady," he replied automatically, following the instructions of the owner temporarily absent elsewhere in the markets.

"My husband would be disappointed if I didn't get any," she said unheeding. "Perhaps I might if they were a little cheaper."

Jojo deftly caught a papaya rolling off the stand. He put it back in a more secure position.

"Would it make any difference if I bought a larger amount?" she asked.

He shook his head. "I'm sorry. That's the owner's policy, not mine."

"Too much," she sighed. "Maybe they'll be cheaper tomorrow." And then, almost confidentially, "If I had half my neighbour's luck I could buy the lot."

Jojo waited to hear of a lottery win or something like that.

"And just for seeing some people in the hall. Imagine that! How lucky can you be?"

"In a hall?" he asked, puzzled.

"Yes, in our boarding house," he replied. "Mrs Cruz saw a companion of the man who was shot last week. She told the police and they gave her a reward."

"Ah," he said in understanding, his heart beating a little faster. "When did that happen?"

"Yesterday. She came in and told me straight away."

"Then she is lucky," he agreed, deciding on the spot that this would be his last day at the markets. It would be safer to lie low at the pension till he had finished his business.

"I wish I'd been in her place," the woman was rambling on. "But I never seem to notice anything. I didn't even see the man occupying number twelve. Just how do you get so lucky?"

"Your turn could be next," the Igorot said in silent contempt. "You never know."

The woman shook her head emphatically.

"No, I don't think so. I'm not lucky," she replied and wandered away among the surrounding jumble of stalls.

*　　*　　*

The station wagon bounced along a rutted street lined with dilapidated, unpainted houses outside which idle groups of sullen, staring people congregated.

"I don't like the look of this place," Ian said to Zac, hanging on tightly to a grip above the back window.

Zac nodded in agreement.

"We'll be through here soon," the bull-necked driver of the vehicle said. "The resort's not like this."

"It wouldn't want to be," Ian exclaimed, feeling the hostility of the poverty-stricken town.

"All the guests I've driven down here say the same thing," the driver admitted. "It's put a lot of our customers off a second visit."

"That's no surprise," Ian said.

As the vehicle turned into another rutted street, a rusty can struck the bonnet and bounced off, landing with a clatter on the roadway.

"Let's get through here quickly," Ian urged the driver.

"I'm going as fast as the road will allow," the man said.

"I don't think the road has been repaired ever since it was built." Zac told Ian.

"What a place," Ian commented, shuddering a little.

"Poverty's not your piece of cake, is it?" Zac said sharply.

"You know my views."

"There's plenty more of it too," he replied, determined not to apologise for what they were passing through.

Ian studied a map in his hand. "I'd rather see the nicer things, thank you."

"Not thinking about it won't make it go away, you know," Zac said, with a trace of anger at his companion's attitude.

"Thank you for the lecture," the Scot said as the town gave way to dry paddy fields either side of the now elevated road. "The subject is henceforth closed. Kindly take note."

The vehicle came to a stop at a road barricade and guard box. Burly figures in blue uniforms emerged. They were all armed with holstered revolvers.

"The beginning of the resort," the driver explained, breaking off for a window conversation with the guards.

"The place reminds me of a prison," Ian confided to Zac.

"It is in a way. A prison for the rich."

"Oh, there you go again," the Scot snapped as the station wagon was cleared for entry. "You're like a bloody parrot."

Zac was about to reply but let the moment pass with heavy silence.

The ruts gave way to a smooth bitumen surface that gently curved through a grove of coconut trees planted with mathematical precision. Picking up speed they swept past a sign saying, "Welcome to Silken Sands Resort." After another curve the wagon passed under an archway of stone. Masses of bright flowering shrubs and trees replaced the palms before they in turn parted to reveal bold structures of stone, timber and glass. Nearby lay a circular turquoise pool that overlooked a beach and the South China Sea beyond. Around the pool tanned figures reclined on deck chairs shaded by striped umbrellas.

"We hope you like it here," the driver said, stopping and getting out to unload the bags at the back.

Ian stepped to the driveway and gazed appreciatively at the pool.

"This looks better," he said, notably more cheerful. Ian could already see himself lounging under canvas, a cool drink in hand.

Zac came to his side and whistled. "No wonder they threw a can at us."

The Scot wheeled on his companion. "For God's sake, will you shut up on that subject. Ever since yesterday you've done nothing but harp on that one theme. Can't you ever think of anything else to say?"

"What did I say?" Zac asked innocently.

"You know damn well."

"I wouldn't if I did, would I?"

"Yes, you would. Just to spite me."

"Is that what you think?"

"You're quite capable of it. Like this morning's ridiculous behaviour. Damn idiot way to remember the slaughter of babies."

"Oh, Ian. I told you that's our tradition on Innocent's Day. Can't you take a joke?"

"About as well as you can take a hint."

"A hint on what?"

"To keep off that bloody subject."

"Oh, we're back to that."

"You never got off it?"

"Don't shout at me, Ian."

"I'll do what I damn well like. I'm not shackled like you."

"We're in a public place. You don't like scenes in public. And neither do I."

"No one is telling me what to do, particularly in this country."

"People are beginning to notice."

"Then let them if they have nothing better to do."

"Stop acting the fool, Ian."

"A fool, am I? So, that's what you really think of me."

"I didn't mean that."

"Oh, don't apologise now. You've already said your piece. Anyhow, I'm going. I have better things to do than be insulted all the time."

"What?"

"Yes, I'm going back to Manila. And then back to Spain."

"I don't believe this," Zac said. "It must be a bad dream."

"Reload my bags," Ian instructed the embarrassed driver.

141

"And mine too," Zac said.

"You're not coming with me," Ian objected.

"How else do you expect me to get back? Walk?"

"Get another vehicle of course."

"There's only one. This isn't a taxi rank. We're not in Manila."

"Very well. But I'm sitting in the front."

"Ride on the roof if you wish," Zac muttered.

The two lapsed into an angry silence. The sound of laughter reached them from the pool side.

"Excuse me," the driver said to the mute pair. "The wagon is loaded. Er, are you sure you want to return?"

Ian strode towards the vehicle. "I've never been surer of anything in my life," he said and got in, slamming the door.

*   *   *

In his office, Felipe studied a computer print-out received earlier that afternoon from Army Intelligence. It confirmed what he thought: the Igorot had been in the service but had provided him with a misleading name. That fitted in with the bogus addresses as confirmed by Jurado. All the same, he was puzzled by the Igorot's apparent non-involvement with anything at all since the discharge, though the report had little in it of those years. It was a trail into nothingness.

Felipe perused again data pertaining to the Igorot's background and service. The father's name was unknown . . . mother died giving birth to her only child . . . raised by a grandfather now dead . . . enlisted at eighteen . . . excellent marksman . . . disciplined and of exemplary conduct . . . refused participation in Fernandez-Batobato tongs . . . bravery citation for rescue work in Mindanao floods . . . promoted to corporal . . . first among nine-hundred in a race over a seventy-kilometre course carrying full pack . . . contracted mumps, no known complications . . . girlfriend . . . rifle accident . . . hospitalisation . . . inquiry finding . . .

Felipe paused and returned to the section immediately before the description of how the man had lost his fingers.

"Bangse-il was seen increasingly in the company of one Pricilla Mendoza while on leave. A subsequent check of her antecedents and background revealed no criminal record and no known links with radical or subversive individuals or organisations. Mendoza was employed as a shop assistant with Alemar's at the time and . . ."

Felipe raced ahead till he came to Mendoza's last known address. He scribbled it on a pad and, ripping free the paper, walked briskly from the room. In a corridor he found his rookie assistant by a coffee dispenser and announced almost triumphantly, "Get your cap Jurado. We're going to see a lady."

* * *

Santos closed the door on his departing attorneys, still undecided whether he would be seeing them in the morning. He had not compromised their professional integrity by confiding Ricardo's plans. He reasoned that they had enough to worry about. As he sank into an easy chair in the evening quiet of the *sala* he could hear the upstairs chatter of the children being put to bed by their mother. Ricardo had quietly gone out that afternoon and would be back soon wanting an answer. What would it be? Stay or go? Spend his last days in a prison or be an exile in a strange land?

Santos turned his attention to a now rather bedraggled Christmas tree. Despite its appearance it had been left standing. Ricardo had wanted to remove it but Hilaria and Sabina had protested at their father's order to clear it away, along with the candle altar and stale cake offering on the shelf behind. Fermina had sided with the children saying, "A little longer won't hurt, Ricardo." Santos had thought the same. He remembered the Christmas trees of his childhood. Then they were wonderful Baguio pines, fragrant with the aroma of their mountain home. Today, people had to make do with paper imitations. And to think that was called progress! The children had done a splendid job with the green crepe and wired stick that Ricardo had brought home. Why, it almost looked like a tree! Till you got close enough to smell it for the phoney it was. Newspapers were much the same now, he reflected. Anyone could buy one on the street and scan its pages and think they were holding the real thing. It had all been so different before those first terrible days. Days in which freedom was replaced with servitude. And how he had hated those slogans carried daily in the newly ordered press!

> *Ang pagsunod sa magulang,*
> *Tanda ng anak na magalang.*
> To obey the parent is a virtue
> of respectful children.

Yes, they had overnight become a nation of children!

> *Sa ikauunlad ng bayan,*
> *Disciplina ang kailangan.*
> For the progress of the country
> it is necessary to have discipline.

143

El Caudillo would not have spoken differently!
   Para sa kaunlaran,
   Tayo'y magtulungan.
   So that we may progress,
   let's help each other.
But my children, help my cause first!
   Ang paglamang sa kapwa,
   Ay gawaing masagwa.
   To take advantage of others
   is a despicable act.
Particularly if it is in the guise of saving a nation!

Santos got up and went to a side cabinet where he poured a small glass of wine. As he returned to the chair and sipped from the tulip glass, he thought at length of his God, his country, his family and the morrow. By the time he had drained the last drop he had come to a final decision.

*   *   *

The Usher's renewed activities had caused bad feelings at Singalong. In less than two days he had successfully intercepted six foreigners. One was looking for Bongbong. As the callboy was still in Mindoro there had been no repercussions. Jessie did not care about the Belgian. However, the loss of the four others had prompted a war council. Lito, Carlo and Max were all upset. Max was the angriest because he had lost two. One had unexpectedly turned up in Manila from Port Moresby, and the other was the Christmas macho who had come to the pension after another Dubbo man, whom he knew as a poofter basher, had booked into the same hotel with a local chick.

Poaching was a cardinal sin in the callboy world. That did not stop it happening constantly. At gay bars many of the older clients who had already made a choice of companion for the night nevertheless enjoyed sitting like King James I on a throne while other callboys swarmed around, hoping to dislodge the rival. A standard technique was the bad mouth. If the companion said something a competitor would catch the eye of King James and mouth the words, "Not true." If the companion was not on his guard he might have to contend with whispers in the royal ear of, "He has VD" and "He's been in jail" and "His cousin has leprosy." If the King was a Louis or Frederick a smattering of French or German could tip the scales in the boy's favour. And many of the boys had considerable linguistic ability, speaking English, Tagalog and several other dialects.

The washroom ambush was also effective. After several drinks a client would feel the need to relieve himself. A smart callboy who had timed the drinker's frequency would be at a washbasin as he walked in.

Hopefully the client would, on entering, say, "Call around to my hotel tomorrow after I've got rid of Nino."

"In the morning or afternoon?"

"Make it midday . . . We'll have lunch together."

"I've been hoping you'd notice me."

"I couldn't help it, er—"

"Carlo."

"It suits you," the customer would say. And then, after a pause, "How old are you?"

"Eighteen," the young Narcissus would reply, dropping the last two years.

"Uh-huh. Well, Carlo, I'd better get back or Nino might suspect. He's nice but very jealous. Don't forget, my hotel at midday."

More secret rendezvous were made in washrooms than in bars. The appeal of a washroom deal was that no one else knew of the breach of ethics. A callboy could casually rejoin the others at the bar and a few hours later on the way home in a shared taxi say to a buddy at his side, "That was a dead old night."

"Yeah. Only good for poachers like Jet and Chit."

"Disgusting, wasn't it?"

"They'd do anything to get a client."

"They tried hard enough tonight."

"So commercial. I'm glad we're not like that."

Of course, lack of deceit was the Usher's big mistake. He was too open. If he operated in washrooms, as did Carlo and most of the other boys he would not now be in trouble. Neither would he be hiding once again in a toilet cubicle, but this time trembling at the angry voices in the hall.

"Where is he?" Max demanded of Jessie and Santiago as if they were personally responsible for his disappearance.

"We haven't seen him since dinner," Santiago replied.

"The coward," Carlo growled.

"We should get Perla to kick the little darling out," Lito said indignantly.

"What's it got to do with Perla?" Santiago asked.

Carlo snorted. "He's robbing us of our business. How can we pay the rent?"

"He has rent problems too," Santiago said quietly. "I know his Adelaide cheque is late."

"That's *his* bad luck," Max shot back. "Why pass it on to *us*?"

"Yeah," Carlo fumed. "The little blood sucker."

"I know where to look," Lito exclaimed, moving down the hall.

"Let's go then," Carlo said, beckoning to the others. Max followed, but Santiago and Jessie trailed reluctantly.

Outside a closed cubicle, Lito put a finger to his lips in a gesture of silence and gently pressed the unyielding door.

"Wait," Max whispered cautiously. "Let's get him when he comes out."

But Carlo pushed the others aside and took command. "Come out you thieving rat!" he yelled, rapping loudly on the cubicle door.

"Ahhh!" screamed the rat. "Who's that? How dare you!"

But even before an enraged Perla could pull up her panties the boys had fled.

*   *   *

Jurado brought the police car to a stop under a street lamp at the third address that night. They were in the dormitory suburb of Sampaloc, near the university belt. Few people seemed about.

"I hope we've found her this time sir," he said. Felipe got out saying, "Me too," and slammed the door irritably.

The officer crossed to a long narrow staircase between shop fronts and climbed quickly to the women's dormitory he presumed was behind a door at the top.

An unsmiling woman with glasses answered his knock and said coldly, "Oh, the police. What do you want?"

"I'm looking for a Pricilla Mendoza," he said edgily. "I'm told her mail is being forwarded here. Can you confirm that?"

"Yes, that's correct," the woman said. "She moved into the dorm about two weeks ago."

The lieutenant relaxed a little. "Could I speak to her?"

"I'm sorry. That's not possible. She's not here just now."

"I can wait if it's not too long. When will she be back?"

"Not for two days. She's at her parent's place in the provinces."

"I see," he said, his irritation returning. "Would you have her address so I can get in touch with her?"

The woman said bluntly, "I can't help. I don't know it."

Felipe jotted down a telephone number and gave it to her. "Could you tell Miss Mendoza when she returns to phone Lieutenant Felipe."

"I'll advise her if she comes back."

The officer frowned. "Is there some doubt about that?"

"She mentioned that her mother was ill. That's all I know."

God damn! Another delay, he cursed. "Well, tell her when you see her."

"Is that all, officer?"

"For the moment," he said curtly.

"Good night," she replied with equal severity, closing the door in his face and leaving little room for him to turn around and descend the steps. He had just got to the bottom and was making a mental note to order a security check on the unfriendly woman when the street was plunged into complete darkness. Sampaloc was having its fourth blackout in twenty-two hours.

*　　*　　*

It was dark at the Santos household later that night, too, but not because of a blackout. All inside were finally asleep after much tossing and turning with thoughts of the day to come. Downstairs, the Santos cat was on the prowl for food as usual. However, tonight its search had an extra urgency. In the absence of the maid no one had thought to throw a few scraps on the kitchen floor. The ginger animal had meowed and meowed in vain. Now the big house was quiet as the cat sat in the *sala* doorway, its eyes transfixed on a candle flame poking above the lip of a high shelf from where the odour of food came. Only fear checked its advance. Only hunger urged it on. At length the cat got up and edged cautiously forward. It paused at the sofa, tail twitching. It moved past the paper Christmas tree. It stopped and paused in the shadow of the high shelf. And waited. And waited. Then leapt.

By the time soldiers outside had smashed in locked and bolted doors those within were beyond help. It was not so much the flames that claimed the Santos family as thick, suffocating smoke. Horrified neighbours watched the drama, their faces a flickering orange. Then the firemen arrived amid the dying wail of sirens. One brigade, two, three, four.

"Save our places," they implored the silhouetted figures unravelling hoses before the already collapsing Santos residence. "It's too late for them."

"We can't do everything at once," a fire chief directing operations called back. "Don't expect miracles."

"But our houses!" they protested, approaching the man.

"Overworked and underpaid," the chief muttered.

The neighbours knowingly looked at each other, one of them about to object. "Don't argue," the others said, digging into pockets. "There's no time."

147

Later the chief was to look back on the night with particular satisfaction. He and his men had done very well. It was a pity about the Santos family, especially the children. But the old man had been a troublemaker. No one who mattered would miss him. The only thing to really spoil the night had been when Fireman Bagatsing tripped and broke his ankle. And all because of a stupid, ginger cat!

· CHAPTER EIGHT ·

As the morning sun rose above the tree line, Martin and Roderick glided down a river on an outrigger canoe. Fore and aft, muscled arms sliced calm waters with glistening oars.

"One more day," Martin murmured, his back resting on the American's chest.

"I'll miss all this," the voice behind Martin's ear said softly.

"Then why go? Get another contract or something."

"No. It's not possible."

"I thought engineers could walk into any job here."

"It's not the job. I'm going back for another reason."

Martin glanced behind but the narrow hull made it too difficult to turn sufficiently to see the expression on Roderick's face. The canoe rounded a narrow bend and banks became cliffs.

"Are you going to tell me why?" Martin asked, fully expecting more silence or words amounting to the same thing.

"I wasn't," he heard Roderick say. "Now I think differently." And after a long pause, "I'm going home for an operation."

Martin did not move but felt instant alarm. He asked, "Is it bad?"

Another pause. "I'm afraid so."

"Will the operation help?"

"It may but I'm not counting on it too much."

"How long have you known this?" Martin asked quietly.

"A while," the voice came vaguely.

"Before our separation?"

"Around about then."

"So that's why y—"

"I had to, Martin. I couldn't hide it if we had continued to live together. I've been having treatment regularly. It was only a matter of time before you noticed. And that wouldn't help me. Unfortunately, things have been getting worse lately."

"And that also explains the moods, cancelled lunches and outings," Martin said.

"I've had some pretty bad days."

"I don't understand why you've been keeping this to yourself."

"It's just the way I am, Martin. I know it has been hard on you. I'm sorry. Try to understand."

Martin could not. Instead he asked, "When's the operation?"

"The week after I get back."

"How will I know what happens?"

"Don't worry. A friend in New York will keep you informed. In case things don't work out a trust fund will be set up in advance and —"

"Don't talk like that," Martin groaned.

"And you'll have no financial worries."

As they entered a spray-filled chasm above which brightly coloured butterflies danced, it was difficult to tell whether the moisture on their cheeks was from a surrounding cascade or their eyes.

*   *   *

Ian stood in a busy Manila street and in smog looked around for transport. In his pocket was a new airticket. The Scot had found a travel agency willing to arrange an early return. He had been lucky and got a flight scheduled for the following day. Now, he only wanted to get back to the protection of his airconditioned hotel suite. A vacant yellow and white taxi approached. The driver honked the horn. Ian ignored it, looking for a cheaper jeepney. He was about to walk farther along the street when a Filipino of similar age appeared at his elbow and said, "Excuse me, are you British?"

"Er, yes," Ian hesitantly replied, vaguely aware that he had seen the man near the travel agency earlier.

The Filipino flashed a warm smile. "I thought so. I heard you speaking. The British people have such nice voices."

"Do they?" Ian said stiffly, dismissing the man as a snoop and now looking down the one-way street for even a taxi to take him away.

The man continued brightly, "I would love to see London. I hear it is a very beautiful city. Do you live there?"

"Well, actually I don't," Ian said in the temporary absence of transport. "I live somewhere else."

"My sister is in London," the man was saying, apparently not understanding the last statement of the foreigner. "She's a nurse. We haven't heard from her for months. We're very worried."

"Why?" he asked with vague curiosity.

"We hear there is much trouble in London with the I.R.A. We fear for her safety."

"Don't worry about that," the Scot assured. "She's probably safer there than here. In fact, I'm *sure* she is."

"Do you really think so?"

"No doubt about it old chap."

"I hope you are right."

"Of course I am. She'll write soon enough."

"That's my problem. I wish my mama could believe Baby was safe. Mama has a bad heart and she's been worrying too much." He gave another brilliant smile. "Baby's my young sister."

"Well, tell your mother that she's worrying about nothing. London is quite safe."

The Filipino seemed relieved and said, "I'm glad to hear that," and, after a lull in the conversation, added, "do you think you could tell my mama? She would believe you. It wouldn't take long. We don't live far from here. It's only a short walk."

Ian frowned. "What could I tell her? I don't know why your sister hasn't written. I only know that London is a safe city."

"But if you came to my house and spoke with my mama it would make her feel much better."

Ian edged nearer the kerb so that he could be better seen when he signalled the first thing he saw.

"But you could help my mama," the stranger persisted. "It won't take long. Only a few minutes."

"I really can't help," he said curtly, looking elsewhere in an attempt to dismiss the man. Up the road he saw approaching traffic. He raised an arm and held it high, regretting the absence of Zac's protection from street harassment.

"My mama hasn't slept properly for months," the man was pleading to the back of Ian's sweaty shirt. "Can't you spare a few moments of your time?"

"There's nothing I can do," Ian said tersely. "Don't bother me any more."

"Please," the stranger begged as the first of a line of jeepneys approached and squealed to a crawl. "Please come with me."

Ian was unable to see the vehicle's destination but did not care. It would take him away from the man. In any case, it was going in the direction of his hotel. He clambered aboard a back entrance and sat down next to a Filipina wearing a top with the message, "Parking space available." The Scot paid no attention. He was just grateful to have escaped.

After a distance he became aware of a sign by the driver's cabin.

Leaning forward he made out the words, "God Knows Judas Not Pay." Hastily, he dug a coin from a pocket. Others passed it forward. He heard the driver call out something in Tagalog and felt the vehicle lurch around a corner.

If Ian had spoken the language he would have known the driver was making an illegal route change, first checking with passengers. All the drivers of the fifty or so thousand jeepneys in the metropolis did that sometime or other. Only when the vehicle passed under an unfamiliar, elevated concrete roadway did Ian become uneasy. He suspected the need for a taxi and felt for his back-pocket wallet. He paled. It was not there. He felt in another pocket for his airticket and with relief found it. He was thankful that he had few notes in the wallet, heeding hotel advice about street pickpockets. Then he thought of the man and cursed. As the jeepney was going farther and farther from the hotel he decided to get off and ask for directions.

In a grimy street Ian searched for a samaritan. He did not know it but he was in *Maynila*, another world within the metropolis where fluent English was not so common. Even outside the confines of *Maynila*, English was slowly breaking down after enjoying a long reign since its introduction at the turn of the century by the Americans. Already there was Taglish, a combination of English and Tagalog, and Bamboo English.

In newspaper columns: "British in winter is never short of rain. It is the time of the year when people Don MacKintoshes and gumboots almost daily."

To foreign investors inspecting a rural site proposed for grain production: "This is a corny area, gentleman."

Or a headline in a movie magazine: "Not an ethnic movie, *nagkaluwagan sa* boobs."

Just to make matters a little worse Ian truly spoke the Queen's English. After his fifth uncomprehended request for directions he was becoming a little alarmed. It was then that he spied nearby a curly-haired youth in shorts waving at him while standing under what appeared to be fern baskets.

"Hi," called the youth.

"Hullo," replied Ian.

"Can I help?"

"You certainly can," a relieved Ian replied. "I'm looking for my hotel near Rizal Park. Can you tell me the way?"

"Sure, no trouble."

"Oh," Ian said. "That's splendid, uh—"

"Efren."

"Tell me, Efren," Ian said jovially. "Where do I go?"

The Usher took the foreigner's hand. "You look terrible. Come with me first. I'll get you a drink."

"Oh, I'm perfectly all right, old chap," Ian protested.

"You'll feel better if you drink something," the Usher insisted, tugging at the Scot's sweaty hand.

"Very well, if I must," Ian murmured, remembering his manners.

"What's your name?" the Usher asked, leading him up a stairway and along a maze of halls.

"Ian."

"Where do you live?"

"Spain."

"Do you speak Spanish?"

"Not really," Ian replied, entering a tiny room.

"What would you like to drink?"

"Oh, the same as you my good fellow."

"I only have orange."

"That will do nicely."

"How long have you been in Manila?" Efren asked, pouring the lukewarm liquid.

"Two days."

"Do you know anyone here?"

"I know one person."

"A boy?" Efren asked, placing the drink by his guest's side.

"Well, actually a man," Ian replied, suddenly feeling hot in the tiny room and reaching for the glass.

"Do you like men?" Efren said, moving a little closer.

The Scot coughed, slopping his drink.

"Would you like to see my photo album?" Efren asked, suddenly producing one and sitting down close by.

"That would be nice," a relieved Ian replied. He did not like discussing his sexual preferences with just anybody, though the youth did have appeal.

"Here's me at a party," Efren said proudly.

"Oh, very jolly."

And turning a page, "Me under the fern baskets."

"Uh-huh, I see."

"And me at the beach," Efren said, putting an arm around his guest's waist.

"The beach," Ian echoed weakly.

"And me skinny dipping," Efren said sliding a hand down the inside front of Ian's pants.

"I say —"

"And me sunbathing without my swimmers," Efren said, his hand active.

"Don't, please," moaned Ian.

"Do you want me to stop?" Efren whispered into his guest's ear.

Ian was silent, his eyes closed. The Usher smiled in triumph. He had claimed another foreigner, though he would find to his later amazement that this one had *no money*!

*   *   *

Tommy had exciting news for Danilo when he called in at the penthouse for brunch.

"I'm going to be a dancer," he announced proudly, dumping a soft bag on the floor and pirouetting gracefully.

"But you were going to do that before," Danilo said. "And then you gave up your lessons."

Tommy laughed. "Oh, that was so boring. Every day exercises, exercises. This is on stage. This is the real thing."

"Where?" Danilo asked suspiciously.

"At the Milky Way. They want us to put on a show to fill a spot."

"Us?" the other queried, a little relieved at the location.

"Santiago, myself and some of the other boys at the pension." And smiling broadly, "Why don't you join us? We need one more."

Danilo looked doubtfully at his friend. "What would we do? I'd feel so silly."

Tommy emphatically shook his head. "No, don't worry. I've thought of an act." He bent to the bag and pulled out two wigs.

"Here," he told Danilo. "Try one on."

The two went to the bathroom and before a big mirror arranged the curly, brunette hairpieces which in both cases came down to their shoulders. They rummaged through the bathroom cabinet and, sure enough, found a make-up box. Whose it was they did not care. A lot of laughs later they surveyed the result.

"Darling," gushed a mascaraed Tommy to a heavily rouged Danilo, "you look so divine."

"Thank you so much," he said demurely, planting a kiss on his friend's lips.

They laughed again and moved back to the lounge room.

"I've got more," Tommy said, producing from the bag two lurid dresses. "Let's try them on."

"Give me the red one," Danilo instructed, now enjoying the game. "It suits me best."

They were into the dresses in minutes and in the bathroom once again. Tommy looked sidelong at his reflection, a strapless shoulder raised provocatively. Danilo pouted, a parody of a courtesan.

"Count me in," he told Tommy.

"Oh, good. I'll tell the others."

"When's the show?" Danilo asked as they drifted back to a couch.

"New Year."

"New Year? But we hardly have any time to get ready."

"Oh, Danilo. It's easy. We only have to be out front a few minutes. We can all come here for rehearsals." And, as an after-thought, he asked, "When's Jan coming back?"

"The day after New Year," Danilo said, suddenly remembering their food was about cooked. He made for the kitchen, shedding his wig.

Tommy followed and helped with the plates. The lot was taken into a dining room.

"Aren't you going to take the wig off?" Danilo asked in his red dress as the two tucked into the food.

Tommy spied himself in another, smaller mirror opposite. "No," he replied at length. "I like it on."

And it remained on till he showered later and left.

* * *

When Carlo awoke after a bad night at El Torro he was still mad at the Usher. Unlike Max and Lito, who had declined to take part in another pension posse, he was determined to avenge his loss. He got out of bed and, pulling on a singlet and shorts, went into the hall and along two doors to Efren's room. He slowly tried the knob. It was locked. He put an ear to the door and listened. He could hear moans.

"The little rat's at it again," he muttered. "I wonder whose guy he's snatched this time."

Folding his arms, he lent on the wall opposite the Usher's door and waited. He did not care if he stood there all day. And all night. He would even the score. The sound of feet ascending stairs and the memory of an outraged Perla prompted him to change his mind. From the safety of his bedroom he heard a knock down the hall. Checking, he saw Jojo's door closing. Carlo quickly resumed his post. He had not waited long when the Usher's door opened. Carlo stepped forward and blocked the exit.

"Morning session over?" Dumbell jeered.

Ian looked embarrassed and confused. The Usher paled.

155

"Get your money's worth?" the angry callboy asked a now red-faced Scot.

The pair took a step backwards.

"You're not getting away with it this time," Carlo said and, stepping forward, swung a badly-aimed fist at the Usher, hitting Ian just above the jaw.

The thump of the Scot collapsing on the floor soon brought Santiago, Jessie and Lito to the doorway.

Santiago whistled. "What have you done, Efrenita?"

"Nothing," the Usher sobbed. "It's all Carlo's fault. He went beserk."

"Don't blame me. The Usher ducked behind that," Carlo said and pointed at the bundle on the floor.

"An Afam," Lito gasped when he got a better look over Jessie's shoulder. "There'll be trouble over this."

Ian groaned and groggily sat up. "What happened?" he slurred as more footsteps sounded in the hall.

"He's all right," Carlo growled, secretly relieved.

Jojo and Zac joined the spectators at the door.

"What's going on?" Zac asked Santiago.

"Carlo socked an Afam," he laughed.

Zac peered between heads and saw the Scot sitting dazed on the floor.

"Ian," he gasped. "What are you doing here?"

"I'm lost," the dazed figure mumbled.

"That's right. He got lost," the Usher sniffed. "I was just helping him back to his hotel."

The boys in the doorway sniggered. "Sure you were, Efrenita," Santiago said. "And holding on *tight*."

Zac pushed past the boys and helped Ian to his feet. "I'll look after this now," he told the others.

"I really did get lost," the wobbly Scot insisted as Zac supported him down a hall. "I couldn't find my hotel." Mid-way down the stairs he asked, "How did you know I was here?"

Zac ignored the question and instead said, "I'll take you back to the hotel." Then he added lightly, "But don't expect any of Efren's extras."

* * *

The lieutenant had only just put the phone down when it rang again.

"It's Pricilla Mendoza," a hesitant voice said. "My landlady said you wanted to see me."

156

Felipe leaned forward in his chair. "I'm very glad to hear from you, Miss Mendoza. But I understood you were in the province and not due back for a few days."

"I'm not needed there anymore. What is it you want?"

"I'm trying to locate a Jojo Bangse-il. I believe you may know him."

"Who told you that?" she asked with an edge to her voice.

"We have our sources," he said, sensing resentment at the intrusion.

After a pause she said, "We were engaged for a time."

"Would you know where we can contact him?"

"I'm sorry. I haven't seen him for nearly a year. I'm not even sure of where he lives. He was always moving. He was . . . a restless person."

Felipe swore silently. "Do you know where he worked or what he did for a living? I ask because it might help us locate him."

The other end of the line was quiet.

"Miss Mendoza? Do you—"

"Yes, I heard you, lieutenant. First, may I ask if Jojo is in any sort of trouble?"

"Oh, this is just a routine inquiry," the officer lied a little too smoothly. "We thought you may be able to help. That's all."

"I don't want to do anything to hurt him."

"On the contrary, Miss Mendoza," he assured the suddenly anxious voice, "this is simply to clear up a small matter. Anything you know that would be of some help would be appreciated."

After yet another pause she said, "He was in several jobs while I knew him. When he left the army he became a security guard at a Makati bank."

Felipe began taking notes.

"Then he left and did casual work including a spell behind a hotel bar somewhere in the tourist belt. About the time we broke up he was working at a market stall."

The officer tensed. "Where at?"

"I think it was at San Andres."

"Not Cubao?"

"Oh, no. I'm sure of that."

"That's been a big help Miss Mendoza."

"Lieutenant, there's someone else who may be able to help."

"Oh? Who's that?" The pen was poised.

"Jojo had a friend. But it was so long ago I can't remember his name."

He decided on a punt. "It wouldn't be Laya by chance?"

"No, it was something like Zamora."

"Can you remember his first name."

"Yes. It was Zac."

The officer wrote down Zac Zamora in capital letters and underlined them.

"That's all I can tell you," she said, quite unaware that it was enough.

Ringing off, Felipe was sure that the girl still loved the Igorot and he had no time to waste.

*   *   *

Khaki uniforms swarmed through San Andres markets. Late afternoon shoppers looked on with apprehension. Sensing trouble, many left.

"Lieutenant," a sergeant called to his superior. "This man says he is the proprietor of the stall where the Igorot worked."

Felipe strode quickly to a nervous man, obviously of Chinese origin, standing by a fruit display.

"Where's the Igorot?" the officer asked brusquely.

"He never came to work today," the proprietor answered. "I thought he might be sick."

"Do you know where he lives?"

"Somewhere in the district, I think," the man said, his hands visibly trembling. "He never says much. He always keeps to himself."

The lieutenant appraised the man before finally ignoring him.

"Not very fruitful," a sergeant by his side observed.

"This isn't the time for jokes," he snapped, growing irritable at the Igorot's continuing luck.

"What did I say?" the sergeant whispered to Jurado, as ever at hand.

Felipe wheeled on the sergeant and said. "If he lives in the district he must be in a pension or boarding house. We might just find him if we're quick."

"There could be hundreds in the immediate area sir," the chastised sergeant said, anxious to get back on side with his superior.

"I don't care if it's thousands," the officer replied crossly to the hapless man. "I want a check on the registers of all boarding houses and pensions in the area. Is that understood?"

*   *   *

Ian looked out of his hotel window at the park lights below. They had just come on. He could see figures strolling along pathways, balloon vendors among them. It looked inviting but he had decided to stay in his suite till he left. That way nothing unexpected would happen again. In any case, he enjoyed the atmosphere of the hotel and the quiet efficiency of its staff. He had checked out yesterday with Zac and returned alone later the same afternoon. No one at the reception desk had made a smart remark. He had been silently thankful. They could not manage to give him his former room but had done the next best thing. One floor down in the same position.

Ian felt famished and looked for a room menu. Running a finger down the list he came to Paella a la Madrilena and immediately was transported in mind to his Spain. He could feel his mouth watering in anticipation. He picked up a phone and gave his order, adding a Flan de Chocolate for sweets. He had only just hung up when he thought of cheese and biscuits and a small bottle of red wine. He picked up the phone again and made the addition. He switched on the colour TV. Liza Minelli was being seduced by a wavy-haired man. It seemed familiar. He switched it off. He put his empty suitcase on a bed and went to the wardrobe to begin packing. On the rack inside he saw Zac's bathrobe. He slid shut the wardrobe door. The fairyland of lights beyond the window beckoned again. Looking at the park below he could just make out soldiers posted around a monument. Rifles were on their shoulders. He returned to the TV and switched it on but this time to a different channel. A boxer was hammering an opponent. He changed to another channel. A compere at a variety show was speaking in Tagalog. He switched it off. He wandered over to a mirror and inspected Carlo's handiwork. A bruise had appeared on his cheek.

"Dammit," he asked his reflection. "Why do I feel so ill at ease?"

It was then that he realised he was on the thirteenth floor.

*　　*　　*

Felix's debut was not being well received at El Torro. The Singalong boys had first been amazed to see the teenage cleaner accompany Lito through the front door to the bar. When they realised Felix was there for business and not pleasure the spite poured forth.

"What does Lito think he's doing?" Carlo hissed.

"Making things harder for everyone," Santiago replied.

"Felix is not even gay," Max exclaimed.

"That's right," Jessie agreed. "He has a girl friend."

"I'll have a quiet word with Lito," Santiago said, breaking away from the group.

159

"Shit," Carlo fumed. "It's bad enough competing with the hotel room boys—"

"And school kids," Max said.

"Don't forget the stand-by boys," Jessie contributed.

"Right. Them too. And now we have the cleaner from the pension. Maybe I should go over and ask him where's his mop."

"Why don't you do that?" Max egged on Carlo. "See how he takes it."

"I'll wait till he's trying to hook a customer," Carlo replied. "That'll be more fun."

"Some wait," the Superstar said. "He's getting one now."

They watched as a scaled-down King Farouk chatted with Felix.

"Right," said Carlo. "Let's spice things up."

They wandered over to the bar.

"Another three," the Arab said, enjoying his growing audience. "Tonight must be my lucky night."

"It is now that I'm here," Carlo said with his usual modesty.

"You're a bit late," Lito said protectively. "Our friend and Felix are about to go."

"Oh, there's plenty of time yet," King Farouk said expansively. Then, with a meaningful look in Carlo's direction he added, "There's always room for one more."

Felix looked uncertainly at Lito. "Felix doesn't mind that," Lito said blandly, ignoring the boy's fallen face.

Max gave Carlo a wink and a nod of unnecessary encouragement.

"Where's your mop, Felix?" Carlo asked triumphantly.

"M-Mop?" Felix stammered.

Santiago shook his head. "No, Carlo," he whispered.

"Yeah, mop," Carlo repeated. And in a confidential aside to the king, "He's a cleaner at our pension."

"Why don't you go and play with your weights, darling," Lito said, taking over from his unblooded pupil.

"Why don't you go and pop a pill," Carlo retorted.

"Christ, a *pusa* fight," Santiago muttered.

"Now, now boys," the king jovially interceded. "Let's not be unpleasant."

"Do as the man says," Dumbell told Lito. "Take the bucket boy back to the toilets where you found him."

Lito slowly eased off his bar stool. "Dumbell," he purred, bravely prodding the muscled chest opposite, "why don't you go and pick on your dirty nose instead."

"Keep your claws off me," Carlo growled, pushing Lito away.

"Cool down both of you," Santiago urged, trying to separate them.

"Mind your own business," Lito snapped, giving Carlo a retaliatory shove before the horrified eyes of Felix.

"Excuse me," the king said, heading in the direction of a washroom.

"You little pimp," Carlo taunted.

"Muscle brains," Lito shot back to the accompaniment of laughs from a nearby table.

"Felix has connections," Santiago hissed to Carlo.

"He won't have any by the time I'm finished with his pimp," Carlo retorted, casting a dark look at the frightened teenager.

"He knows the pension owner," Santiago persisted.

"So what?" he replied, warily watching Lito.

"So there could be trouble," Santiago said. "Come on. Let's quit this place and try the disco up the road," he said looking around for the Superstar and Aussie Max.

"Hoy," Carlo said, suddenly noticing their absence. "Where are the others?"

"They were here a minute ago," Lito said.

"They've left," Felix said flatly.

"Left?" Lito repeated suspiciously.

"Yeah, that's what I said."

"What d'you mean?" Dumbell asked.

"They left with the fat man," Felix replied, now thoroughly disillusioned with the whole business.

* * *

Climbing wearily into bed once again, Fortunato cursed his relatives for the ordeal he had endured over the past two days. From the moment Crispina had answered a knock on the front door and in had burst his country cousin George, gossipy wife Carmen and five brats, he knew he wouldn't have any peace till he had seen the last of them. And he was so right! Within the first hour of their arrival, the brats had succeeded in blocking the new toilet with newspapers and banana skins. He had to get a suction stick from a neighbour because the kids had hidden his. They wouldn't even tell their weak-kneed father where it was. Then Crispina had dropped and smashed a jug of chilled raspberry drink in fright. She had been taking it out of the refrigerator when she saw a cockroach inside. The refrigerator was brand new and the rubber seals intact. So the only way it could have got there was for the brats to have put it there. After cleaning up the mess he had to go to the store. Naturally, his cousin had tagged along. And he should have guessed why! He had put up with George's weak jokes and back-slapping for two whole days before his cousin had finally come out with it: he had wanted a loan for his backyard factory in Tarlac. Huh, some business! Who wanted to buy candle sticks these days? Only those subversives dressed up as priests! He had laughed at George. What did his cousin think he was, a Rockefeller? And when he had finally got his relatives out of the house and taken them to the bus depot what had that freeloader said before boarding? "Fortunato," George whispered out of the hearing of the women. "You're a hard man. The only thing soft about you is between your legs." How dare he say that to him! No respect at all! After that he didn't bother to stay and wave them off. He couldn't care less if he never saw them again. Fortunato snorted in annoyance. Two wasted days! He hadn't even had time to see his friends at the police station about that Igorot. The fat vendor was probably wrong again. Still, he couldn't be sure. Better to leave that decision to them. Yes, he would call in at the station in the morning on his way to Rizal Park. It would only take a few minutes.

Turning off the bed-side light he thought of George's insult. "I'll show him," he muttered and, feeling a twitch between his knobbly legs, commanded, "On your back Crispina."

· CHAPTER NINE ·

The last poem of Jose Rizal, written in a military cell a few hours
before his execution on the morning of 30 December 1896:

> I die just when I see dawn break
> Through the gloom of night, to herald the day
> And if colour is lacking my blood thou shall take,
> Pour'd out at need for thy sake,
> To dye with its crimson the waking ray.

Ian could not sleep. He turned sides for the umpteenth time in
the big unfamiliar bed, unable to forget winter in Spain. Or rather,
all the winters without Zac. He tried to think of something else but
always drifted back to his dread of loneliness as though magnetised
to a nemesis. He knew he could survive the summers by submerging
himself in surf and business. Afterwards, in the comfort of his
apartment and drink in hand, he could take in the view he never
tired of. He could sit for hours and gaze at the rock, the sweep of
the bay and, at the south end, the pale orange headland fringed at
the base with whitewashed villas. Even a hated twenty-storey
hotel, which had stolen part of his view when it was erected nearby
a few years earlier, had a transient fascination in its mosaic of
balconies, about four hundred in all. In the summer every room
was occupied. He could tell this at a glance by the presence of
damp towels and costumes draped on all the balcony railings.
Flags flew from there too. Some of the guests, particularly the
Swiss, seemed to delight in proclaiming their origin as though their
nationality was a personal triumph instead of the lottery of life he
knew it represented. In any case, he was always amused at Nature's
ignorance of Swiss neutrality. Often a flurry of air would spring up
from nowhere and, catching guests unaware, send their belongings
tumbling to the street below. Once he saw a red towel making an
erratic descent towards the moving figure of a Spaniard he knew
to be a nearby caretaker. Without breaking stride the man scooped
the towel into his hand before it touched the footpath. That was
the fate of most things blown from the balconies and it never
ceased to entertain him. He had been tempted on occasions to

take a stroll in the street and add to his wardrobe but had thought of what his neighbours might say.

Then, the season would abruptly end; the streets empty of crowds; the beaches, which had seemed like antbeds by turquoise honey, desolate expanses of nothingness; the hotel a shell, its balconies deserted and swimming pool a white hole with a bottom of dirty rain water. At night the change was more depressing. The view became a black void in the absence of the illuminated pool and neighbourhood neon. A yelping guard dog replaced the strains of the hotel band and its frequent renditions of "Feelings". The barking had almost been too much at times and after sleepless nights he had wandered along windy promenades, close to tears of self-pity. The first sightings of aged pensioners arriving in bus loads from Britain and northern Europe for a cheap winter holiday had not helped either. Wrapped in thick clothing and scarves, they stood on the sandy promenades gazing blankly past wind-whipped palms at a bleak and uninviting sea. It had always reinforced his fear of loneliness and death.

Ian shifted position in the bed once more. In the darkness he brought his watch arm close to his myopic eyes. Two glowing spots indicated it was five o'clock.

*   *   *

Zac and Jojo were up by five. On the lower floor, Zac had the shower cubicles to himself. In a hall on the way back to his room he met Reggie whose averted eyes revealed self-embarrassment at having being seen going to a cubicle even though wrapped in a towel. All the males in the pension wore towels to and from the showers but Reggie was shy and always washed early in the lower floor cubicles which had better pressure.

"Up for the Rizal ceremony?" Zac asked mischievously, knowing the man's real motive.

"Uh," he grunted, hurrying by.

"Your towel's slipping," Zac called out, watching a rear view of Reggie hastily clutching at a covered buttock.

The man cast Zac a dark look and disappeared around a corner.

Back in his room, Zac dressed. Then he threw his few possessions in a small, soft bag. He looked around for what he knew would be the last time and went upstairs, slipping a letter under Perla's office door on the way. Jojo was lounging on the bed, apparently waiting. Seeing Zac's bag he looked up quizzically.

"I'm going home afterwards," Zac said, parking his bundle on the floor. "And on the first bus I can squeeze on to."

164

"For how long this time?"

"As long as I have a good reason for staying there."

The Igorot sat up straight. "This is a bit sudden, isn't it? What caused the decision, the Christmas visit?"

"Oh, that and other things," Zac replied. And thinking he owed Jojo a better explanation said, "I'm needed back there."

The Igorot nodded slowly as if in thought. In the distance the first of the day's firecrackers spluttered. Then he said, "So we won't be seeing each other for a long time."

"It looks that way," Zac answered, feeling no particular emotion and wondering why.

The other was silent. He rose gathering his own shoulder bag. They moved towards the door. In a hallway, Zac said, "Have you got th—"

"Yes," he replied and tapped the bag. "It's here, ready for the balloons."

The pair had just passed under the fern baskets when they heard the distant wail of sirens in the pre-dawn quiet.

Zac counted at least two and noticed they were getting closer. His partner strode ahead in the gloom towards the laneway and canal.

"What's the hurry?" Zac asked.

"We don't want to be late."

"No chance of that. The ceremony doesn't start for over an hour."

"Traffic might be heavy."

Zac caught up in the laneway. The sirens were louder. "Something's going on in the neighbourhood. Maybe a fire somewhere," he suggested.

Their rapid footsteps rang hollowly as they crossed the footbridge.

"Or, some big shot going home in a hurry," the Igorot said tersely.

"No, I don't think so," Zac differed. "Sirens aren't necessary this time of the morning."

They were nearly across when the squeal of brakes from somewhere behind caused them to turn in time to catch a glimpse beyond the laneway of a slewing police car, its roof light flashing. Then a second and a third car flashed past the gap, their brakes protesting and sirens dying. Zac and Jojo heard the slam of car doors, then shouts. Lights came on in the pension now silhouetted against a steely eastern sky.

"Let's get out of here," the Igorot whispered hoarsely, tugging his companion towards another laneway beyond.

"*Christ*," Zac said gravely. "What's that all about?"

"Let's just get away. Someone else can worry about them."

A block away from the footbridge Zac asked again, "What do you think is happening?"

"How would I know? Maybe it's another drug raid."

Zac sidestepped a dead rat on the road. "But the boys don't use the pension anymore. Not after their last scare."

"Then it's another wasted raid. That's nothing new."

"Perla won't like it," Zac said as they turned a corner. "This is the third raid since I've been back. Was it like this before?"

"I don't remember."

Zac sensed his partner's reluctance to talk but nevertheless asked, "How could you forget *that*?"

The Igorot ignored the remark.

Zac was about to speak when he became aware of a vehicle behind. It still had headlights on. He saw their faint leggy shadows on a wall race towards them as the car swooshed by, its suspension springs squeaking in protest at the rutted surface.

The car turned left at a nearby intersection. They had reached the point where they last saw it when Zac said breathlessly, "Slow down for God's sake."

The Igorot eased the pace a little. "You're out of breath because you talk too much. Do you know that?"

Zac scoffed, "And you don't seem to want to talk at all. Just why are we in such a hurry?"

"I told you. We don't want to be late. We want to be able to pick our position. Have you been to a Rizal Day ceremony before? No? Well, you'd be surprised at the crowd. I was in an army guard once. We were there an hour before and so was half the city."

They saw a bus approaching from another street and, when it drew level, jumped aboard. As it lumbered through back streets and entered an already busy Taft Avenue, a rim of brilliance edged into a colourless eastern sky. It was six-twenty.

*   *   *

Felipe tightened his grip on Efren's curly mop.

"I know nothing," the callboy whimpered from his bed for the third time at the room full of police, some of whom still had their guns drawn.

"That's not what your friends around here say."

"They're not my friends, not anymore," Efren said sullenly. "They're just lying to take the heat off themselves. Sweet Jesus, I'm

166

telling you the truth. Can't you see that?"

Felipe released his hold. He stared at the teary face of the near-naked youth lying tensed on the bed. Outside the room he could hear the muffled sobs of the woman who had identified herself as the manageress before dissolving into hysteria. He knew it would be hours before anyone could get any sense out of her. The officer swore silently. Why was the Igorot always a step ahead? The man had more luck than the sea had fish! If only that fool of a *barangay* captain had reported his suspicions sooner!

Jurado put his head in the room. "Uh, lieutenant, there's a boarder who thinks he can help."

"Then send him in," the officer said curtly.

Reggie appeared in the doorway. The lieutenant impatiently gestured him to the room's only chair. The boarder sat down, eyeing the officer warily.

"I hope you can help more than him," Felipe said tersely with a backward nod of his head at the figure of Efren trying inconspicuously to slip on a singlet over his naked chest.

"I think so," Reggie said, suddenly aware that for the first time in more than a decade he was a participant in something of consequence. He glanced at the expectant faces now flanking the officer and decided it was possibly even a matter of great importance. A matter that, if handled properly, might bring an overdue change of fortune.

"What can you tell me," Felipe said, concealing with some effort the considerable irritation he felt over the Igorot's continued elusiveness.

Reggie cleared his throat. "Well, I used to be a newsman till—"

"Damn it mister!" the officer exploded. "I don't want your life history. What do you know about the Igorot?"

"He left twenty minutes ago," Reggie said hastily, quite taken aback by the man's rudeness.

"Where was he going? Did he say?"

"No, but he works at the markets. Maybe—"

"Forget it. He doesn't work there anymore."

"Oh, I didn't —"

"Just what *do* you know mister?"

"He left with a man who boards here too."

The lieutenant's eyes narrowed. "What's the name of that person?"

"Zac Campora."

Well, well, Felipe thought, the friend. Turning to his offsiders he ordered, "Search Campora's room."

167

"Ground floor," Reggie volunteered promptly, now in tune with the situation. "Room seven."

"Does Campora have a job?" the lieutenant asked, the room now seeming almost empty with only a sniffling Efren and the two men.

"No, but he's looking for one. He told me that."

"What does he normally do?"

"He seems to travel a bit. He only returned from Europe a few months ago."

"To live in this place?" The officer looked around contemptuously.

Reggie shrugged. "Maybe he has spent all his money."

"Did he ever say which part of Europe?"

"Yes. He mentioned Spain and England."

"Nowhere else? Like Eastern Europe?"

Reggie swallowed hard, not liking the direction of the interrogation. "He never talked about anything like that. He said he had spent almost a year in Spain with an English friend."

"And do you know his friend's name?"

"He didn't say. But the friend is now in Manila. He's staying in some hotel. That's according to the boys here."

The officer looked at a silent Efren and raising an eyebrow said, "Well, which hotel?"

"I'm not sure sir. It's somewhere near Rizal Park."

Felipe was debating whether to jog the callboy's memory with another tug of the hair when Jurado re-entered.

"Campora's room has been cleaned out too. The only things in it are a fan and a picture of Rizal. The boarders say they're pension property, unlike that carving the Igorot left."

"Did the boarders say anything else?"

"They don't know anything."

Reggie cleared his throat again before venturing in a small voice. "Maybe they went to the ceremony."

Jurado and Felipe exchanged glances.

Reggie sensed a response and continued, "Campora mentioned the Rizal ceremony when I passed him in the hall on the way to the showers. Later when I saw them leaving the Igorot's room I heard something about balloons."

"Balloons?" the rookie echoed.

"Yes. They sell them in the par—"

"Of course!" Felipe exclaimed. "It makes sense. The President will be there!" And bundling Jurado into the hall, commanded, "Get the others. We're going to the park."

Reggie was quickly at the doorway. "I used to be a newsman," he called to the retreating policeman. "I covered the palace. I noticed things. I was good at my job."

But the hall was now empty. Reggie dipped into his hip pocket and pulled out the wallet. Unfolding it, he gazed at the familiar photo.

"Too good," he muttered.

Then he saw his nightgowned wife emerge from their room down the hall and crankily beckon him inside to find out what was going on in this madhouse pension.

*　　*　　*

Roberto finally found a parking spot for his big Ford in an alley near the park. He looked for a mind-your-car boy in vain.

"This will have to do," he told his children. "I'll look after my door. You lock the others. And make sure they're locked."

Chito, at fourteen the eldest of five, organised his brothers and sisters. "All locked," he reported solemnly to his father.

The six walked to the end of the street and turned a corner.

They had disappeared from sight for only a few seconds when two men stepped from a doorway to the alley.

"It's just the model we want," one said. "And the owner's a Chinese too. He can afford the inconvenience."

The other laughed harshly, replying, "Yes, but keep away from it for a minute in case they come back for something. I've seen it happen before."

They lingered by the door then, certain they would not be disturbed, swiftly approached the vehicle. One man deftly slid a wire loop between the driver's side window and the door panel. He gave the wire a little tug as though he were fishing and was rewarded with a "click." In a trice he was behind the wheel and had opened the opposite door. Next he fiddled under the dashboard with some wiring and the engine sprang to life.

"Let's get out of here," the driver said to his companion, engaging the transmission.

Within twenty minutes the car was on the northern side of the Pasig and inside a large workshop with three other stolen vehicles. Work on Roberto's car started almost immediately.

*　　*　　*

A flower clock in Rizal Park indicated six-forty-one when a curiously silent Zac and Jojo appeared at the eastern entrance, a low sun already warm on their backs. They strode purposefully

169

and shared a wide concrete path with a stream of humanity moving in the same direction. On each side were lawns sprinkled with slumbering bodies. Sheets of newspaper had been steepled over heads. A few stirred and one peeped at the flow which had disturbed the usual morning quiet of the park.

The pair pressed on, outpacing slower family groups and passing a policeman untwisting his belt. They crossed a road cutting through the park and entered the central section. Here, national flags fluttered from poles. Columns of helium-filled balloons quivered above vendors. Zac started in their direction but his companion said, "Not yet."

In the distance they saw the back of the Rizal monument. Khaki, black, red and white figures milled around the base and within a roped-off area. They held metallic objects which glinted in the morning sun.

"Bandsmen," Jojo said as they neared on their right the familiar façade of the Chinese Gardens, a triple archway behind which lay curved pavilions and shrubbery.

The Igorot gripped Zac's arm in guidance. "There's a breeze from the south. Let's take that side of the monument."

They veered towards a crowd gathered behind ropes. Another of equal size was opposite, creating an area of privilege in between. This space was reserved for officials. Foreign representatives were already seated on wooden chairs. Also inside its perimeters, but standing, was a contingent of ever-vigilant men, all tall and wearing white shirts over pants. They had formed a rough line of about sixty paces from the monument to the flagpole by Roxas Boulevard, along which thousands of armed soldiers had assembled.

The two pushed into the crowd to a point immediately behind a large party of schoolgirls over whom they had a good view of the monument and pathway.

All the girls held flags and chattered excitedly. One immediately in front of Zac giggled and said, "See? Now some of them are looking at us."

"That's their job, silly. They're supposed to do that," one next to her said.

"But aren't they tall," the other prattled on. "And so big. They look like giants."

"They have to be big to be in the Presidential Guard," said the girl with all the answers. "If anyone fires a gun they will be his shields."

"Ooh! Do you think that will happen today?"

"Don't be silly. It's just in case."

"Oh," the chastised girl said, as if somewhat disappointed. Then in an abrupt change of subject she confided, "Do you know Gregorio is dating Celeste now . . ."

Zac ignored their chatter and looked to his left and right and behind. He was surrounded with faces, all expectantly awaiting the start of the ceremony. He sharply returned his gaze to a spot scanned seconds before. He was almost sure it had been a face he knew. He was about to tell his companion and suggest they move elsewhere when Jojo whispered in his ear, "Wait here. I'll be back with the balloons," and was gone. Zac looked again for the face in the crowd but it too had vanished. Zac frowned. He felt suddenly uneasy. He looked towards the flagpole and fidgeted absently with his watch.

Then Zac became aware of a tall building beyond the flagpole and realised with mild surprise he had been inside it only a short time ago. It seemed like years since he'd left Ian's suite for the last time. Poor, pathetic Ian! Probably he was looking down on the scene at this moment. Or more likely in bed asleep. He checked the time. Six-fifty-four. Where was Jojo? It would have been better to get the balloons earlier. It would be even better not to be here, he thought. In fact, now that he was finally here in the park surrounded by all these people the whole idea seemed stupid. Even insane! What was he doing here? Waiting for what? Abruptly, he stopped fidgeting with the watch, having come to a realisation. He looked again at the dial. It was six-fifty-five. The ceremony would begin in five minutes. Time enough to pull out. Time enough to quit. Yes, he was sure! He scanned the crowd behind. There was no sign of Jojo. And he was glad. He threaded his way to the back of the crowd. He broke through to green space. He began striding for a park exit. Then he felt a hand grip the back of his shirt. He half turned to see Jojo holding with the mutilated hand a bunch of red balloons.

"Where are you going?" the Igorot demanded roughly.

*   *   *

Not wanting to miss the unfolding spectacle in the park below, Ian had phoned room service and ordered breakfast. He was seated by the window again and wishing he had brought his binoculars along on the trip when the bed-side phone rang.

"Yes?" enquired the Scot, mildly annoyed at being interrupted.

"Room service sir. Do you require hot or cold milk with your porridge?"

"Oh, didn't I say? Hot, thank you."

171

"Very good sir. Breakfast will be up shortly."

Ian heard a click and replaced the receiver on its stand. He adjusted his spectacles and then checked his watch. It was nearly seven. He unlatched the chain on the door in preparation for room service. He moved back to the window. The crowd seemed to have swelled even in the brief time he had been away. He estimated there were thousands of people. Some of them seemed to be schoolchildren and held little flags. Clusters of balloons here and there gave the gathering a festive atmosphere. How *jolly* it all was! He switched his attention to a wide road which was lined with armed soldiers. Now he could see approaching between their ranks a fast-moving phalanx of shiny limousines.

Nearing the flagpole the vehicles slowed and finally stopped. Burly figures tumbled out and surrounded a black Cadillac. Eventually a smallish man in a white shirt and dark pants emerged. He was quickly followed by a taller woman with a piled black hairdo and a full-length orange dress with short butterfly sleeves. As the pair stepped on to the kerb Ian heard the dull eruption of artillery fire from somewhere in the park.

*   *   *

Zac flushed with guilt then, resenting the angry grip of his companion, said firmly, "First let go of my shirt."

The Igorot's face was set in ugly lines. "Not till you tell me what's going on."

Zac tried to pull free. "Let me go," he said a little louder. "I'm leaving. I've had enough. This whole thing is ridiculous."

The Igorot's grip tightened. "We're in this together," he growled. "Or that was the idea."

"Count me out," Zac said sullenly.

"Worm," the Igorot hissed as artillery fire signalled the beginning of the ceremony.

"Say what you like. I'm quitting. Now *let go*."

Heads turned in their direction.

The Igorot ignored them and stared coldly at Zac. "I should never have bothered with you," he sneered contemptuously.

"I said let go!" Zac shouted angrily, pushing his adversary backward so that not only did the offending hand lose its grip on the shirt but the helium balloons jerked free of the other. The cluster rose rapidly skyward.

"Oh, look," a small child nearby cried, pointing for all to see.

More heads turned towards the pair, now glaring at each other in hostile silence. The crump of artillery continued but another

172

sound was beginning to intrude, the strengthening wail of approaching sirens.

The Igorot became aware first. He broke off the staring contest, his eyes darting elsewhere.

At that moment a small monkey-like man in a white shirt appeared by the two and commanded, "Hoy! The President's in the park. Behave yourselves."

The Igorot turned to see the *barangay* captain. Their eyes locked. Fortunato gaped.

"Y-You," the *barangay* captain spluttered. "The p-police want—"

The Igorot did not dally further. Shoving Fortunato roughly aside, he began sprinting in the direction he had entered the park, his shoulder bag flapping wildly before dropping to the grass. He did not stop.

Zac watched amazed till he heard Fortunato's quivering voice. "You're under arrest."

Stunned, he asked weakly, "What for?"

"Terrorism," snapped Fortunato, beginning to see the prospect of rehabilitation in the eyes of his police friends who had mercilessly abused him that morning at the station for his slowness in reporting the suspicious activities of citizens.

"Me, a terrorist?" Zac said incredulously. He was almost inclined to laugh but for the sick feeling in the pit of his stomach.

"Yes! A terrorist just like your companion. We'll have him soon too. Now come with me—"

"Like hell," Zac said, nimbly averting Fortunato's grasping hands. "I've done nothing wrong."

"Help me," the little official ordered a group of spectators who had now turned their backs on the distant ceremony in favour of something less mundane. "I'm a *barangay* captain."

"I'll get the police," a man volunteered and quickly slipped away. The others did not move, save a woman who protectively put a restraining hand on the shoulder of the child first to see the ascension of the red balloons.

"You'll all answer for this," Fortunato said to the onlookers, turning away from Zac and wagging a finger at them. "You're helping the enemy."

Zac knew it was his last chance. With a spurt he was away, fleeing in the trail of his vanished companion. He heard a child's voice pipe, "That bad man's running away," but did not look back. Nor did he when he heard the *barangay* captain yell, "Stop!" Instead, Zac ran harder. He flew past a man asleep on the grass. He swerved to miss a park cleaner carrying rubbish to a bin. Then he saw the Chinese Gardens and, forsaking the open park, veered under the archway and into the protection of Oriental-style structures and scattered shrubbery. He bypassed an artificial pond spanned by a rainbow bridge and ran through an open-sided pavilion with curved green roofing. No one was about. He slowed his pace, needing desperately to catch his breath. He stumbled to a stop in a pavilion, leaning against a pillar for support.

Gasping, he looked around. Beyond was an open square of grass with a centre clump of shrubbery and stacks of upside-down earthen pottery. Beyond that was a spiked metal fence which separated the park from a deserted, leafy street. Zac glanced back to see if anyone had followed into the gardens. He saw nothing. He knew the fence could be scaled with ease. He stumbled through the pavilion and was about halfway across the grass when he heard shouts from the vicinity of the pond. Zac scrambled into the shrubbery and crouched, mindless of the scratches and stings on his face and arms. He had no sooner done so when he glimpsed through the foliage and pottery several khaki figures coming into sight. He could make out they had their guns drawn.

*   *   *

The Igorot slowed to a quick stride, having just raced out of a park exit. Now that he felt out of immediate danger, his priority was to appear less conspicuous. He put all lingering thoughts of his companion's fate out of his mind. He coldly concentrated on finding the fastest way out of the metropolis. He was on the parkside of T. M. Kalaw, a broad thoroughfare. Opposite were commercial buildings. He looked for a bus or jeepney in the light traffic. A taxi approached and he promptly signalled.

The driver's radio was blaring music as the Igorot got in the back and said loudly, "Chinatown." The driver swung the vehicle into a U-turn and accelerated. The Igorot checked the rear view. Certain he had no pursuers, he began formulating a plan. At a red light he became aware of the driver watching him via the rear vision mirror. Horns blared behind as the light changed. The taxi jerked forward, now part of a thicker stream of traffic. An old truck ahead belched fumes and the Igorot wound up his window through which he could see part of the Walled City. Traffic slowed again, then stopped. At length, the driver irritably turned off the radio and joined a chorus of horn-honkers before dabbing his forehead with a dirty cloth kept on the dashboard. Outside a grinning boy carrying a tray of cigarettes was finding customers at almost every window. The taxi driver brought some and the chirpy explanation, "An accident ahead. Part of the road is blocked." The Igorot lent forward and read the meter. He handed the driver the correct amount and got out, threading his way through idling vehicles to the kerb. He strode towards the Central Post Office which was in the far distance, occasionally looking over his shoulder. A jeepney came by and he hopped aboard, sharing the front seat with the driver and a passenger. The jeepney was nearing the post office when he saw that traffic farther ahead on the Jones Bridge had slowed to a crawl. With cool surprise he saw the reason. Soldiers had set up a checkpoint midway along the structure. Wearing helmets and with rifles strapped to their shoulders, they were quickly scanning the barely moving vehicles and, apparently satisfied, waving them through to Chinatown on the north bank. The Igorot got off near the plaza fronting the post office and wandered almost to the base of the lone statue bearing the inscription, "Andres Bonifacio." Beyond he could see that the approaches to the MacArthur Bridge on the far side of the building were similarly banked up. He knew it would be the same on all the bridges and strategic points in the metropolis. A net was drawing around him.

The Igorot hesitated, unsure of his next move. Quite abruptly, he wheeled and strode towards the approaches to the Jones Bridge. There, he feigned an interest in the riverbank below while leaning against a railing. Not many people were about. A boy fished absently with a hand line while absorbed in a comic. A bent man of indeterminate age meandered slowly by, carrying a pole and hessian bag. Much farther along the waterfront someone was rummaging through a collection of large, lidless drums, their sides streaked with rust. On the river itself a customs launch was making its way towards the unseen bay. He glanced at the bridge checkpoint but averted his face at the sight of several soldiers turned in his direction. He looked again at the bent figure. The man had stopped by a small punt moored off a concrete apron and was in the act of throwing his burden into the craft.

Realising the figure was a canal scavenger, probably on his way to ply some backwater, the Igorot descended nearby steps and walked swiftly to the punt. The man was about to cast off.

"Can you get me to the other side?" he called from a height to an uplifted face, not bothering to waste time with pleasantries.

The man, unshaven and hollow cheeked, eyed him without expression. At length he said, "Why should I?"

"I'll pay you for your trouble," the Igorot replied, tossing him a few pesos.

The scavenger caught the money and said, "Get in."

Halfway across, the man stopped rowing.

"Why do you stop?" the Igorot asked coldly.

"Just looking at the bridge," was the knowing reply.

"Haven't you seen it before?"

"*Much* too often."

They drifted towards the structure on an incoming tide. The Igorot shifted uneasily. He could see the soldiers checking traffic. Soon one would turn to the river and see him.

"Row on, junk man," he hissed menacingly.

"I'm tired," the scavenger said. "I think I'll rest a little longer."

"If you start rowing again I'll give you more."

"How much?" the man asked with an evil grin.

"More than you would earn floating the river today."

"That's nothing. I think I'm worth a thousand pesos."

The Igorot clenched his fists. "I don't have that much money."

"Then this is your unlucky day, isn't it?" the emaciated face sneered.

They drifted nearer the bridge. So near that no one above could see them till they passed under and to the other side.

"Here," said the Igorot digging into a pocket and throwing the contents between their feet. "It's all I have. Take the lot."

The scavenger scoffed, "It's not enough," but bent forward to scoop up the offering. Too late, he stiffened in realisation. The Igorot's hand chopped viciously down, breaking the man's neck with a loud crack.

Quickly the Igorot retrieved the money and arranged the hessian bag over the lifeless form. He took command of the punt which was now under the bridge and by a pylon. He scanned the river banks but everything seemed as before. He began rowing casually to the Chinatown side, avoiding a line of moored motor cruisers on which he could see some signs of life. Alongside a dilapidated barge he pulled the oars in and with a length of rope already tied to a metal ring in the bow fastened the craft to a rusty bollard. The Igorot clambered ashore unchallenged. Without looking back he said softly, "Goodbye greedy one. No hard work now." Then he set off in the direction of the Chinatown Arch and somewhere beyond.

*　　*　　*

Zac could feel his heart pounding furiously. Police seemed to be in all directions but incredibly he had remained undiscovered in the shrubbery. He was almost at the point of surrendering when he was shocked to hear a nearby voice say, "It's been confirmed. They're N.P.A. One of the terrorists dropped a bag with a guerrilla banner in it." Another voice replied, "Well, thank God it doesn't look like they're here. I don't get paid enough to get shot." He heard the two laugh and the conversation trail off with something about "roadblocks." After that the gardens seem to empty of police. Zac remained crouched a few minutes more till he became aware of a terrible cramp in his right foot. He could bear it no longer and stood, pressing the ball of his foot hard into the ground. Gradually the cramp subsided. He thought he heard approaching voices and ducked again but after a few minutes no one had appeared. He decided it was time to make a move. He cautiously emerged from the bushes, checking in all directions. Then he crossed swiftly to the metal fence. The design made it easy to climb. He was straddling the top and bracing himself for a short drop to the deserted street when his shirt snagged on a spike. He unsuccessfully tried to free it several times, feeling increasing panic. Finally, he wrenched it away, tearing the fabric. Zac dropped heavily to the pavement and, glancing around to make sure his unorthodox exit from the park had not been seen, quickly set off along the tree-lined street. He was cautiously nearing a corner made blind by high stonework when there came into view the back of a policeman standing hands on hips. Zac momentarily froze before turning and running in the direction he had come from. In the far distance through tree boughs he could see Ian's hotel. He heard a shout from behind. Suddenly, the hotel became a symbol of refuge, a sanctuary in an insane world. He pumped his legs as fast as he could but they seemed incapable of serious effort. It was as though he were in a slow motion nightmare. Then his heart seemed to explode. As he pitched forward into an enveloping black blanket his last thought was of his murdered mother.

*   *   *

Ian turned away from the window, repulsed at what he had just witnessed. He had not had time to eat all his breakfast, so many were the distractions. Now he did not even have the appetite to finish it.

Breakfast had arrived just after the artillery had begun. He had set up the trolley before the window and was preparing to eat when he noticed a big bunch of red balloons drifting towards his hotel window. He thought they would even bump the glass but at the last moment the balloons were sucked higher in a violent current and disappeared. Then he became aware of what appeared

177

to be police fanning out in the back section of the park. The ceremony had continued. A man whom he realised could only be the President had laid a wreath at the base of the monument before standing back with head bowed. The President had in time returned to the side of the woman in orange, obviously the First Lady. Next, the couple and an entourage had walked to the flagpole where the President raised a flag. After inspecting an honour guard on the road, the two had got back into the limousine which sped off, followed by some of the other vehicles. Not so many police were in the rear section of the park by that time though he could see knots of them in some surrounding streets. He had half consumed a lukewarm bowl of porridge when he thought he heard a dull pop. He looked down just in time to witness someone falling to the ground. He was about to search elsewhere for a possible explanation of the sound when he noticed a spreading dark stain on the back of the still figure. In the following minutes the body was surrounded by police and he realised it had been a fatal shooting.

Ian pushed the trolley away from the window. He considered eating the now cold and brittle toast with some butter and marmalade but decided against it. Instead, he went to the closet, took out his suitcase and clothes and began packing. He had a sudden urge to get out of the city as quickly as possible even if it meant sitting in an airport lounge for a few hours. He thought Zac might have phoned by now to at least say goodbye a last time. Secretly, in his inner heart, he had hoped for something much better. But here he was, preparing to return home alone. In an hour he would be heading for the airport and by noon on his way to Spain.

Ian tried not to think of Zac too much. The depression he had felt in the early hours before sunrise was beginning to overwhelm him again. He showered and dressed, thankful to do anything to keep himself busy and his mind off unwanted thoughts. Later, downstairs in the foyer, however, he made a final check for messages while his statement was being prepared at the other end of a marble counter. An attendant peered at an empty box hole and shook his head with a polite, "Sorry sir, nothing." Ian drifted dejectedly back to accounts. During the taxi ride to the airport he entertained the idea of diverting to Singalong pension till he dismissed it as being pointless. At the airport he wandered through the structure, up and down every escalator and from end to end. Finally the counter responsible for the flight to Madrid opened for business and Ian joined a short queue. About twenty minutes later he was sitting in a tastefully furnished lounge awaiting a monochrome monitor to signal that passengers could board. He donned his spectacles and scanned the travellers, apprehensive of seeing children among their numbers. Surprisingly, there were none. In an opposite row of seats sat a middle-aged man who vaguely reminded him of an Abraham Lincoln, a garland of delicate white flowers around his neck. The man became aware of Ian's attention, accepting the intrusion into his private world with a sad smile. Ian looked elsewhere in embarrassment, the sweep of his gaze falling on an arresting and friendly face. The stranger had apparently been watching Ian for, immediately their eyes met, the man was ready with a wink. Ian turned his attention elsewhere again, though this time not in embarrassment but as a ploy to give him time to consider a response. The readiness of a flight to the United States via Tokyo was announced on the screen. The Lincolnesque figure gathered his belongings and moved towards an embarkation gate. Ian casually surveyed the winker again, now flicking through a glossy magazine. Ian liked what he saw. Very much. So he got up with his possessions and walked over, spectacles and all.

"How far are you going?" Ian asked.

"Madrid," the stranger replied with the friendliest of smiles.

"Marvellous," he said, taking a handy seat. Already to the Scot Spain seemed much less lonely.

· EPILOGUE ·

Even an hour before that year had been swept away by time, the metropolis was a pyrotechnic Armageddon. Flashes of silver rent the heavens. Red flares hung suspended as though unable to penetrate the noise and acrid smoke. Roaring bonfires cast weird shadows and bathed the surrounding dilapidation in shades of red and orange. Streets became seeming extensions of a nightmarish Belfast or Beirut when passengers in passing jeepneys found themselves the horrified targets of lobbed crackers. So did drivers of sedans and taxis and citizens foolish enough to venture out as midnight approached.

Indoor festivities were definitely more orderly. Especially at the police station near Rizal Park where Captain Felipe celebrated with colleagues his recent promotion for the destruction of an international communist cell. At Singalong pension Perla enjoyed a few drinks with a gentleman friend in her room. Upstairs, Yolanda read in bed and nibbled a chocolate while Reggie talked in a hallway with a sleepy Gilbert. At the Milky Way, Tommy and his friends prepared in a dressing room for the show to come. All the other boys, excepting Martin, were either on the dance floor or at El Torro, hell-bent in the pursuit of fortune and fun. Some of the older boys seemed to celebrate with almost forced gaiety. Perhaps they had heard of a superstition holding that whatever one did on New Year's Eve would be repeated throughout life and knew it to be cruelly untrue.

At the luxury hotel where Ian had stayed, a capacity crowd filled the Oriental Fantasy Room. Exactly at midnight streamers flew and whistles blew. A band struck up "Auld Lang Syne" and the well-to-do of Manila and the outside world embraced each other with cries of "Good Fortune" and "Happy New Year."

There was much festivity, too, at gracious Malacañang Palace by the Pasig. In fact, confetti on a dance floor was so thick that when a diamond clip fell from the silk gown of a guest it was quite difficult to find.

Decidedly sombre at that moment was the atmosphere in the

Tondo shack Jessie had visited. Sickness was present once again, but this time fears were held for the life of a younger brother. A priest had been called and Jessie's family urged to pray, but somehow they lacked the spirit. Elsewhere in Tondo smoke eddied from a charred pile of rubble which thirty minutes before had been home for a family of eleven. A spark from a nearby bonfire started the blaze. Neighbours had worked feverishly to prevent the destruction of their shacks. If they had had access to a handy tap the fire could have been put out with a few buckets of water.

Far to the north in Baguio, Judge Garcia had gone to bed, deciding earlier he had seen the birth of enough new years and would not miss anything by passing this one up. He was quite right, as usual, Baguio's fireworks being miniscule by Manila standards. However, they were not so insignificant that they went unnoticed by a band of guerrillas encamped on a mountain slope. One of the band had, that last day of the year, been appointed by the region's Revolutionary Committee as commander of the squad, in view of his previous military experience and proven daring in the cause of the people's revolution. At the same time it had been ruled that henceforth he be known to fellow revolutionaries as Kummander Lobo, a code name honouring his fearless Rizal Park exploit only two days before, in which a valiant partner gave his life in opposing the forces of reaction. Kummander Lobo had evaded military roadblocks and eliminated a dupe of the reactionaries to reach Baguio where he quickly contacted forces that had been made known to him previously by Revolutionary Hero Laya for use in emergencies. Within hours of arriving in Baguio he had been taken to a safe house on the outskirts of the city and, after an overnight rest, to an outlying village where he attended the committee meeting that had resulted in his triumphs.

Kummander Lobo was now encamped in special territory. The guerrilla hierarchy regarded northern Luzon as a training ground for its forces because of the rugged terrain. Thousands of guerrillas roamed the Cordilleras and tens of thousands more lent support to their cause. Outside the Cordilleras too, their numbers were growing. Already the southern island of Mindanao, once called the Land of Promise, had become the Land of Turmoil as a result of guerrilla activity. In many provinces of the nation, officials had called for more troops to keep roads open, patrol remote villages and most importantly, separate the dissidents from the farmers and the rice harvests. The guerrillas had amassed a huge stockpile of weapons with which to support its forces. In the parry and thrust of the deadly duel many lives had been lost on both sides. The

Church was snared in a crossfire, with scores of its priests and nuns from the more radical lower ranks on the run from the regime. The guerrillas had an efficient intelligence network which kept track of efforts to trap and capture the underground leadership. Many times, though not always, warnings had come just in time. The task of the revolutionaries had been made increasingly difficult by the regime harnessing the forces of poverty. Big rewards had been posted for information leading to the capture, dead or alive, of key rebel figures. The rewards were more than a peasant could hope to earn in a lifetime of sweated labour. Yet, insurgency continued to grow. The tide of history was lapping at the regime's ramparts.

And now the movement's newest warrior stood alone on a rock shelf in the crisp night air. He gazed at a horizon of city phosphorescence, above which silently ascended an occasional red flare. He heard one of his men call from the camp, "A happy New Year, Kummander Lobo," and then the others in ragged chorus. He smiled faintly but did not echo the words. This was not the year. Instead he raised a mutilated fist towards the myriad stars and shouted, "To the revolution."

other recent fiction from GMP:

Agustin Gomez-Arcos
THE CARNIVOROUS LAMB
translated by William Rodarmor

Into a shuttered house in Franco's Spain, where the ghosts of past rebellion and present defeat still taint the air, Ignacio is born, the carnivorous lamb of the title. His father stays locked in his study, amid memories of political failure. His mother, vague but implacable ruler of her shadowy domain, refuses to acknowledge her son's existence. Only his brother Antonio is real – father-surrogate, teacher, protector and eventual lover. Their relationship is the centre of this story of one family's suffocation under an intolerable regime, which is also an incisive, savagely funny, but not entirely despairing look at post-Civil War Spain.

Born in 1939, Agustin Gomez-Arcos has been living in France since 1968. Before his exile from Spain, he received the Lope de Vega Prize for two of his plays and was widely acclaimed for his translations from French. Despite this, his works were banned and he left the country. *The Carnivorous Lamb*, written in French, appeared in 1975 and received the Prix Hermès for the best first novel of that year.

"A carnal poem, frank, provocative, triumphant . . . and a dirge for Spain" – *Le Monde*.

"Extraordinary, beautifully constructed. Agustin Gomez-Arcos extends and deepens his sexual themes until we realise that the entire bizarre tale is a metaphor for the future of Spain" – *San Francisco Chronicle*.

ISBN 0 85449 018 3 (paperback)   £4.95
     0 85449 019 1 (cloth)   £12.50

Tom Wakefield
THE DISCUS THROWERS

Considered by many critics to be one of Britain's most original contemporary writers, Tom Wakefield's *Mates* and *Drifters* have been widely praised for the way they depict the humour and pathos of human relationships. His latest novel continues in the same vein, following the progress of five everyday figures who react against the social conventions that shackle their lives.

"Wakefield is an accomplished narrator; detached, witty and knowing" – *The Times*.

"There can be no doubt that we are in the hands of a finely perceptive and sensitive writer" – *Guardian*.

"Delicate marquetry of the domestic and everyday in his characters and plot, richness of detail, and sheer, irrepressible humour of character and viewpoint. This is a lyrical, magical novel, and a warming shot of sentiment in a climate of cool" – *City Limits*.

ISBN 0 907040 79 9 (paperback)   £3.95
       0 907040 80 2 (cloth)   £9.95

GMP is the world's leading publisher of books of gay interest, with a wide range of titles including Fiction, History, Art, Photography, Health, Biography and Memoirs. Send for our full catalogue to GMP Publishers Ltd, P O Box 247, London N15 6RW.